DATE DUE

DEC 15 1992			
MAY 27 1997			

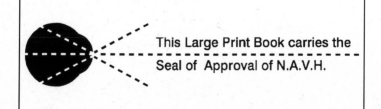

This Large Print Book carries the
Seal of Approval of N.A.V.H.

SPRING BRIDES

SPRING BRIDES

A YEAR OF WEDDINGS
NOVELLA COLLECTION

RACHEL HAUCK,
LENORA WORTH AND
MEG MOSELEY

THORNDIKE PRESS
A part of Gale, Cengage Learning

GALE
CENGAGE Learning·

Farmington Hills, Mich • San Francisco • New York • Waterville, Maine
Meriden, Conn • Mason, Ohio • Chicago

GALE
CENGAGE Learning®

LIBRARY OF CONGRESS CATALOGING-IN-PUBLICATION DATA

Spring brides : a year of weddings novella collection / by Rachel Hauck,
   Lenora Worth, and Meg Moseley. — Large print edition.
      pages cm. — (Thorndike Press large print Christian fiction)
      ISBN 978-1-4104-7797-2 (hardcover) — ISBN 1-4104-7797-5 (hardcover)
      1. Christian fiction, American. 2. Weddings—Fiction. 3. Large type books.
I. Hauck, Rachel, 1960– II. Worth, Lenora. III. Moseley, Meg.
PS648.C43S67 2015b
813'.01083823—dc23   2014049811

Printed in Mexico
1 2 3 4 5 6 7 19 18 17 16 15

CONTENTS

■ ■ ■ ■

A MARCH BRIDE

RACHEL HAUCK

■ ■ ■ ■

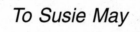

To Susie May

KING NATHANIEL II AND AMERICAN SUSANNA TRUITT ENGAGED!

KING NATHANIEL: "I'M MARRYING THE LOVE OF MY LIFE"

Brighton Kingdom
The Liberty Press
2 June
King Nathaniel will achieve what few of his ancestors have been able to: the right to marry the love of his life, American Susanna Truitt.

Less than a day after he convinced Parliament to amend the Marriage Act of 1792 forbidding marriage between foreigners and royals in line to the throne, he winged his way to St. Simons Island, Georgia, and proposed.

Was it romantic?

According to Truitt, "Very. He strung white lights from this old, old oak tree, got

11

down on one knee, and even produced fake snow." Truitt blushed as she glanced at King Nathaniel. "I told him I wouldn't fall in love again until it snowed in Georgia."

"She never stipulated it must be real snow," the king said, his arm around his bride-to-be as they sat in the Crown Room of the King's Office, fielding questions from select reporters.

The king never intended to fall in love eighteen months ago while on holiday in southern Georgia. But "God," he said, "had other things in mind."

Truitt, a landscape architect, designed the king's American cottage garden. While she presented garden ideas, romance bloomed.

"I'd just ended a long relationship where I thought marriage was the end game," Truitt said. "But instead of proposing, my boyfriend broke up with me. That very same day, a year-and-a-half ago, I met Nathaniel under this ancient tree, Lovers' Oak."

The king proposed under the same tree. The newly engaged couple plan a March wedding.

"Susanna needs time to adjust to Brighton as well as royal life."

"It's very different from slinging barbecue in my mama and daddy's Rib Shack," Truitt said, going on to say that joining the royal family is daunting and that the notion of being "a royal" has not completely sunk in.

From Stratton Palace, Dowager Queen Campbell declared she was "thrilled" for her son. "True love comes along so rarely these days."

Prince Stephen, the king's younger brother, issued a statement from his rugby club. "Susanna is quite the sport. She's good fun and a solid match for Nathaniel. I'm profoundly jealous. But happy for my brother."

Truitt will be the first foreigner to marry a Brighton ruler since Princess Paulette of Lorraine, the wife of Crown Prince Kenneth, nearly destroyed our military forces by urging her husband and father-in-law to aid her uncle, King Louis XVI, during the French Revolution.

What's the word on the street of this "American invasion"?

"I don't care who he marries," uttered a customer at a Cathedral City Starbucks.

Others exude more enthusiasm. One university student said, "My friends and I think it's grand. She's a lucky girl. We wish them joy."

Wedding plans are just beginning as Truitt transitions from America to Brighton Kingdom. Designers are frothing to be the

Chosen One for the future queen's wedding gown.

But who knows what this American will choose for her dress or her wedding venue? Traditionally, all Stratton House royals have married at Watchman Abbey, where the king's coronation was held this past January.

"We don't know what Susanna will do," said Penny Pitworth, a royal reporter for B-TV. "She may not want to marry in Brighton at all."

Hold your collective gasps. The king and future queen of Brighton may not marry on our sapphire isle at all but on her home isle of St. Simons in Georgia.

"Either way," Pitworth said, "we've a royal wedding upcoming and all of Brighton should rejoice."

And so we shall.

ONE

For the first time in her life, Susanna Truitt was uncomfortable in a garden. As a landscape architect, she viewed gardens as her sweet spot, her place of rest and peace, but standing among the esteemed guests of Lord and Lady Chadweth's seventeenth-century ivy-covered stone and glass atrium, she felt the arrow of doubt spear her heart.

Three weeks before her wedding, and anxiety rumbled in her soul.

She cut a glance toward her fiancé, King Nathaniel II of Brighton Kingdom, as he laughed with his old university mates.

What in the world was she doing here? Surely Nathaniel had changed his mind about marrying her.

Susanna breathed out, collected her fears, and shoved them aside as she tipped her face toward the bright rays of sun slicing through the glass pane ceiling. After a long Brighton winter, she was homesick for

15

Georgia.

"You know you did, mate . . . We were there, eye-witnesses . . ."

Susanna tuned in to the conversation around her.

"No, no, you've got it all wrong, Nigel." Nathaniel's protest launched a jovial debate among his friends, an aristocratic group of eight who seemed to look to Nigel as their leader.

Susanna smiled, rocking from one high-heeled foot to the other, exhaling. She had no idea what they were going on about, but lately Nathaniel seemed to have many things in his life that excluded her.

Which led to her feeling a bit like an outsider, even among her garden "friends" — the potted palms, hydrangeas, lilies, and royal maples.

"So, Susanna, how is every little thing?" This from Winnie, Nigel's girlfriend.

"Every little thing is just fine." It was the bigger things that concerned her.

He's changed his mind. Of course. It would be on par for her love life. Adam had changed his mind. Why not Nathaniel?

"I can't imagine all you're going through for this wedding." Winnie chortled. "It's the wedding of the century."

"So they say." Susanna's legs wobbled a

16

bit as she pushed her smile wider.

First lesson in being a royal? Smile. Be cordial. And stand a lot. Who knew royal life included so much standing? And handshaking. Lots and lots of handshaking.

And pulling out the hand sanitizer was considered ill form.

Susanna had rallied the King's Office to let her wear sneakers or flip-flops for long receiving lines, but the protocol officers flatly refused.

"Tell me, are you nervous?" Winnie pressed her hand on Susanna's arm. A move, she'd learned, that was acceptable for family and close friends, but not others. "I'd be a nervous wreck. The *Liberty Press* is reporting a telly audience of over a billion."

Susanna's smile faltered as a fresh wave of nerves washed ashore. "Well, then, we're going to need a bigger cake."

Winnie stared at her, then tee-hee'd. "You're quite droll, Susanna. I like that in a woman."

With that, Winnie returned to reminiscing with the men and Susanna was back to feeling alone and aching for home. For warmth. For unobstructed sunlight.

Aching for her own folks with whom to reminisce. She'd not been to Georgia since her best friend Gracie's wedding last October. She'd finally said yes to her boyfriend, Ethan.

But even then, it wasn't really like being home. Nathaniel couldn't get away, so Susanna traveled with a security officer and stayed in a hotel.

She returned to Brighton, a North Sea island gem, and enjoyed a lovely, mild October only to have November descend with gray days and an early snow.

For four long months, Susanna hibernated in palaces and castles, enduring the Brighton winter while being schooled on Brighton law, customs, traditions, and how to be the wife of a king.

So today as the sun crested the first pure blue, cloudless sky of March, she felt ready to burst with longing for south Georgia's heat and balmy breezes.

She missed the wind in the live oaks and the jaunty sway of Spanish moss, the fragrance of Daddy's barbecue sauce simmering on the Rib Shack's stove tops, the feel of a surfboard under her arm, and above all, the ability to move about town without a gaggle of photographers on her heels.

She longed to hear Daddy's "Hello, kitten" and Mama's "Susanna Jean, need you to pull a shift at the Shack." She missed hearing her baby sister, Avery's, exuberance about . . . *everything.*

"Susanna —" Nigel leaned toward her. "Surely Nathaniel told you the story of the skiing bear." Nigel's laugh bent him backward and he seemed more like a frivolous playboy than the CEO of his own shipping company.

"A skiing bear?" She glanced at Nathaniel, who smiled, shaking his head and sipping from his champagne flute. He didn't care much for champagne, but he held a glass out of respect for his host and hostess. "No, he didn't."

"It's an old story, love." He peeked at her, then away, down the wide aisle of the warm, bright atrium, toward the open doors. A fresh breeze sauntered in and rustled a few maple branches, spraying the atrium with the saline fragrance of the bay. "I'd nearly forgotten all about it."

"Forgotten it?" Nigel's tone contained no reserve. "Please, Nathaniel, it was the most extraordinary thing I've ever seen. I can't remember when I laughed so hard, I'll tell you that, old chap."

There, she caught a hint of Nathaniel's laugh. Something he'd not done much of lately.

Susanna regarded him for a moment, trying to figure what bothered him. What bothered her.

As their wedding drew near, her man looked . . . sad.

He's changed his mind and he's afraid to tell me!

Her heart crashed and her lungs strained for a pure breath. It took every ounce of her will not to run out of the atrium.

"Susanna, you should've seen him." Nigel's story reeled in the rest of the circle — Winnie, Blythe and Morton, Lord Michael Dean and his wife, Lady Ruthie, and her sister, Lady Becky. "The lot of us went skiing on a spring holiday from university. Michael, Mortie, you were there, remember?"

Skiing on spring break? A luxury in Susanna's world. She'd spent every spring and summer break from the University of Georgia at her parents' barbecue place, waiting tables and running the back of the house just to earn enough of her living expenses for the following semester.

And if she ran out of money before the semester's end, she cut Friday classes, drove home, and worked nonstop all weekend.

". . . on our last day we determined to take in as much skiing as possible." Nigel geared up from storyteller to entertainer. "We'd spent all day on the slopes, you see. Our boy Nathaniel here was the most determined to ski the day away, like a man facing a life sentence or some such."

"He was set upon graduation to enter the Royal Fusiliers as an infantryman like all the crown princes before him," Michael said.

Susanna knew about his military days. Nathaniel was quite proud of serving his country. He'd even briefly served during the war with the Royal Fusiliers Intelligence Corps.

"So this holiday was his last as a free man."

"I was born a crown prince," Nathaniel said to his glass more than to his friends. "I've never been a free man."

Susanna leaned to see his expression. What happened to the man of confidence and security who'd come to embrace his divine destiny?

He'd been at great peace over his calling as a king. So why the snarky comment?

When his gaze met hers, she smiled, searching for the teasing glint he reserved just for her beneath his blue eyes.

He nodded to her and she waited for *that* tug to appear on the side of his lips when he wanted to kiss her in public but couldn't.

However, his eyes did not twinkle, nor did his lips twist.

She could live with his dull eyes and sober expression, but she could not live without his look of love. The one that sparked a warm twinge of lover's passion. The one that made her tremble with longing when he kissed her.

For well over a month now, she'd missed his tender glances and wooing warm words. Yes, he'd been busy, traveling, distracted and distant with his kingly duties. But when they were alone, he remained distant. Lost in a world she could not enter.

Their typically lively and deep conversations were now of mundane things like a late winter snow or the unusual prediction of sun and refreshing temperatures in early March.

Nathaniel no longer spoke about their dreams, hopes, and plans.

"So there he is, love. Susanna, are you getting this?" Nigel nudged her again, catching an eye from Nathaniel. "Pardon, I see your fiancé didn't take kindly to me calling you love or my elbow in your ribs. Anyway —"

"If you're going to tell the story, Nigel, tell it," Nathaniel said, gruff and irritated.

"Mate, you can't deny me the luxury of milking this fabulous story."

"Go on," Susanna said, reaching out to set her champagne flute on a tray carried by a black-tie server. "I'd like to hear this."

"So there we are, having a grand time. Nathaniel is flying down this slope, I mean *flying*." Nigel crouched down into a skiing position. "It's a fantastic hill and a fantastic run. There he is at jet speed when a bear — a big, blasted black bear — ambles out of the woods right onto the run."

"Hungry. Just out of hibernation." Nathaniel came a bit more alive. Nigel's storytelling had a way of turning off the silence and chasing away the blues. Even in Nathaniel. "He looked square at me like I'm his lunch, heaven sent."

"The lot of us are right behind him, pulling up, skiing off to the side," Michael said.

"In the meantime" — Morton's laugh was low and cool, the sound of a stuffy blueblood — "we're watching our friend and crown prince ski to his death."

"You should've seen it from my vantage point," Nathaniel said. "I've nowhere to go but into the trees, square into the beast, or off the side of the mountain."

"And people tell me surfing is dangerous," Susanna said, laughing, finally feeling a bit more at ease, realizing it wasn't the garden making her uncomfortable but Nathaniel's surly silence toward her.

He regrets his proposal. What else could it

be? Enough. She'd confront him the moment they were alone.

Theirs had not been the easiest of engagements. Not only were they blending lives and hearts, getting to know one another as a couple, but they were blending cultures and expectations, all before the eyes of the world.

Most of the adjusting fell on her shoulders because she wasn't merely marrying a man, but a king. She wasn't getting to know just a new family but one with deep roots in ancient European history.

She wasn't just learning the ins and outs of her new country, but a whole different way of life.

And the press . . . nothing can prepare one for the press. Behind Duchess Kate in the United Kingdom, Susanna was now the most photographed woman in the world. She found it exhausting.

"We're yelling for him to stop, but he keeps plowing down the hill," Nigel said.

"I couldn't stop, ole chap."

"Then we start debating," Nigel went on. " 'Who's going to tell the king? And shall we say his son died bravely, doing what he loved?' "

"Fine lot, that, having me dead before seeing my great plan of escape." Nathaniel

24

broke out of his somberness with a heartfelt laugh.

"What's all the hilarity? I wasn't invited?" The raven-haired beauty, Lady Genevieve Hawthorne, boldly inserted herself into the group as a spark of jealousy ignited a prickly heat in Susanna.

"Ginny, love, where've you been?" Blythe leaned forward to air-kiss Lady Genevieve's cheeks.

"Bowing out of another engagement."

Lady Genevieve was everything a crown prince-turned-king would want in a wife. A former Miss Brighton *and* Olympic lacrosse champion, she was stunning, sexy, and intelligent. Worse yet, she had once vied for Nathaniel's heart.

He'd refused her, choosing Susanna instead. But perhaps now, as the wedding neared and he had a chance to watch Susanna function in royal situations like this hoity-toity garden party, he wished he'd made a better choice.

Susanna flipped her gaze up at Nathaniel. Was he staring at Ginny with any longing or affection?

No, he was staring down at *her.* Susanna finally felt a bit of warmth in his expression. He smiled and her knees went weak.

"We're telling the story of the skiing bear,"

Nigel said.

"Oh my word." Lady Genevieve rolled her eyes. How did she make even *that* look alluring? "What a grand time we all had." She ha-ha'd like she ate diamonds for breakfast and flossed with spun gold. "Of course I knew you'd escape, darling. Naturally." Lady Genevieve fell against Nathaniel, caressing his arm. Then she shot Susanna a sly glance. "Susanna, darling, gorgeous dress. Love the orange flowers and vintage vibe. A Molly Turnwalt design or I'll turn in my fashionista card."

Susanna smoothed her hand over the ivory skirt with its splash of orange blossoms. "From her spring line, yes."

"In college, I only wore Molly Turnwalt." Lady Genevieve laughed with Winnie. "Remember her T-shirts and peg-leg jeans? Oh, to be twenty-two again."

Susanna burned with embarrassment, breathing deep, refusing her soul the sweetness of firing off a sour retort. Lady Genevieve was trying to make Susanna look out of touch and childish.

"Ginny, darling —" Nigel shoved her aside. "I'm telling a story."

"Oh right, Ni, I forgot it's all about you." Lady Genevieve rocked back, folding her arms, pulling a face. "Do go on."

A twittering laugh floated through the group with familiar, longtime-friend glances. Susanna hated feeling like a wallflower. She peeked up again at Nathaniel to discover he was watching Ginny, a slight smile on his lips.

Susanna felt sick. Weak. She'd been here before. Two years ago. On the beach at home with her longtime boyfriend, Adam Peters. She had expected him to propose, but instead he toiled with the words to end their relationship.

"I've found the right ring but not the right girl." Adam Peters's confession still pierced through her heart at the oddest times.

But she'd been so committed to her plan to marry him that Susanna had refused to see the truth. They were *not* right for each other.

Well, she refused to be so naive this time. If she and Nathaniel had wandered down a dark romantic dead end, then she'd be the one to turn on the light.

However, she'd not give up just yet. She joined the conversation, turning to face Nathaniel. "Since clearly you lived, I suppose you found a way out of this bear collision?" Susanna stepped closer to her fiancé, sending a signal to Lady Genevieve to back off.

Susanna was the one wearing Nathaniel's ring.

"Yes, I managed to calculate an escape."

"Escape?" Nigel laughed. "Susanna, he performed a feat only Houdini would attempt. To the right there was a thick stand of trees. An option worse than running into the bear. Trees don't frighten and run off. To the left" — Nigel arched his hand through the air — "was a tumble over the side of the mountain with a straight drop down to the rocks."

"I had no choice but to ski into the bear," Nathaniel said.

"You really skied *into* the bear?" Susanna smiled, searching his expression for truth. For hope.

"Not exactly. As I whisked closer and closer, going faster and faster, I started yelling for the bear to move, but he merely stared at me as if I annoyed his sleepy thoughts. I braced for impact when I hit one of nature's moguls and —" Nathaniel whistled, slicing his hand through the air.

"He went airborne," Nigel said.

"You jumped the bear?" Susanna liked the mental image of a young prince soaring through the air, his regal, chiseled features cutting through the icy breeze as he hurdled a sleepy, hungry winter bear.

28

"Cleared him by a good four feet," Nigel said.

"It was spectacular. You should've seen it." Genevieve's tone carried a subtle reminder. *I'm a part of Nathaniel's inner circle, and you, Susanna, are an interloper.* "We sat around the fire talking of it all night."

"Say, Nig, didn't Hampsted film it with his camera?" Morton snapped his fingers, remembering. "He was always sticking that thing in our faces."

"By George, I believe he did." Nigel stretched, searching over their heads. "He's round here somewhere with his new wife. Ah, there he is . . . Hammie."

Nigel and Lord Michael scurried off to hound Hammie about his home movie while the distinguished Henry Montgomery, Brighton's former prime minister, approached Nathaniel.

"Pardon, Your Majesty, might I have a word?" He bowed slightly, then smiled at Susanna. "You are looking lovely as ever, Susanna."

"Thank you, Henry."

"Excuse me, darling." Nathaniel turned to Susanna. "I'll return momentarily."

Susanna watched him walk off with Henry, their heads bent together. What could Henry want in private at a garden

29

party honoring the king and his future bride?

The unease in Susanna's heart surfaced and burned. Did Henry want to discuss something about Brighton? About Nathaniel? Or maybe his upcoming marriage?

Perhaps it had to do with Nathaniel's mother. In public, Henry was the former prime minister. In private, he was Nathaniel's stepfather, married to his mum, the Dowager Queen Campbell. They wed last July after the one-year anniversary of King Leopold V's death.

Susanna scanned the atrium garden for Campbell, who was unmistakable in a bright yellow spring dress with a matching coat, shoes, and hat. Once she had taken off her mourning clothes, nothing but bright colors would do. The press was starting to notice, calling her Colorful Campbell.

"So," Lady Genevieve began, interrupting Susanna's thoughts. "Your wedding dress. We're all dying to see it." She wrinkled her nose. First at Susanna, then Winnie, Blythe, and Lady Ruthie. "Aren't we? I don't suppose I could get a sneak peek?"

Susanna marveled at the woman's boldness. Asking to see her gown like they were best friends. They hardly knew each other, and Susanna trusted her about as much as

30

sticking her hand into a dark hole in the ground. Never knew what might bite back.

"I'm afraid not." Susanna gazed past Lady Genevieve's slender shoulder, eyes fixed on Nathaniel's back, his dark suit accenting his wide shoulders. "The designer and I are bound by an agreement of mutual exclusivity."

"Really? Merry Collins made you sign an exclusivity?"

"I offered, if you must know. I wasn't going to require something of her I was not willing to take on myself."

Genevieve arched her brow. "She must love you."

"We have a mutual respect," Susanna said, irritated by this conversation. Irritated by the fact Nathaniel seemed to be in some sort of deep discussion with Henry — indicated by his pinched brow and squinting eyes. What was going on? This was supposed to be a party. A joyous celebration of their upcoming wedding.

Instead, Susanna felt a certain dread.

Nathaniel shoved back his jacket as he anchored his hands in his pockets. A sure sign he was frustrated. Annoyed. His signature move — hands in his pockets — was considered ill form in Parliament and at state events, so he'd broken the habit.

31

Except in moments like now.

He nodded once. Then glanced back at Susanna.

Something was definitely wrong.

". . . do you think you'll work, Susanna?"

She switched her gaze to Winnie. "Work? Yes, as time allows. I've been consulting with AGH Partners, landscaping a new garden in tribute to King Leo."

"Fantastic. Good for you. I always think the wife of the king should have a job, you know, hold on to her own identity."

Hold on to her own identity? Winnie had no idea of what she spoke. Susanna had *long* given up on such an idea. She'd all but lost her identity the moment she said yes to Nathaniel and moved four thousand miles away to Brighton.

The only thing that remained of her was her American heritage. Which the press loved to point out.

A woman with a large pink hat stopped to talk to Lady Genevieve, but kept one eye on Susanna as they whispered and laughed.

Never mind. Nathaniel was coming her way, so Susanna excused herself.

"Nathaniel, what's going on?"

His gaze communicated a raw, vivid fear. As if he were about to do something he didn't want to but must.

32

Yep, she felt his cold glance all the way to her bone marrow. He was dumping her. Adam had the same look on his face that stormy afternoon on the beach.

"I've something to tell you." He hooked his hand around her elbow and steered her toward the open French doors.

"You're scaring me." She walked with him, her strength draining.

"Your Majesty!" The party director hurried toward them with determined strides, waving her clipboard in the air. "We're ready for the formal pictures now."

"Thank you, Mrs. Janis." Nathaniel sighed, looking down at Susanna. "We'll talk after this."

No, no, she couldn't take it anymore. "We'll talk right now. What is going on with you?"

"Susanna, please —" He smiled at Mrs. Janis, who waited with a frozen smile. "Let's get the photograph. The Chadweths went to a great deal of effort to have this party for us."

"What's the point of this party or a photograph if you're breaking up with me?"

"We'll be right over here, Your Majesty." Mrs. Janis backed up, pointing to the corner of the atrium where marble fountains spewed crystal water from angel wings.

"Just say it." She became forthright when she was nervous. With Adam, she used their twelve-year history to launch an argument, but she only had eighteen months with Nathaniel. Ten of which they spent apart. "You regret proposing to me."

"I what?" Nathaniel reared back. "What are you talking about, Susanna?"

"Well, do you? You're distracted and distant. You've stopped talking to me about your life. You hardly smile or laugh when we're together."

"I realize that government business has gotten in the way a bit, yes."

"This is not about government business. Look, I've been dumped before, Nathaniel. I'm aware of the signs."

"Susanna, I am not Adam Peters."

"Then what?" She grabbed his arm. "Do you think it's not going to work with me as your wife? Are you sorry —"

"No, Susanna, no." He grabbed her shoulders as he peered down at her with blue sincerity, his chest rising and falling with each deep breath. "Quite the opposite. I fear *you* will regret saying yes to me."

Two

Nathaniel tried to relax the tension from his bones as he walked Susanna up the broad, grand staircase to her Parrsons House suite.

They had put off talking after their small confrontation at the Chadweths'. It wasn't the place or time. Since then, they'd barely had a moment to themselves. They'd departed the garden party for a dinner at the American ambassador's home with only enough time to change wardrobes. It had been a long Friday.

"Are you coming in?" Susanna stood in the doorway, waiting.

Nathaniel tried to discern from her tone and posture whether his answer should be yes or no. "Actually, that'd be lovely."

She led the way in, slipping off her jacket, passing through the suite's teakwood foyer to the living room.

The clock on the fireplace mantel chimed eleven bells.

For three more weeks, this would be her home. Then she'd move to Nathaniel's palace apartment and this suite would become their private living quarters for Christmas and holidays when they traveled to the family's country estate.

Already Susanna's influence was changing this place, changing the palace — his former bachelor pad — in small, gentle ways. Above all, she was changing his bachelor heart.

He could *not* lose her. Must not. Yet he felt as if he'd been holding his breath for so long he had to let go and let life deal him the hand it must. He had to tell her the truth. After that, she might very well want to leave.

Could he blame her? She'd given so much already. This one final request could push her to the royal edge.

Slipping out of his tuxedo jacket, Nathaniel gestured toward the tea cart that Rollins, the Parrsons House butler, had set out for them.

"Would you like some tea?"

"A small cup. Thank you." Susanna sank slowly to the cocoa-colored sofa she'd recently selected as part of the apartment's remodel. It was one of the only expensive pieces she had authorized, saying that the apartment suited her just fine without spending a lot of money to remake a room that already looked "splendid."

Her simplicity was just one of her many qualities that endeared her to him. And one more reason why he was so desperate not to lose her. She kept him grounded in everyday reality.

Pouring her tea, Nathaniel added the dollop of cream she'd come to love. "Here you go, love." He handed over her cup. "Rollins left some biscuits too."

"I couldn't eat another thing." She patted her stomach, settling back against the couch. "Ambassador Riddle went all out, didn't he? I can't believe he brought over Michael Baggio."

"He's always been a classy chap."

Tyler Riddle and his wife, Kate, had hosted a fine evening of food and wine, topped off with a very special guest: the American standard singer Michael Baggio, whom Susanna adored.

And he openly adored her back, aiming his musical charms right at her.

But why not? She looked stunning in a midnight blue gown, her long blonde hair flowing over her shoulders in wide curls.

Nathaniel tried to give her space throughout the evening, grateful for the distraction of the other guests and his need to circulate.

Yet he let her know he was there for her and in no way did he regret asking her into his life.

For his own sake more than hers, he held her hand at Mr. Baggio's miniconcert. The blasted singer stirred his jealousies.

Halfway through Baggio's first number, "The Way You Look Tonight," Nathaniel caught an emotional mist in Susanna's eyes and he knew. She was homesick.

Well, perhaps that was the gist of it all. She needed to be free to fly if her heart so dictated. He had grasped too tight, suffocating his precious bird. Perhaps he needed to let go and be willing for her to fly away.

And if the bit of news he carried in his chest caused her to doubt her decision to marry *him,* then so be it.

Nathaniel poured his own tea, snatched up a chocolate biscuit, and settled in the wing chair adjacent to Susanna, noting that his thoughts were far more courageous than his heart. He wasn't willing to let her go. Not in the least.

He took one bite of his biscuit and tossed it to his plate. He wasn't hungry. And he had no taste for tea.

"Susanna —"

"Nathaniel, I've decided it's okay if you don't want to marry me." Her blue eyes were steady on him. Wide. Without guile.

He set his tea on the table and rose to his feet. "How can you say such a thing? What makes you think I regret proposing? You do realize I went to Parliament with an Order of Council for the right to marry you. It's the first time a king offered his own bill or amendment in over a hundred years."

"That doesn't mean you haven't changed your mind since then."

She said that with such calm and clarity. "Perhaps it's *you* who has changed her mind." Nathaniel stood behind his chair, hands propped on the curved wings. "Do you regret saying yes to me?"

"Do you regret proposing to me? You've been so . . . weird lately."

"I know, love, I know." He exhaled, returning to his seat.

"And what was that smile you gave Lady Genevieve this afternoon? I thought you wanted to keep her at arm's length after how she tried to manipulate you into marrying her."

"You've heard the saying, 'Keep your friends close but your enemies closer'?"

"You think you need her on your side?"

"I think I need her not to fight against me. Can we not talk about Ginny?" He pressed his hand over his heart. "There's something I've been avoiding discussing with you."

"Like what?" The rosy hue faded from her cheeks.

"Susanna." He stood again, too restless to remain seated. "There was a writ passed in Parliament last week, sponsored by the Liberal-Labor Party coalition, who you know recently took control in Parliament. As it were, they are also a small but loud voice against the monarchy."

"What kind of writ?"

"An addendum to the Marriage Act. Brighton parliamentary procedure allows for a writ to be attached to any law or act by a majority vote in the House of Senate and Commons within a year of the law's ratification."

Nathaniel paced over to the window and stood in the room's shadows, peering into the rich, dark, velveteen night. Parrsons was situated on top of the cliffs surrounding the northeastern bay, and on a clear night the lights shining down from the heavens seemed to be within a man's reach.

"Nathaniel?" Susanna's warm hands smoothed over his shoulders.

He turned around and drew her to him, embracing her, kissing her cheek, working down her long, slender neck to her shoulder, holding on to her for dear life. "I love you so much."

When he found her lips, she rose up on her toes, looping her arms about his neck, returning his affection, matching his ardor.

"Talk to me, Goose," she said, her lips still brushing against his.

"Goose?"

Top Gun.

"Tom Cruise. Anthony Green."

"Very good, Your Majesty."

"If I'm Goose, does that make me *your* wingman?" He lifted his head, grinning, squinting down at her. "I believe you're to be *my* wingman."

She grabbed a fistful of his starched shirt. "Tell me what's going on."

"You have to give up your American citizenship."

"What?" She released him, stepping back. "That's the writ? Susanna Truitt has to give up her American citizenship? Or does this apply to all people wanting to become citizens of Brighton? Brighton no longer welcomes dual citizenship?"

"You've been a good student of Brighton law and history." He watched her, trying to read her changing expression.

"Of course — I want to be a good Brightonian. A good wife to the king. But, Na-

41

thaniel, I also want to remain an American."
She fidgeted, gathering her hair in her
hands, piling it on her head, then letting it
fall loose again. "I mean, it's all I have left
of who I am. I thought it was one of the
things you love about me."

"Indeed, I do love who you are in every
way, and if it were up to me, your American
citizenship would not be an issue. But I'm
not an autocrat. I've a parliament to deal
with and they've come up with their own
constraints. The writ applies only to the
Royal Marriage Act. Not to all Brighto-
nians. The proponents argue that the spouse
of the monarch cannot have divided loyalties. All laws, all treaties, all acts of war are
in the reigning monarch's name. In this
case, mine. If for some wild reason Brighton should find herself on the opposite side
of a conflict with America —"

"They think I'd be a traitor to Brighton?"

"Yes."

"But I wouldn't. And taking my citizenship doesn't guarantee my loyalty . . . if I
were so inclined to be a traitor."

"Agreed. But we can't know what the
future will bring. Surely you see their point,
Suz. They want to protect Brighton and her
people. They want to protect the royal
house."

"Protect them from me?" She laughed, mocking. "Little ole Susanna Jean from St. Simons Island? The American government doesn't even know who I am besides a social security number and a tax bracket."

"Maybe before, but they certainly know who you are now."

"So what? I have no real authority."

"But you have access to people with the real authority. You have access to me. You are an influencer in the world now, Susanna, whether you've grasped that or not."

"Influencer? I'm fodder for fashion magazines, tabloids, and hate blogs." She backed up, a dark shadow flickering across her face. "But to me, I'm just your wife-to-be. A landscape architect, Rib Shack waitress from Georgia."

"Surely you understand your station is far more than 'just a,' Susanna. You're marrying a king. Don't play naive. You understood what it meant when you agreed to marry me. You're on the world's stage now. Every major American television station has crews and broadcasters setting up shop outside of Watchman Abbey, ready and waiting to report on our wedding. We've had hundreds of requests from magazines, newspapers, and broadcast stations in the States and the world for interviews with you. Just you. Not me a'tall. What you say and do will influence nations."

"Okay, okay, maybe I kind of knew that when I moved here." She twisted her hands together. "But now you're putting skin on it. Giving it eyes and ears . . . and a little beanie cap on its newborn head."

"Sweetheart" — he reached for her, smiling — "remember what you told me that day on the grounds of Christ Church? We'd only known each other for a few days, but you so wisely said I was born for a purpose, to have influence in ways most people only dream about. You said of yourself, 'I'm Susanna Truitt, born on St. Simons, for some purpose. I'm not an accident.' Don't let this writ get in the way of what God is doing. With you. With us. The only way my opponents win is if we let this writ come between us."

"So it's done? No way to stop them? At all?" She tempered her voice and Nathaniel detected a small sprinkle of hope.

"What do you think I've been doing the past two months?"

"That's why you've been distant? Distracted? Why didn't you tell me?"

"Because you had enough on your docket, love. If I succeeded, then no harm. If they succeeded, then I'd tell you. That's why

44

Henry pulled me aside at the garden party. The writ was ratified late last night." He regarded her for a moment, waiting for some kind of reaction, his own small fears blipping over the plains of his heart. "I'm sorry."

"Don't you have to sign all the laws?"

"Indeed, but this writ is under the parliamentary jurisdiction on a law I already signed."

Listening to his own explanation, he felt his heart begin to crumble. Why in the world would any woman give up her freedom and privacy to marry him?

His past romantic rejection ghosted through his thoughts. Lady Adel Gardner's humiliating public refusal ten years ago of Nathaniel's very public proposal during his father's birthday party found a fresh breath every now and then, and taunted him.

"Good heavens, no!" she said into a microphone. "If I marry you, my life will never be my own!"

Yeah, he'd walked into that one deaf, dumb, blind, and stupid. Not long graduated from university, he was fumbling to find the "next phase" of his life. So why not marry the lovely and fun Adel?

But she rang the death knell on that plan. And Nathaniel swore off romance afterward, eager to avoid repeating the mistake with another woman. Then he met Susanna under Lovers' Oak and all his fears vanished.

"Then it is done. I have no say. If I marry you, I cannot be an American citizen."

"Actually, *before* you marry me, you cannot be an American citizen. Otherwise, I'm in default of the law."

"You're the king. You can't be arrested or tried."

So, she'd studied much of their laws. "No, but it will fire up my political opponents. And yours." His heart burned in his chest.

"I have to take the Brighton citizenship oath before our wedding?" She bristled, the light in her eyes laser-thin, her lips drawn and tight. "As if I didn't have enough to do. I wasn't planning on taking it until this summer."

"We just have to bump it up, is all. Is it all that much of an inconvenience, love?"

"Yes, it is." They stood inches from one another, but were miles apart. "You fought for me? Tell me you did."

"I fought for you, for our children and their children. But I must admit I see the wisdom of the writ. Not that I doubt your loyalties, but for future generations. It just seems wise that the ruling monarch be married to someone who doesn't have loyalties to another nation. I understand the limitations of the human heart. One can only be pushed so far."

"Nathaniel, just because I give up my American citizenship doesn't mean I no longer love my country. Doesn't mean I couldn't turn into a traitor. Not that I would, mind you." She backed away, turning into the room. "I don't know what to say. I've moved to a new country, spent nearly ten months learning your culture and traditions, the social strata, not to mention the royal life."

"And you've done splendidly, Suz. Marrying me is no ordinary melding of two lives."

"Two lives?" Susanna whirled back around. "There's no two here. Only one life. Mine. I'm the one who was required to do all the changing. I have to fit into *your* life. And gladly, Nathaniel. I love you. But this writ is making me deny the one last thing I have of myself, of what's wholly mine, of what I bring to this marriage as an American. It's as if those in Parliament want to crush me. I'm sorry, but it just seems to fly in the face of why you petitioned Parliament for the Marriage Act amendment in the first place."

"Exactly my argument when I debated the

writ sponsors. But surely you see their reason. The wife of the sovereign must be true to her country in word if not in deed. Yes, you can remain American in your heart, but to the world you are solely Brightonian."

"This is insulting." She paced around the room. "They all but accuse me of being a spy or committing treason."

"No, Susanna, sweetheart, they are really trying to prevent me from expanding my authority by having ties to America. This is more about me than you." He cut her off as she rounded the room again, gently slipping his arm about her waist. "We're a small North Sea nation with rich resources. We've been threatened in the past. We are well aware it could happen again. Especially on the world's current stage. While we value and treasure our allies, especially America, members of the royal house must be devoted and committed to Brighton alone. My own loyalty cannot be compromised because of my wife's nationality. Love, I reasoned at length with the new prime minister, with the leaders of the House of Senators and the House of Commons, trying to win a way for you to be both American and Brightonian, but they passed the citizenship requirement."

"And what if I refuse to accept it?"

He swallowed hard, the sudden jerk of his heartbeat stomping on his next breath. "Then we . . . Are you saying you refuse?"

"I'm asking, what happens if I do?"

Their gazes locked. Anxiety pulsed in Nathaniel's ears. He was going to lose her. Nothing short of abdicating his throne could keep her.

Was he willing to give up his throne and kingdom, his five-hundred-year heritage and destiny, for her love? Could he do what he was asking her to do?

"Susanna, I've not thought that far, if you must know." *Oh, liar.* He'd thought of nothing else. But he needed more time to consider his own response.

Across the room, the ring of her phone pierced the air. She broke away from his arm. "It's Mama's ring tone. We've been trying to connect all week but keep missing each other. I need to answer this."

"Of course." A break in the tension was a relief.

Nathaniel fell against the windowsill, watching the only woman who ever made his heart resound with love answer her phone and greet her mum with a soft, sweet Southern twang.

He loved the way her words bent and

swayed, putting him in mind of Spanish moss swinging from craggy live oak branches on a balmy Georgia evening.

Oh Susanna . . .

THREE

"Yes, Mama, I heard you . . ." Susanna collapsed to the sofa, absorbing Mama's news about Granny. Pneumonia. Can't travel to Brighton for the wedding.

She truly had to give up everything. First the man she loved was telling her she must sacrifice her American citizenship in order to be with him. Now Mama was telling her Granny could not travel? What next?

"Gracie's here too," Mama said. "She's got something to tell you."

Please let it be good news. Susanna listened to the muffled sounds of Mama handing the phone to her matron of honor and best friend since elementary school.

"Hey, Suz."

"Hey, Gracie. How's the baby?"

When Gracie and Ethan married in October, they were set to sail around the world until she found out she was pregnant with a honeymoon baby. So they weighed anchor on St. Simons and charted a new course.

"Good, sort of . . . I'm on bed rest."

Susanna rocked forward. "Bed rest? What happened?"

Gracie detailed her situation as if she were reading from a menu.

Complications. Spotting. Contractions. Want to give the baby a fighting chance. Doctor said she couldn't be on her feet for more than an hour a day. "So Marlee, God bless her, is running the salon for me. She's such a gem."

"If you can't be on your feet, then you can't travel." It wasn't a question. It was a cold, stark revelation. Gracie's news mingled with Mama's and Nathaniel's, creating a cold, chilling cocktail of disappointment in her belly.

Here she was about to marry a *king,* and she wasn't even close to having her *dream* wedding.

Watchman Abbey, while stunningly beautiful, was not the sweet haven of Christ Church where she'd dreamed of having her wedding since she was twelve. She loved the ancient church, and never stepped on the lush grounds without feeling the presence of the Divine.

On top of Granny and Gracie, Susanna had learned in the last two months that her best college buddies, who had all made a pact to attend each other's weddings, could not come. Not one of the seven. Careers, babies, fear of flying over the Atlantic . . . they had their many reasons for not RSVP-ing "Attending."

She mentally scanned the most recent guest list she'd seen. Shoot, most of her family and extended family weren't coming.

Instead, they all informed Mama they preferred to see Susanna and her king at the St. Simons Island reception at the end of April. Asking the kinfolk to fly all the way to Europe? Too rich for their blood.

Fine, fine, she'd see them in April. But her granny and matron of honor had to be there. They must.

Susanna felt ill. This was wrong. All wrong. And she'd best open her eyes to the signs. She refused to cling to a *plan, again,* that was falling apart. She'd not redo her life with Adam Peters.

"Suz? You all right?" Nathaniel's bass voice flowed over her shoulder as he tenderly caressed her.

She shook her head, listening to Gracie apologize ten ways to Sunday, tears bubbling in her eyes.

"Did you hear me?" Gracie said.

"Yes, I heard you." She pressed her hand

53

under her eyes, pushing back her tears. What good were tears now? Crying would change nothing.

"I'm heartsick over this. Ethan and I have been talking for days, trying to figure a way for me to come, wondering if I should just ignore the doctor's warning and —"

"No!" Susanna jumped up. "Don't even think about it. The baby's safety is more important than my wedding."

"I — I can't believe this . . . My best friend is not only getting married but getting married to a real honest-to-goodness king and I'm going to *miss* it." Susanna heard the muffled sound of Ethan saying something in the background. "Oh right, Suz, Ethan says to tell you he's arranged with Reverend Smith to broadcast your wedding on a big screen from the Christ Church grounds." She chuckled. "He worked it all out by himself when he found out most of the parish wanted to watch it together. Everyone is joining in to help with food and setup. Channel 11 is even sending out a news crew."

"I always wanted to get married under the oaks on Christ Church grounds."

"And you'll be there, Suz, kinda. On a movie screen via a projection TV. Your mama assured me she'll get one of your aunts or uncles to get your granny there. I even invited your college friends. We'll be with you, Suz, I promise. If not in body, then in spirit."

Homesickness hooked her heart and furrowed deep. "I miss you, Grace."

"Miss you back, Suzy-Q. Big time. It's not the same around here without you. My baby girl needs to know her Auntie Suz!"

"It's a girl?"

"Naw, we couldn't tell on the first ultrasound. I'm just speaking it out loud in case God hasn't made up His mind yet. We'll know on the second ultrasound. Hopefully."

Suddenly, Susanna wanted to go home. Now.

She needed the sunshine soaking through her skin and warming her cold bones. To walk on the beach. Bury her toes in the wet sand. To get lost in the hubbub of the Rib Shack on a Friday night. To curl up with baby sister Avery on a Sunday afternoon for a classic movie marathon.

"Listen, here's your mama. I'll e-mail you soon, okay? But I know you're going to be so busy, Susanna. My girl, a real-life queen."

"No, just a princess. We decided to let Nathaniel's mom be the only queen."

"Then a real-life princess. Frankly, I like

princess better, don't you? Feels more Disney."

"Yeah. Disney." This wedding felt nothing like a fairy tale.

"I'm really, really sorry about this, Susanna."

"It's not like you did it on purpose. I understand." She did, but it hurt.

"You're going to be a beautiful bride. We'll all be praying for you and cheering you on. Go get 'em. Show the world how a good ole Georgia redneck does it."

In one sentence, Gracie summed up everything twisting and turning in Susanna's heart.

The life she knew was over. Once she said "I will" to Nathaniel, Susanna Jean Truitt from St. Simons Island, Georgia, USA, would be "dead."

She'd be a totally new person. Princess Susanna of Brighton Kingdom. Wife of a king. From private citizen to public.

A Brightonian. A European. She was even changing continents.

Susanna turned to Nathaniel, who'd perched on the edge of the wing chair, waiting. She loved him. She did, and her heart beat with that truth.

But was it enough?

"Shug." Mama was back on the line.

"Don't worry, we'll have things buttoned down by the time of your wedding so Daddy and I can be there with —"

"What? What do you mean so you and Daddy 'can be here'? You have two brothers and four sisters who can look in on Granny."

"Simmer down, Suz. I'm just saying you don't have to worry about us not making it because Granny's sick. Grandpa can take care of the little things, and I'll draw up a schedule so everyone knows when it's their turn to take care of them."

No one in the family dared buck a Glo Truitt schedule.

"Mama, g-give Granny my love. Tell her I'm praying for her." Susanna sank down to the couch cushion, trembling, drained, exhausted.

"Will do, Suzy-Q. She's devastated to miss this, but we want her well enough to see your children. Now don't you worry about a thing. Focus on Nate and your wedding. We'll see you in a few weeks. I hope Gracie's not being able to come doesn't dampen things too much."

"Even so, it can't be helped, Mama."

The conversation moved to small talk. The Rib Shack business was picking up nicely as word got out that the owners' daughter was marrying a king.

Avery was focused on the last months of her senior year and final volleyball season. Another athletic scholarship arrived for her. Ohio State. Which she was seriously considering.

Daddy's heart checkup went smooth as a whistle, but Mama fought him on his diet. "Can't be eating no fried catfish and hush puppies for dinner every week."

But Susanna struggled to listen, to engage. She was busy looking at the signs. Was this marriage really going to work?

By the time the call ended, Susanna was confused, tired, and suffering from a full-blown bout of homesickness.

"What's going on at home, Suz?" Nathaniel asked. "Is Granny all right? Grace?"

"No, I mean, yes, technically they are all right. But everything is going wrong." Susanna recapped the call, working to sound rational and reasonable when she felt like weeping.

"Love, I'm sorry."

"It is what it is." The mantel clock chimed midnight. Susanna fixed her gaze on Nathaniel. "I want to go home."

"Agreed." He moved to sit next to her. "How about I adjust our honeymoon plans? We'll travel to St. Simons Island first thing after our wedding. Stay at my, our, cottage.

Then we can go to our secret destination."
He gave her a wicked smile, sweeping her
close to him, kissing her cheek.

The honeymoon plans were his alone, and
Susanna made a game of trying to lure the
information out of him. Nathaniel played
along, pretending she'd guessed correctly,
or worse, that he'd let their destination slip
from his lips.

*Yes, we're going to Dollywood! How did you
guess?*

In truth, he was a man of steel when it
came to keeping secrets.

"I want to go home now, Nathaniel."

"Now? The wedding is three weeks away.
We have engagements on our diaries. The
last time we coordinated our schedules,
yours was fairly booked. I think you have a
final fitting and wedding arrangements to
approve."

"I don't care." She stood, trembling, shaking from a cold she couldn't define. "I know
it makes me sound loony, but I need to go
home." Unchecked tears now spilled down
her cheeks. "I miss everyone. I miss Granny.
She's eighty-five years old. Complications
from pneumonia could be devastating.
And . . ." She gave him a long, steady
glance. "I need to think."

"Think? About what?"

"What you're asking me to do. Give up my citizenship. I never really thought about it before, but, Nathaniel, I'm literally giving up *everything.* By the time we're married, I won't recognize myself."

"I realize that, but there's no need to run off." He stared away from her, his jaw tensing.

"I need some time. Some space."

"Have your space. Take some time. But flying to America is rather drastic, don't you think?"

"I'm not flying to America, Nathaniel. I'm going home."

He sighed, long and heavy. "Will you come back?"

She pressed her hands beside her temples, her head starting to throb with emotional pressure. "I don't know."

"Susanna, we've been on this course for nearly ten months. And now you 'don't know'?" She could see the passion in his voice reflected on his face and in his eyes. "What is it you don't know?"

"I don't know what I don't know." Her thoughts and reason deflated like a carnival balloon. "It's all coming down to the wire. This is it. Forever. No one from my side of the family is coming except Daddy, Mama, Avery, and Daddy's sister and her husband."

Susanna eyed the tea cart, which also contained an ice bucket of water bottles. She reached for one, twisting off the cap. "Now my granny can't come, nor my best friend. It makes me wonder." The heat of panic crawled across the base of her neck. "Then you bring up my citizenship and I just wonder if all of this isn't some sort of sign. Like I've ignored all the others and God is throwing me one last clue."

"You can't be serious. The citizenship writ is a sign *not* to marry me? Gracie and your granny's health issue are signs for us not to wed?"

"Well, what would you think if you were me?" She knew in her head that she was not making one bit of sense. But her heart said, "Soldier on, sister."

She took a long sip of water, trying to quench the parched place deep in her soul.

"This is ludicrous. Look at everything that's gone well, Susanna. Our wedding plans have fallen into place. The people of Brighton are embracing you. I daresay the citizens of the *world* are embracing you."

"People hate me too. A friend from home sent me a link to the latest Susanna hate blog."

"Blimey, why do they send you those blasted things? Do they think you want to see them?" He paced around the chairs. "I can't believe you're drawing our whole relationship into question. Teach me to fall in love! This is Adel all over again."

"Excuse me, but this is *not* Adel all over again." Susanna intercepted his path to confront him. "Adel never had the challenges I've had. She was only concerned about her privacy, and frankly, she's not done a good job of keeping her life out of the papers anyway. I resent the comparison."

"What would you have me believe? I've no choice here, Susanna. If you marry me, you must be a Brighton citizen and a Brighton citizen alone. The only other option is for me to abdicate —"

"Never." Susanna flashed him her palm. "You abdicate and this wedding is off for sure. I won't be responsible for the crumbling of the House of Stratton."

"Then what are we arguing about?" He pressed his hands on the back of a wing chair. "And by the way, I'm not Adam Peters toying with your heart until something better comes along."

"I know, I know." Susanna downed the last of her water.

"Do you? Because sometimes I believe you're still that girl on the beach waiting for him to propose."

"Yeah, and sometimes I believe you're the terrified lad who proposed publicly and got humiliated. And who started to think that no woman would want you because her life will never be her own."

"And? Am I wrong? That's precisely what you're saying to me now. That nothing of yourself will remain once you become a Brighton citizen and marry me."

Susanna conceded with an exhale. He was right. So what was bothering her? Really? She'd weighed the cost when she said yes to Nathaniel. She'd understood it meant leaving her life behind and beginning a new one in a new kingdom, with a new name and a new destiny.

But then the "Not Attending" RSVPs started rolling in and there was one thing after another. Pile on after pile on.

And something dark hovered over her heart.

"I don't even know what I'm doing here," she said barely above a whisper as she picked at the water bottle's paper label. "Nathaniel, what do you want with me? A plain ole common Georgia girl with red clay on her feet and sea salt in her blood."

"Is that the core of this issue? That you don't feel worthy? Susanna, you've seen me at my worst. You've seen my life. How can you question your value to me? I love you, Georgia girl."

"But don't you wonder? How can we make it? Marriage is hard enough without mixing cultures and nationalities, not to mention social classes."

"This? From an American? Your great melting pot nation was built on cultures and nationalities mixing. On tearing down the walls between social classes." He sighed and pressed his hand to his forehead. "Susanna, I'm beginning to think you really don't want to marry me. All these excuses —"

She set her water bottle down and crossed to the window. "I just feel homesick, like I'll never be myself again. I feel lost in the swirl of you, of the royal family, of the wedding. It's more about you and Brighton than you and me. Every other day I hear a story about how the people are afraid of my influence. How I'll turn you into an American." She raised the windowpane, ushering in a fresh, cold blast that shoved aside the stale, tepid air in the room. "I guess that's what the writ is about, huh?"

"How long have you been feeling this way?"

She shrugged. "I'm not sure I knew until now."

Her confession of doubt opened door after

door of fear, uncertainty, and dread. What if she gave up everything, even her citizenship, and the marriage failed?

"For now, please, I need to go home. Go back to ground zero, get my bearings, and sort out what I'm feeling."

"All right." His heavy exhale revealed his hurt. "But you fly on *Royal Air Force One.*" Nathaniel reached for his jacket and headed for the door. "Just tell me you're coming back, Susanna." He paused at the door, his blue eyes wet and shining.

"I think so." She twisted the antique diamond ring around her finger. "But I don't know."

Nathaniel regarded her for a moment and opened the door. "I'll have Jonathan make the arrangements."

Susanna knew Jonathan, Nathaniel's aide and friend, would call within the hour to discuss details, searching for details that went beyond a proposed departure time and which Georgia airport she preferred. He'd want to know what was going on. All without asking outright.

"Nathaniel," she said with almost no volume. "Thank you."

"Thank you?" He shook his head. "I already regret agreeing to this."

The sound of the door slamming as he

took his leave echoed in Susanna's heart
the rest of the night.

FOUR

On Monday afternoon Nathaniel muddled through his daily routine of scheduling and correspondence.

In truth, he thought of nothing but Susanna. His mood drifted toward an ever-widening, swirling black hole of fear. At any moment, he might collapse within himself, never to be seen again.

Like the time he leapt foolishly into the murky, cold waters of Roose Lake his frosh year at university. He sank beneath a quagmire of roots and weeds and barely found his way to the surface. His lungs nearly burst for want of air.

She'd been gone three days, and try as he might, he couldn't clear himself of the blasted, dark foreboding creeping through every molecule of his body: *She's not coming back.*

But she must. She simply must. However, the velvet pouch in his pocket warned him otherwise.

Rollins, the Parrsons House butler, had found Susanna's engagement ring on her dressing table the morning of her departure for home.

When he brought it to Nathaniel, his heart nearly stopped. Was she actually planning to stay in America?

Settle, mate.

Susanna had also left behind her favorite shoes, the gold Louboutins she wore to his coronation ball. And pictures. All of her family photos remained in her suite parlor and her bedchamber.

Surely she would return to Brighton. He inhaled long and slow. And she'd reclaim her ring.

Yet he could not deny her arguments about royal life. It was not easy. Susanna *was* giving up everything to marry him. Was he worth it?

Since the day she arrived in Brighton as the king's fiancée, the media immersed her into her own murky waters of scrutiny, nitpicking, and faultfinding.

Anything to sell papers or draw in viewers. All three Brighton news outlets sent crews snooping around St. Simons Island, searching for the underbelly of Susanna's American life and family.

One talk show tabloid spent a week, a *whole week,* on her relationship and breakup with the American Marine hero Adam Peters. Only half of the story's details were even partially true.

But despite the downsides of being associated with Nathaniel, Susanna was setting the world on fire. All on her own.

A billion viewers were estimated for their wedding. News outlets who'd all but forgotten about Brighton royalty battled the King's Office royal red tape for permits to send broadcast crews for the wedding.

Once Susanna mentioned in an interview that she loved the Scripture, "The joy of the Lord is your strength," every bookshop on the island promptly sold out of their Bibles. News presenters read Nehemiah 8:10 on air, and a children's choir performed a song based on the verse.

Her very presence boosted Brighton's economy. The fashion designers merely mentioned a frock they'd designed for her and online orders crashed their servers. Tourism was up last quarter by 5 percent.

"Knock, knock." Nathaniel's brother stuck his head inside the office doorway.

"Stephen, what brings you round this time of day?" His afternoons were consumed with rugby practice. He'd been playing for the national team since his return from Afghanistan where he served with the Royal Air Force.

"Came to see you." Dressed in slacks and a shirt, his black hair flowing loose about his sturdy face, he looked more and more like their Leo-the-Lion dad. Stephen crossed the wide, sunlit office and sat in a chair across from Nathaniel's desk. "You look horrible." Tact? Not with his little brother. "Not sleeping, are we? How are things with Susanna? Have you heard from her?"

"We've spoken once, but otherwise we seem to be missing each other." Nathaniel drummed the pen in his hand against the desk and stared at the financial report in front of him. Seeing but *not* seeing. "What are you about today? No practice?"

"My ankle is still bothering me. I'm taking some time off."

Nathaniel glanced up. "Time off? For a sprain? That doesn't sound like you. 'Play through the pain,' you always say."

"Yeah, well, not this time." Stephen stared at the floor, then at Nathaniel. "I came to check on you. Is everything all right?"

Nathaniel looked toward the tall, narrow window where the sunlight dimmed behind a cloud. "I don't know."

"How can you not know? You're getting married in a little more than a fortnight."

"Two weeks and four days."

"Spoken like a man in love," Stephen said. "I'd be counting the days too if I was marrying someone like Susanna. But here's my question for you. What are you doing here if she's there?"

"Giving her space. She's only gone home for a few days to see her granny and her friend Gracie. Besides, I've work to do, Stephen."

"What of this business about her American citizenship?"

"I see you've spoken with Mum, the family crier."

"She said Susanna might not want to give up her citizenship. Pretty bold of Brock Bishop and his party to tack on the writ."

"Yes, but I agree with them. Not because I mistrust Susanna, but for our descendants and the future of the throne."

Stephen whistled, leaning forward on his arms. "She must feel betrayed, Nate. You're no better than our ancestors who authored the Marriage Act to keep royals from marrying foreigners."

"I disagree." Nathaniel rocked forward in his chair, resting his elbows on the desk. "Marry whom you will, but the spouse of a

Brighton royal *must* be a Brighton-only citizen. It's not too much to ask for the spouse of a royal in line to the throne."

"But you must see her side. She's doing all the giving, all the changing."

"I realize that." Nathaniel sighed and recapped his Parrsons House conversation with Susanna to his brother. "She is overwhelmed." He moved to the window. The first of spring's green leaves had started budding on the oaks lining the palace grounds. "Rollins found this. Brought it to me this morning." Nathaniel pulled the pouch from his pocket, dangling it from his fingers. "Susanna's engagement ring."

Stephen whistled again. "She left it behind?"

"On purpose or not, I don't know, but Rollins found it on her dressing table." Nathaniel slipped the ring back into his pocket and it burned like a hot coal. "I don't know what I'll do if she doesn't come back."

"Big brother, snap out of it. Go get her. Don't sit around *hoping* for the outcome you want. It's been three days. I can't believe you're not packing to leave. For pity's sake, you're a king. Act like one. Look at you, pouting like a helpless child."

"Just what do you suggest? I wing my way to St. Simons Island, grab her by the hair, and order her home?" Nathaniel returned to his desk. "You should've seen her face when I told her she had to renounce her American citizenship. She's already put up with leaving her home, her career, family and friends, taking on all the burdens of marrying a royal, but this last request required the only thing she really had left of herself."

"Balderdash. She's plenty left of herself. Her faith. Her love for you, and yours for her. Her talent as a landscape architect, her way with people. Get over there and remind her of those things. For pity's sake, act like a king. Remind her that she's a princess. Remind her that you are worth all she's giving up. Remind her of who she is with or without her American citizenship. Do what needs to be done to win her heart. She loves you, Nate. You need her. I daresay we all need her."

Nathaniel squinted at his brother. "Fine speech, but does she need us? I can't imagine why she'd want to marry me with all the trappings I come with. It can be a privileged life, but also brutal and hurtful. Someone actually e-mailed her a link to a blog dedicated to hating and criticizing her. The blog title is not worth repeating in polite company. And what do you think I've been doing since she moved to Brighton but reminding her of the very things you mentioned?"

Despite his words of protest, Nathaniel had spent the weekend talking himself out of exactly the kind of plan his brother was suggesting. Part of him ached to put his schedule in the rubbish bin and go after her, while the other part convinced himself to leave her be and give her the courtesy of space. She'd come round when she was ready. Right?

"Go get her. Tell her in no uncertain terms. If you ask me, you're not giving her enough credit."

"Really? Then why did she leave?"

He shrugged. "Perhaps she was a bit overwhelmed. What bride isn't? Let alone one becoming a part of our family. But you leaving her be is just confirming all of her fears. I say again, go after her."

"I'm not sure one human heart can love another as much as we are asking of her."

"Blimey, Nathaniel, you're a blasted cynic. Mum wasn't born and raised a royal, but she adjusted to royal life quite well."

"She was the daughter of a lord who groomed her to marry a king. And you know full well she struggled with the press in the beginning. But in her day there was no paparazzi. No blogs. No Twitter. No twenty-four-hour news cycle. There was a barrier between the press and the royal family."

"Nice to see you have your list of excuses memorized. So tell me, are you planning on being a bachelor the rest of your life? Or perhaps taking up Lady Genevieve's offer to marry, produce an heir, then get a divorce?"

"Don't be crass."

"Nathaniel." Stephen stood, towering over his brother. "Do you love her?"

"It hurts to breathe when I think of life without her." Nathaniel rose to his feet, gently pushing his brother back a step. "But I have to be realistic. Maybe I should let her go."

"You are a coward." Stephen headed for the door. "If you lose her, it won't be because of this citizenship writ or all of the things she has to give up to be your wife. It won't be because you're some magnanimous chap who freed the bird who wanted to fly. It will be because you're afraid." He eased open the door. "And that will mark your reign for the rest of your life."

FIVE

"Two days." Mama passed Susanna in the kitchen, her hair wet from her shower, curling in ringlets about her head. She flashed two fingers. "Then I'm kicking you out."

"Kicking me out? Fine, I'll live with Aurora in her tent."

Aurora, a former hotshot DC lobbyist, was a multimillionaire who lived on dimes and nickels in a tent in the woods. A kind of spiritual savant, she doled out her millions as she saw the need, along with divine messages from God.

Real ones. Bone-chilling ones.

She'd been a voice from heaven in Susanna's life when she first met Nathaniel, then only Crown Prince, visiting the island.

"For the life of me, girl . . ." Mama opened the cupboard for a coffee mug, then poured from the big pot Daddy had set to brewing before he headed off to get fresh fish for the day. No fancy machines for them. They still used the old-fashioned percolating kind.

"Besides, I came home to see Granny and Gracie."

"Well, you've seen them. They're fine. Why don't you just go back to Brighton and marry that boy?"

"Really, Mama? You think it's just that simple. That I've not thought this through a hundred bazillion ways?" The smooth, uneventful flight over on *Royal One* had given her entirely too much time to think.

Why did the citizenship request bother her so dang much? And more than that, why did she slip off her engagement ring and leave it behind?

Had her head already decided and her heart was catching up?

Susanna shoved her cereal bowl forward. There was still over half a bowl left, but she'd not really been hungry since she'd left Brighton. Her attempt at having breakfast was merely a reach for some kind of normalcy.

"I just can't help but wonder if maybe I didn't rush into this because I was stinging from losing Adam. Maybe I got swept up in the magic of it all."

"Poppycock. You didn't even know Nate was a prince for two weeks. Y'all were friends. Then he left. Shot out of here when his father died and you didn't see him for five months."

"What'd you do, keep a diary on my love life?"

Mama tapped her temple. "I got more in here than cobwebs and spiders. And never in my life have I seen you 'swept up in the magic' of anything. Not even Disney World." She laughed. "You met Cinderella and like to drove me crazy asking, 'But what's the girl's *real* name, Mama?'"

"Well, she didn't look like Cinderella to me."

"That's what I'm saying, Suz; you're a realist."

"Which is why I'm here now. I'm being a realist. Come on, Mama, in all your life, did you ever see me as a royal princess?"

"No, but when I saw you with Nate, I pretty much knew he was the one. You love him and it's written all over your face every time you hear his name. And the same goes for him. You should see him when you walk into a room. The rest of us are no more than buzzing flies on the wall. He adores you."

"Love. Adoration. Fine. But they don't make an enduring marriage."

"Know what your problem is, Susanna?" Mama rapped her knuckles on the island counter. "You're scared."

"Two minutes ago I was a realist." She snapped a couple of grapes from the fruit bowl in the center of the island.

"A scared realist." Mama snatched hold of Susanna's left hand. "What's this? Susanna Jean, where is your engagement ring?"

Shoot, she'd forgotten about her bare left finger. And wasn't Mama quick on the draw? Susanna had been hiding her left hand since she arrived home, but all this talk of being scared caused her to lower her guard. "I left it in Brighton." She curled her hands into her lap.

"Oh, have mercy —"

"Mama, Nathaniel and I both needed to think about what we're doing. Yes, it's down to the wire, but there's also a lot on the line. I left the ring in my suite at Parrsons House in case, for whatever reason, you know, I didn't go back. Hey, Nathaniel has just as much to think about as me. He could call any second to break off the whole thing. So don't put this all on me. Besides, I didn't want to be responsible for a two-hundred-year-old royal family heirloom."

In truth, her ring finger felt cold and empty, and she missed the beautiful antique designed for Queen Anne-Marie. She regretted her impulsive, childish decision.

She hoped the ring remained safe in her bedroom where she had left it. And that Nathaniel didn't find out.

"I'd like to wring that boy Adam Peters's neck for doing this to you. Making you scared to hang on to anything worthwhile because it might be ripped from your hands." Mama's hand smacked the counter. "Listen to me. You let fear keep you *with* Adam about ten years too long. Now fear is driving you *from* Nathaniel." Mama reached for her coffee cup, her eyes glued on Susanna.

That's the way she did it — she eyed a person until they confessed their deepest, darkest sin.

"Actually, Mama, fear is also making me wise up. This citizenship issue put everything in a fresh light." Susanna leaned against the counter, watching the sunlight wash the kitchen window. "Let's say I do this *one* last thing, in a series of *one* last things I've had to do to marry Nathaniel. There will be no going back. I'll forever be a citizen of Brighton Kingdom and never, ever again a native-born American citizen. Should we break up, for whatever reason, I'd have to immigrate back to my own country."

For a brief moment, she felt justified in

her dramatic exit from Brighton. After all, Nathaniel and the Parliament had asked a dramatic thing of her.

But what hit her afresh in the cozy old kitchen where she taught her baby sister to bake chocolate chip cookies was how bold and rash her move was when she slipped off Nathaniel's ring. Just how true was her commitment? How deep was her love?

"This ain't the kind of fear that makes one wise up. This is the kind that makes a girl run. You always ran to your *garden* as a kid to hide when you were afraid — which is exactly what you're doing now."

"Thank you for that, Professor Glo. I don't need your pop psychology. Besides, I ran to hide from you and Daddy when you got to fighting like wild animals, throwing dishes and four-letter words at each other."

Many of Susanna's girlhood evenings were spent hiding in her secret garden, her closet, hiding from the storms raging *inside* her house.

"I make no excuse." Mama sipped her coffee. "We were young and foolish when we got married. Divorce was the best thing that ever happened to us." Mama smiled. " 'Cause then we met Jesus, got healed, and remembered why we loved each other in the first place. But, Suz, you're grown now. You understand these things. Your teen years were pretty darn good as I recall. Daddy and I both apologized for your childhood. Did all we could to make it up to you. This fear is on you. It's yours to deal with no matter where or how you came by it. You stayed with Adam because you wanted a safe plan. And we see how well that *didn't* work for you. Now you're leaving Nathaniel to hide in your garden — this one just happens to be all of St. Simons. Marrying that boy is probably the *safest* plan you ever came by. Hear me now, Suz. If you let fear clip your wings now, you will never fly again."

Susanna made a face. "Never fly again? Don't be so dramatic, Mama." She moved out from under Mama's stare and carried her soggy Cheerios to the garbage disposal.

But Mama took hold of her shoulders and turned her around. "Fear is nothing but a big ole fake roar. You let it trip you up and, next thing you know, a mewing kitten will have you hightailing it to the hills. That's the way fear rolls. Don't look for it to play fair."

"Fear also teaches you a lesson," Susanna retorted. "Get a swat on the behind, you learn to behave. Touch a hot stove, you learn to keep your hands to yourself. Get burned by love, you understand that nothing, not even the truest of intentions, is a sure thing in this life."

"So this is how you're going to be? Cynical?"

"I prefer the term 'realist.' "

Mama started to reply, but her old Motorola cell phone buzzed from the counter. "Hold that thought. This might be your granddaddy with an update from the doctors." Mama answered as if it might be granddaddy, but her expression and tone changed as she conversed in low, clipped sentences. "Yes. Certainly. Of course. I see."

"Who is it?" Susanna slipped her arm around Mama's shoulder. "Is it Granddaddy?"

"Shhh." Mama waved her off, shaking her head, pinching up her face as she listened. "You can send it to my e-mail address. Yes, that's the one." Snatching up her purse from the kitchen table, Mama started for the garage. "We can manage from our end, yes."

Susanna trailed after her, unhooking her old bike from the pegs on the garage wall. "Mama, who is it? Is everything all right?"

She nodded, holding up one finger, closing her eyes, moving her lips as if memorizing what she heard on the other end of the call. "Thank you for calling."

"Who was that?"

"Restaurant business." Mama hopped behind the wheel of her truck without a backward glance at Susanna and fired up the engine. With a push of the remote, the door rose, creaking and moaning. Mama shifted into reverse. "See you later, Susanna Jean."

"Yeah, sure, see you later."

Susanna watched her leave, straddling her bike, feeling unsettled about their kitchen conversation. As if there were more to be said.

Was her commitment to Nathaniel true? Strong enough to endure criticism from bloggers and royal watchers? Strong enough to give up everything, including her citizenship? Susanna pedaled down the driveway onto Stevens Road, heading for Frederica.

What she didn't know, the Lord did. *If any of you lacks wisdom, you should ask God.*

The saline island breeze carried a lingering hint of winter, but the early morning sun promised a clear, warm day.

Susanna slowed as she approached the low stone wall surrounding the Christ Church grounds, her heart aching for a touch from the Spirit.

What was it about the unseen that made sense of the seen?

Settling her bike against the wall, Susanna passed under the ivy-covered entrance — a pitched roof covering over wooden seats — and stepped into the glorious atmosphere of the historic church grounds.

Tears flashed in her eyes as she cut across the lush, green lawn, still damp with the morning dew. She breathed in the crisp air, absorbing the sense that the Divine waited for her.

She found a sunny but secluded spot at the far corner of the yard, away from the activity of parishioners arriving at the white clapboard church for morning Bible study, and settled down against the trunk of a maple.

She waited before speaking, listening to the sounds around her — the distant voices going into the church, the cooing of mourning doves, the rustle of wind in the leaves.

"Father," she began, low and slow, addressing her prayer to her one true King, peace descending upon her soul. "Give me wisdom. Help me make sense of my own heart."

At the end of her petition, the world fell dramatically silent. No voices. No cooing. No shuffling leaves. Her thoughts remained tangled and knotted.

Talk to me, Lord.

Surely when she was stuck, God had a way out. An answer she never imagined.

Stretching out her legs, Susanna folded her hands over her middle and studied the blue patches of sky through the tree limbs.

The same blue as Nathaniel's eyes. She missed him. Mercy, what must he be thinking of her right now?

A fly buzzed around her ears and she batted it away.

In the distance, she heard the slap of a car door followed by a murmur of voices and the crunch of heels on the brick path.

If she were Nathaniel, she'd be doubting this relationship about now. What groom wouldn't, with a fiancée who was so dramatic and over the top as to leave her engagement ring behind?

If he found out about that, and she hoped he wouldn't. She opened her eyes and sat forward. *What was I thinking?*

Fear. Such a rude counselor.

God, wisdom! Please . . .

"I like to come out here myself to think and pray."

Susanna glanced right to see Reverend Smith approaching, dressed in khakis and a blue button-down shirt, his graying hair cropped close to his head.

"Reverend! Hey . . ." She started to rise but he dropped down onto the grass next to her.

"Mind if I join you?"

"Not at all." A fresh wash of tears flooded her eyes.

"Beautiful day." He propped his arms on his raised knees. In his midfifties, Reverend Smith had a youthful air, but his demeanor, his sermons, reflected his wise, contemplative life.

"Yes, it is." One more word, and she'd burst. Tears. Gushes. Sobs.

"Mind if I ask you a question?"

She shook her head.

"What are you doing here? Aren't you getting married in two weeks?"

She brushed away the slight trickle of tears twisting down her cheeks. "Two weeks and three days." She peered at him. "I think."

"You think?" He arched his brow. "Have you changed your mind? Because the hospitality ministry is very excited about the live broadcast we've planned for your wedding. There's going to be a pancake breakfast. We expect a big turnout." His soft laugh made her smile. "What's going on? Care to tell me?"

Susanna yanked at the blades of grass

beside her legs and recounted the events of last Friday to her pastor, right down to her argument with Nathaniel and her impulsive decision to leave her ring behind.

"Ah, I see. So the details were piling on, and then Nathaniel lit a fire under it all when he told you about your citizenship."

"Pretty much."

"But, my word, Susanna, you're marrying a king."

"Not as easy as it sounds. It's no movie, I tell you."

"Nor should it be. There's a lot of responsibility with marrying any man, let alone a king." The reverend patted her back.

"Yeah, I guess so." More tears.

"Tell me, why is the citizenship issue holding you back?"

"Because it means *everything* of me is gone. My nationality, my people, my culture. Is our love really worth it?"

"Jesus felt it was."

"I'm not Jesus."

He chuckled. "But you're called to be like Him. He gave up His citizenship in heaven to become a citizen of earth. He is wholly God, and wholly man, for the rest of eternity."

"Then Nathaniel should give up his citizenship for me." She was being a brat and knew it, but just for the moment, she wanted to sound out this idea.

"I don't know much about royalty, but I guess he'd have to abdicate his throne to surrender his citizenship."

"Exactly." More grass pulling. "And it's not an option. I can't be responsible for a nation losing their king. I'm no Wallis Simpson."

"Susanna, take a moment and raise your thoughts heavenward. What is God saying to you in this juncture?"

"I don't know. Why do you think I'm sitting here? I feel all jumbled up."

"Because you're trying to understand with your head." He patted his belly. "Listen here, in your spirit to the Holy Spirit. You're familiar with the biblical character Esther."

"Jewish refugee in ancient Babylon. Very beautiful, married the king and became a queen."

"Sound familiar? Could you be a modern-day Esther?"

"I don't see how. My marriage to Nathaniel won't likely save America from her enemies."

"But your marriage to Nathaniel may save other people. You'll have access to leaders the rest of us can only dream about. You are stepping onto the world stage, Susanna.

Your very presence influences people. Don't you see what God is doing?"

"Now you sound like Nathaniel." She peered at the reverend. "But how can a redneck girl from Georgia be an influence?"

He smiled. "Maybe you're exactly what the world needs. You're putting limits on yourself that God is not. Want to know how I see you? A woman who makes the whole world her backyard barbecue. You make people feel warm, welcome, invited. You're also a truth speaker. In all the good ways. As you move into the role of Nathaniel's wife, you're going to make royalty more accessible and therefore, in my humble opinion, make God more accessible."

She laughed, a bursting, scoffing sound. "Please, Reverend."

"Do you think you just stumbled into this relationship without any divine intervention? That the Lord was out to lunch when you met and fell in love with Nathaniel? You both overcame great odds to be together. Can you allow yourself to consider the idea that God is promoting you to royalty, like Esther, for such a time as this?"

"But I'm not worthy." She hung her head, letting her hair curtain her face.

"Ah, there's the rub." He bent to see her eyes. "You're making this about your worthiness instead of God's. None of us are worthy. Do you think I'm worthy to be a reverend? To pastor His flock?"

She raised her head, combing back her hair with her fingers. "You're a good man."

"I used to be a very bad man, Susanna. You've not heard my testimony?"

She squinted. "I thought you went to Bible college out of high school. Never did drugs, smoked, or ran with those who did."

"You're right. I went to Bible college, then seminary. Waited until I was married to Bren to have sex. Never dabbled in pornography. But oh, I was jealous and envious of my fellow scholars, a gossip, judgmental. Selfish."

"All right, I get it." She held up her hand. "None of us are righteous."

"No, not one." He fell silent for a long moment and his confession echoed across her mind. Then, "Susanna, I implore you to keep your ear near His heart. He'll speak to you. I understand your reserve about giving up your American citizenship. It's kind of the last thing that is solely yours as you go into this marriage. But may I remind you, you are first the Bride of Christ. You've already given up everything of who you are to be married to Him. You are more than an American. You are a citizen in the kingdom of God. A princess in His household. So don't put limits on yourself based on a natural citizenship when, technically, you've already given it up to be a member of a higher world — one that is and is to come. What if you're called to be a part of ushering in some aspect of God's kingdom here on earth by being a Brighton royal?"

Her heart burned with each of his challenges.

"You still think of yourself as the scared little girl hiding from her parents while they brought the house down on each other."

She nodded, her tears unstoppable. Reverend Smith was hitting on all cylinders today.

"But God sees a redeemed woman bought by His blood. One with a renewed heart and mind. Susanna, it's extraordinary. He's entrusting you to be a Christian example to people around the world. For such a time as this. Are you sure you want to give it all up to remain that scared little girl? Because I see a woman who broke out of her past, reached for the brass ring, got it, and is now letting fear rob her of her destiny."

"I thought I was over all of that." Susanna fell against him, her head resting on his shoulder, sobbing.

"Sometimes pressure brings up the last of the yucky old residue." He slipped his hand into hers, a soft prayer humming from his chest.

She wept for all the hours she'd hidden in her closet, pretending it was her magic garden while Mama and Daddy screamed obscenities at one another.

She wept for all the years she waited for Adam Peters, only to find out he wasn't her one true love.

She wept for her soul, her heart, her country, and all she was surrendering for the sake of love.

"You're saying good-bye to a life you've known up till now." The reverend shoved a worn, soft handkerchief into her hand. "Press on to what lies ahead, to the upward call of Christ, the apostle Paul told us. And forget what lies behind. Something better awaits you."

The reverend's final words cut through every cloud of confusion and a blip of joy smacked her heart.

Susanna sat up, mopping her face with his white hankie. "I asked the Lord for an answer and He sent me you." She smiled, peering at him. "Thank you, Reverend, thank you."

"Did I help?"

"Very much." Weird, now that the tears had dried up and the confusion had lifted, she felt so much lighter. Free.

Standing, she dusted the grass and leaves from her jeans. "I know what I need to do. I only hope it's not too late."

Six

Nathaniel tossed his suitcase in the master suite of the St. Simons Island cottage. This had been the royal family's American getaway since 1902.

"Liam," he said, jogging down the stairs. "Let's head to the Rib Shack, see if we can locate Susanna." His chief security officer fell in step off of his right shoulder.

They'd arrived on the island an hour ago, set up the chief and staffers he'd brought along at the Prince and King Hotel before heading for the family cottage.

Listening to their syncopated footfalls scuff over the gravel drive as they made their way toward the SUV, Nathaniel second-guessed his decision to not ring up Susanna with his plans.

He thought to surprise her, but now he wished he'd told her he was coming.

Oh, how he missed her, ached to hear her voice, to see her face. Back in Brighton, he had often met her for luncheons and they dined every evening together, spending weekends touring Brighton's glorious mountain retreats or walking the winter shores.

He was addicted to her being in his life. Living without her would be unbearable. Susanna brought him gifts he hadn't realized he was lacking: ease, courage, and the joy of feeling comfortable in his own skin.

Liam headed down Frederica toward the Rib Shack as Nathaniel stared out his window, Wednesday's soft evening light flickering past.

Being back on the island made him all the more homesick for Susanna.

He prayed that three days had been enough time for her to think. To perhaps miss him. To decide he was worth her everything.

Nathaniel's thoughts came round as Liam turned into the Rib Shack's sand-and-seashell car park.

As he stepped out into the evening shade of the guarding oaks, he scented the heady fragrance of grilling meat and sweet barbecue.

The sight of the Shack, the fragrant aromas, put him in mind of the summer he came here on holiday, met Susanna, and signed on to work for her mama as she enlisted the aid of anyone and everyone to share her daddy's workload after his heart attack.

Nathaniel warmed with the memories of his days at the Shack. He'd spent several *happy* evenings scrubbing grease vats and Cloroxing toilets as an ad hoc employee. No one knew he was a prince.

He'd do it again to be near Susanna. To be a normal bloke.

Cutting around to the back of the restaurant, Nathaniel took the deck steps two at a time, the warm sea breeze shoving against his back, and drew open the kitchen's screen door.

"Glo?" he called, scanning the kitchen for his future mother-in-law. The place was hopping, with two chefs on the grill and two at the prep table.

Bristol, a lean, ponytailed Shack employee, stood at the service window calling out orders. "Keri, pick up, table ten."

When she turned to garnish a plate of ribs, she caught sight of him standing in the doorway.

"Well, I'll be." She curtsied, smiling. "Welcome, Your Majesty."

"Bristol, it's a pleasure to see you." He

97

nodded, returning her smile. He checked the urge to tell her that since she was American, protocol dictated that she didn't need to curtsy. But she looked rather practiced and polished. He'd not deny her the effort. "Tell me, is Glo about?"

"In the office." Bristol tipped her head to the kitchen's back corner. "Y'all hungry? I'll pull you a plate if you'd like. Liam, you cotton to baby back ribs if I recall."

"You remembered." Liam checked with Nathaniel before passing through to the dining room.

The big chap was all but licking his chops at the mention of baby backs.

Nathaniel rapped lightly against the office door frame. "Permission to enter?"

"You made it." Glo popped up from her chair, reaching for him, wrapping him up in a hug. "How's my favorite son-in-law?" Stepping back, she held him at arm's length, her warmth and down-home goodness embracing the weariest places of his being.

"Better now that I've seen you." He eased down to the chair adjacent to her desk. A bit younger than his own mum, Glo was a beauty with a bit of brawn in her soul. He could see Susanna in her features, in her actions. And he admired her.

"Ha! You didn't fly four thousand miles to

see *me*."

"Well, not expressly, no." He leaned forward. "Have you seen Susanna? I thought to surprise her, but now I wish I'd rung her."

"She headed out on her bicycle this morning, just as your assistant called saying you were on your way. I've not seen her since."

"She doesn't know, though, about the plan?" The plan he prayed worked. That he'd not set himself up, once again, to be rejected by the woman he loved. Though his "love" for Adel was nothing more than youthful infatuation and lust.

"She does not. I only told the *necessary* folks, just like you asked." Glo shot him a sneaky smirk as she reached down, tugging open a bottom desk drawer. "Got the specifications from your assistant —"

"Jonathan, my aide." Of course she *knew* Jonathan, but he was nervous, filling the void with words.

Glo passed him the printed checklist. "As you can see, I conquered half of them today. The food has been ordered. Still waiting on some of the bigger ticket items."

Nathaniel scanned the checked items, excitement blooming in his chest, clouded only by the realization he had yet to speak to his beloved. He passed the list back to Glo. "Thank you for your help. I know I imposed upon you."

"Pshaw, boy, it's for my Suz. We've not been able to do much for the Brighton wedding. It's my honor to help with this."

"Spare no expense. I'll pay whatever to have the turnaround we need."

"Dollars and cents? Now you're speaking southern Georgian. But Gib and I got most of this. A few folks got so excited about your plan, they offered their services for free."

"No, no, Glo, I insist on paying. Otherwise it is meaningless if it cost me nothing."

"I could say the same thing." She slapped her palm against the desk, then slipped the paper back into the bottom drawer. "We should be good to go by Friday evening. We got tonight and all day tomorrow to tidy up this list."

"Whatever remains unaccomplished, remains. It is only important that Susanna is there. Speaking of my true love, where should I look for her? Your home? Might she be at the hospital? How is your mum?"

"*Mum* is doing just fine. She went home this morning. She's sitting up, taking food on her own. She'll live to be a hundred, God willing." Glo reached for the desk phone. "Let me see if I can't track her down."

While Glo made a few calls, Nathaniel paced the small office stuffed with supplies and old lamps.

On a whim, he'd put forth this idea, his only idea, to woo back Susanna.

He could not abdicate his throne over the citizenship debacle, but he could meet Susanna on her side of the world and do his level best to prove he loved her and wanted to marry her no matter what her citizenship.

Now if only she still wanted him.

She didn't seem the kind of woman to run out on her commitments readily. But all bets were off when one was challenged right down to the core of her identity.

"Nathaniel!" Avery dashed into the office and roped him in a big hug. No pretense. No inhibitions. Just love. "You're here. I'm sooo excited. Mama, I found the dress in Granny's things."

"Good girl." Glo dialed another number. "Did you drop it off at Morgan's? Nathaniel, she's not answering her phone — let me try her granny's."

"Yep, and they're putting the bum's rush on it." Avery perched on the edge of the desk, her eyes bright. "Is Colin coming?"

Ah yes, his young cousin. The prince who was stealing another Truitt girl's heart. "He's on his way with Mum and Stephen as we speak. We're running out of royal aeroplanes. Susanna has *Royal One.* I flew on *Royal Two* with the accompanying staff. Mum, Stephen, and Colin along with Jonathan had to charter from a private carrier."

Avery twisted up her lips, snapping her fingers. "And to think, the rest of us have to fly coach."

"All right, missy." Glo poked her in the back, holding the phone receiver to her ear. "You have homework? If not, I could use an extra hand in here tonight. Sue Ellen called in sick. Hello, Marlee, Glo Truitt here. Susanna's not around the shop, is she? Getting her hair done?" She listened with a grimace, then hung up. "Well, no one's seen her since this afternoon. She visited her granny around noon. Then popped by Gracie's a little after two and left there before three. She's not at Gracie's salon nor at the house —"

"Y'all looking for Suz?" Avery said, popping up from her perch on the edge of the desk. "Mama, I can't stay. I've got a team meeting." She tugged her phone from her rucksack. "Did y'all try to call her?"

"Did you just hear me say she's not answering her phone?"

"Yeah, Mama, you have a different ring tone — Suz, hey, it's me. Where are you?" Avery grinned at Nathaniel. "When are you coming home? I want to order a large cheese pizza from Sal's." Avery's eyes widened with surprise. "You're in Savannah? Waiting to take off for Brighton? You realize you love Nathaniel and want to go back to Brighton? Why am I repeating everything you say?"

Avery shot Nathaniel a visual plea. *What do I do?*

He motioned for her to keep talking as he retrieved his phone and dialed *Royal One*'s satellite phone.

"So," she said, elevating her tone with a bit of merriment. "I bet Nathaniel is excited you're coming back. What? Right, right, you want to surprise him. Cool, way cool." She made a face, shrugging at Nathaniel. "Well, I'm sorry you won't be home for pizza. But hey, the only thing that trumps hot cheese pizza is true love, right?" *Ha-ha.* "Okay, I'll tell Mama you've left. We'll see you in a couple of weeks."

"Here, let me talk to her." Glo took the phone from Avery, whispering to Nathaniel, "If she's fixing to take off . . . you best hurry and do whatever it is you can do to stop that plane. Mercy, I sound like I'm in a movie or something."

Nathaniel was on it, his chest buzzing with untethered emotions, aware of the ramifications. Her plan was ruining his.

But Susanna was returning to Brighton. Of her own accord. He smiled, then stepped out of the office, through the kitchen, and onto the back deck.

Fabian Rainwater, a former pilot for the RAF before joining the king's service, answered the sat phone.

"Fabian?"

"Your Majesty, is everything all right?"

"Listen, please don't react if Susanna is in hearing range. But do not take off."

"I'm in the cockpit now. What reason shall I give her? We're wheels up at eight o'clock."

"I'm here. On St. Simons Island to surprise her."

"I see. Under the radar, I imagine."

"Very much so."

"It's not easy being a king in moments like these, is it?" A soft, humorous lilt bent his words. "What reason shall I give her for the delay?"

"You're the pilot, Fabian. Make something up."

"Mechanical?"

"Perfect. But one that cannot be solved easily. No waiting round in Savannah overnight. She must return to the island."

"Will do, sir."

"Fabian, you must come along as well.

And your copilot."

"For any special reason?"

"Indeed. A very special reason."

Nathaniel rang off and tucked his phone in his jeans pocket, his stomach rumbling for the tangy taste of barbecue, his heart churning for her love.

SEVEN

Susanna thumped her suitcase back up the back deck of the Rib Shack, exhausted and disheartened and discombobulated, the ordeal of the past few days weighing on her.

The citizenship writ in Brighton. Her decision to come home. The lack of communication with Nathaniel. Her morning conversation with Mama. Her encounter with Reverend Smith at Christ Church.

Her subsequent decision to return to Brighton.

Visiting with Granny one last time before flying home. She was comforted by the light in Granny's eyes and the color on her cheeks.

A final stop by Gracie's.

Scurrying home to pack and get down to Savannah, meet up with the pilot, and wait for wheels up.

The disappointing news that the plane had mechanical problems.

Hiring a car to return to St. Simons with the pilots, Fabian and Roark.

She had spent the car ride with her forehead pressed to the dark window, hiding her tears.

See, this was exactly why she *planned* things. She wore spontaneity like a wet sack. Thin and falling apart. She should've never left Brighton. Now it seemed as if she'd hit a brick wall on returning.

Lord, please, tell Nathaniel I love him.

She'd tried to call — forget surprising him — but his phone went straight to voice mail. So instead she rang Rollins and asked him to arrange for a car to meet her at the Brighton airport.

Then Susanna instructed her lady's maid, Ansley, to make sure the emerald green Alexander McQueen party dress was ready to go. She would surprise Nathaniel at dinner.

But not tomorrow night after all. Darn plane.

"Well." Mama stepped onto the deck, a dish towel in her hands. "Just where have you been?"

"Believe it or not, trying to get back to Brighton."

Mama snapped the air with her towel, tipped back her head, and raised her hand toward heaven. "Thank You, Lord. Finally."

"I'm not in the mood, Mama." Susanna kicked her suitcase against the deck rail to let a young family pass.

Mama hollered toward the kitchen door. "Bristol, you got customers on the deck." She joined Susanna at a table. "So, you were heading home?"

Home? Brighton *was* home, wasn't it? "I wanted to surprise Nathaniel."

"What happened?" Mama ran her strong, soft hand over Susanna's hair, brushing it away from her neck. Her unexpected tenderness brought Susanna's tears to the surface. "What made you decide to go back?"

"I prayed a prayer." Susanna recapped her conversation with Reverend Smith, leaving out the part where she cried over her childhood. Mama didn't need piled-on guilt.

"So why aren't you winging it toward Brighton?"

"Mechanical problem. The part won't arrive until Friday."

"It's going to be all right, Susanna."

"You don't know that, Mama." She vaulted off the picnic table bench. "The more I think about it . . . the longer I'm away from Nathaniel, he's not going to want me back. What kind of woman slips off her engagement ring because the life of her intended comes with certain requirements? I mean, if he was the head of Apple and I was a peon at Microsoft, I wouldn't think twice about resigning."

"But he's not asking you to quit your job, Suz. Like you said, he's asking you to give up your very identity. You'd no longer be an American citizen with all of our family's heritage and tradition. You're moving a long way from the poor Irish farmers who came to this country looking for a better way of life."

"Wait, now you're saying I did the right thing by leaving?"

"No, I'm saying I understand why you panicked. You were right to take time to think about it. Did you overreact? A bit, but you've made a lot of very big changes in the last year and a half." Mama flicked the towel at Susanna's legs. "I'm proud of you."

"I'm not so proud of myself, but —"

"Susanna!" She whirled around to see Aurora emerging from the pines and palmettos that lined the path to the beach. "What in the world?" Aurora called out. "You're not supposed to be here." The woman scurried up the deck steps wearing a mismatched outfit of a summer dress over jeans with an oversized men's sweater that might have been the style in the 1950s.

"Came home to think."

Aurora, with her white-blonde hair and bright red fingernails, circled the picnic bench where Mama sat and glared at Susanna through narrowed eyes.

Her testimony was a simple one-line pitch. "I went crazy and returned to my right mind, and to my God."

"Listen to me." Susanna flinched as Aurora jumped up on the bench, startling Mama. "You belong in a palace." She fired her hand in the air, pointing east, toward the Atlantic and Brighton's shores. "You don't know, Susanna. You don't know . . ."

"What don't I know, Aurora?" The woman wafted so much between the natural and the supernatural that at any given moment she might be speaking from the Spirit or from the craziness of her own soul.

Let the hearer beware . . .

"Such a time as this." She wagged her long, skinny finger at Susanna. "Such a time. Such a time."

"That's what Reverend Smith said."

"Then there you have it." Aurora jutted her hand to her waist, standing on the bench like a skinny, worn-out Wonder Woman. "Glo, what's cooking?" She sniffed the air.

"You know what's cooking, Aurora. You

hungry?" Mama exchanged a glance with Susanna. She always leaned toward Aurora being crazy. But Susanna knew better. Aurora had declared, "The prince is coming," just days after Susanna met her prince under Lovers' Oak.

She didn't know he was a prince, but somehow Aurora knew.

"I am, Glo." Just like that, Aurora shifted gears, jumped down off the bench, and followed Mama through the kitchen door.

But when she glanced back at Susanna, the glint in her eye ignited a flame in Susanna's spirit.

"Don't be afraid," she said. "Fear is the opposite of faith. And without faith —" She shook her head. "You can't please Him."

For moments after Aurora went inside, Susanna burned with the fire of truth, leaning against the deck rail, exhaling the embers of doubt and fear.

This wasn't about giving up her citizenship but about giving up *all* of herself. The final call of God was to surrender all of her plans to Him — her identity, who she thought she was and wanted to be.

What did it matter what country she belonged to in this world when she was a citizen of God's glorious kingdom?

And how many times in her life had she

been willing to surrender her heavenly citizenship for the momentary pleasures of this world?

Far too often.

Her heart churned with a blend of joy and grief. Joy at what Jesus afforded her. Grief at how little she understood its power. Loving Nathaniel was also about loving her Lord and being true to Him above all else.

As she made her way down the sandy path to the beach, Susanna's heart whispers came to life. "I know You can fix the mess I've made, but help my heart to believe," she prayed. "Tell Nathaniel to call me? Or listen to my gazillion voice mails? Lord, help my weak, frail heart."

Heading north on the beach, into the wind, with the light of the stars and waterfront houses guiding her, she struggled to keep the flame of truth alive.

She now added guilt to the battle of doubt and fear. She should've never left Brighton.

Up ahead, a small light bounced over the sand. Someone was walking her way. A man. He had broad, square shoulders and a long, even gait.

She knew that stance. That stride.

Nathaniel?

She picked up her pace, and when she caught the glint of his glossy black hair in the bold white light burning from the edge of the Island B&B, she kicked up her heels and began running on the smooth wet sand.

"Nathaniel!" The crashing waves roared against the shore. She saw him quicken his own pace. She fired into his arms the moment she reached him. "Oh my gosh, you're here. You're here."

He caught her up, lifting her off the ground, swinging her around, kissing her cheek. "I'm sorry, love, I'm sorry. I should've never let you go."

"No, no, it was me, babe, all me."

He buried his face against her neck, and his warm breath sent chills skirting over her skin. "I was scared of losing you. I wanted to tell you." He set her down. "I promise not to hide things again. Especially in matters of your heart and mine."

"I promise not to overreact. This is a whole new life for me, Nathaniel, but I'm ready." She exhaled. "I'm ready."

"But if you aren't, we can postpone —"

She rose up on her toes and kissed him, pressing her hands against the sides of his head, weaving her fingers through the silky threads of his hair. "I don't want to wait. In fact, I was flying home to you —"

His kiss stole her breath and invoked warm waves of passion, each crashing sensation eroding her fears and awakening her love. When he broke the magic of the moment by lifting his lips from hers, she swooned against him.

"It feels like forever since I've seen you."

"Susanna, two years ago when we stood on this beach, right after Adam broke things off, I told you I could never marry you." He lifted her chin, and by the way he tipped his head, she could see love reflected in his eyes by the beachside lighting. "The law prevented me. But tonight I tell you I am desperate to marry you. Even if you don't renounce your American citizenship, I will marry you."

"Nathaniel, your political enemies will have you for lunch."

"And I'll have them for dessert. I must have you in my life. I've no doubt the Lord brought you to me, and I'm going to trust Him for the outcome of our union. If they destroy me, then let Him see to them."

"Funny." She smoothed her hand over his chest. "But I was flying home to tell you I will do what you and the law ask. This morning Reverend Smith reminded me I'm more than a citizen of the US or Brighton, but a citizen of God's kingdom." She stepped out of his embrace, collecting her feelings, gathering them into words. "It's like . . . wow . . . the largeness I've felt in my heart for the past two years, like there was something more, suddenly made sense. I'm not just Susanna Truitt, American girl, or Brighton princess, I'm a daughter of the King of Heaven."

With each declaration of truth, joy carved a new path in her heart.

"And I'm a son of that very same kingdom."

"So it doesn't matter if I'm American or Brightonian as long as I'm following Him. Serving my Lord."

"Susanna, my American love." He dropped to one knee. "Marry me. Please." He fumbled for something in his pocket. She smiled when the cool sensation of platinum slid down her finger.

"My ring! You found it." She knelt in front of him.

"Rollins brought it to me. I thought I was a goner until Stephen came along and kicked me in the britches."

"Oh, God bless Stephen. Nathaniel, I've been so foolish. Please forgive me —"

"Forgive me."

"Absolutely, and yes, I'll marry you. I'll become a full-blown Brighton citizen. What does it matter as long as we are together?"

His kiss was tender and sweet, then ardent

115

and passionate as he enveloped her in his arms and sank down on the beach.

When the doorbell rang in the middle of Friday afternoon, Susanna opened the door to find Jonathan, Nathaniel's aide, standing on the veranda in knee breeches, waistcoat, cravat, and white stockings with gold buckle shoes.

"You've got to be kidding me."

"Milady." The man bowed, presenting her with a sealed envelope. "An invitation from the king. I will await your reply."

"When did you get here?" She took the envelope, flipping it over to see the back. It was plain and white, but composed of thick, pressed linen. "We're meeting for dinner at six. What's this about?"

"Does the lady wish me to read the invitation for her?"

Susanna laughed. This was over the top. "No, the lady does not."

"Suz, who's at the door?" Avery shoved in next to her, pressing her shoulder against the doorjamb. "Jonathan, dude, Halloween isn't for seven months. But *kicking* costume."

"Whatever do you mean?" He speared her with a long, hard gaze. "I'm delivering a missive for His Royal Highness, King Na-

116

thaniel II."

"A missive? Well, la-te-da." Avery draped her arm over Susanna's shoulder and tapped the invitation. "What does the missive say?"

Susanna turned toward the living room as she tugged the stiff stock card from the envelope. Inside was an elegant invitation engraved in navy script.

It would be my honor
if you would join me
this evening
7:00 p.m.

Goose bumps ran down her arms and tingled over her scalp as she studied the words, trying to read between the lines. "Jon, what's he up to?" she said, returning to the door. "Join him for what?"

"What answer shall I give His Majesty?" Jonathan remained in character, stiff and unemotional, keeping his eyes fixed on the far corner of the veranda. Yet he was not quite able to hide the twitch on the edge of his lips.

"Tell him yes, but just exactly for what will I be joining him?"

Jon snapped his fingers at a nearby SUV with tinted windows. Liam popped out wearing his customary dark suit — thank goodness, something that made sense in this scene — carrying a large box tied with an enormous purple bow. He dashed up the steps to hand it to Susanna.

"And this is?"

"For this evening, milady. Your carriage will be along at six forty precisely."

"Carriage? Six forty? Jon, Nathaniel is ten minutes away. Five if there's no traffic. I can drive myself."

"Six forty, milady."

She made a face. Something was up. "All right . . . Does he require anything else of me? This isn't about the citizenship oath, is it?"

Jonathan stepped off the veranda with a bow, still very much in the role of royal footman. Inside the house, Avery hovered, begging Susanna to open the box.

"Hold your horses." She set the gift on the kitchen table, thinking, wondering, fingering the silky purple bow. "What do you think this is about?"

"Suz, he's romancing you. Go with it. Don't overthink it. Heck, you never know how long this kind of stuff will last."

Susanna made a face. "How would you know, Dr. Love?"

"Locker room talk." Avery shoved the box toward Susanna. "Open it!"

Susanna grinned, her expectation pinging. "This is kind of fun." She loosened the ribbon and lifted the box lid. Shoving back a layer of white tissue paper, she sighed, tears springing to her eyes when she saw the pale mauve satin gown. "Oh my, Granny's wedding dress." She slipped her fingers through the spaghetti straps and lifted the sixty-four-year-old dress from the box. "Aves." She drilled her sister with a steely stare. "Where did he get this?"

"Me, of course." Pure. Without guile.

"And why did you give him this dress?" Susanna held the gown against her with trembling, adrenaline-charged hands.

"I was digging around in Granny's things and —"

"You found the dress and gave it to Nathaniel?" Susanna inspected the lace and sequin flowers and the gold cord appliqué. "It's been cleaned and pressed."

"Well, you didn't want to wear it wrinkled, did you?"

"Avery Mae." Susanna reached out to pinch her sister's arm. "You tell me what's going on right now."

But the lithe volleyball star ducked out of the way. "You know what? You need to learn to live in the moment." She scooped a handful of M&M's from the dish on the kitchen counter. "I'm out of here. Volleyball practice." She scooped up her gym bag. "Hey, Suz, your gold Louboutins will go great with that dress."

"Yes, but they're in Brighton. And I'm only hanging out at Nathaniel's cottage, right?"

"Suit yourself." Avery shrugged, reaching for the doorknob.

"*Right,* Avery?"

"Whatever." The door clapped behind Avery.

"Avery!" But she was gone.

Susanna turned back to Granny's gown. It was beautiful. Expectation bloomed into excitement as she dashed upstairs to try it on.

She'd discovered Granny's wedding dress when she was eleven and begged to try it on. When Granny finally relented, Susanna stood in front of the hallway mirror, her lean preteen body lost in the bodice and wide skirt, but her womanly heart was mesmerized.

She'd promised herself then and there she'd wear the gown for her wedding.

Someday. When true love found her. But once she became engaged to Nathaniel and started taking appointments with Brighton designers, she knew she'd never be able to wear something this simple and vintage to marry a king.

In her room, she turned on the light and closed the shades. Shimmying out of her jeans and top, she stepped through the crinolines and tulle, drawing the silky skirt over her hips, sensing the history and tradition of her grandparents' devotion slide along her skin.

The dress fit without her needing to suck in her gut or her breasts flowing over the top. Dashing to the closet, she shoved open the door for a pair of shoes. Maybe Avery had a pair she could wear.

She gasped when she flipped on the light. Oh bother, more tears.

There on the tile floor, neatly posed, were her gold-bedazzled Christian Louboutins. All the way from Brighton.

Susanna grinned, hugging the shoes to her chest. *Thank You, Jesus.* She didn't care how they got there, just that they did. Whatever Nathaniel was planning for this evening, she would embrace it.

Because love was proving itself over and over, and conquering all her fears.

EIGHT

On Friday evening precisely at six forty, Susanna stepped onto the veranda, her gold Louboutin shoes resounding against the wide boards.

She breathed deeply, filling her lungs with the fragrance of the island. With the fragrance of love.

For the first time since she had said yes to Nathaniel, she *felt* like a princess.

The breeze dipped a bit lower and swished the hem of Granny's gown, twirling the folds against her legs. She glanced down to see the gold and crystal shoes sparkling in the early evening light.

Gracie had insisted on sending a stylist from her salon to do Susanna's makeup and hair. Lexi arrived at three thirty with her bag of magic tricks to fashion Susanna's hair into a loose updo with long golden curls dangling about her neck, and to apply her makeup.

A laugh rumbled in her chest. She pressed her hand over her lips, keeping her smile inside, growing wider and warmer.

I am in love with a king. With Nathaniel of Brighton.

She'd been so overwhelmed with moving to Brighton — adjusting to a new country and culture, developing her young relationship with Nathaniel, and planning a wedding — she'd not considered her own royal reality.

Susanna raised her chin to the breeze as it twisted her curls about her shoulders. Reverend Smith was right. Her new station in life afforded her such great opportunities for good.

Oh Lord, use me to make Your Son's name famous.

She had no idea what Nathaniel had planned for this evening — he'd been unavailable all day today. Something about kingdom business. But she'd planned to surrender her heart fully to him tonight.

If love demanded her whole identity and being, then she'd give it. Unreservedly. Fear had no place in the heart of a princess.

The sound of horse hooves resounding against the asphalt drew her attention to the road as a pair of matched white mares with gleaming coats turned down the driveway drawing a glossy black and gold open carriage with red spoke wheels.

Susanna gasped, pressing her hand over her heart, falling against the porch post.

Jonathan, still dressed in his footman costume, rode on the back. He hopped down when the carriage stopped at the veranda steps, bowing and offering his hand. "Your carriage awaits."

"This is too much . . . too much. Jon, where are we going?" She slipped her hand into his as he aided her into the carriage, settling her onto the rich red leather seats.

Jonathan patted the side of the carriage and spoke to the driver. "Be off with you now." He hopped onto the back as the driver chirruped to the horses.

"Burt, hey." Susanna leaned forward, glancing up at the man steering the horses. "How'd you get this gig?" Burt, a longtime family friend and customer of the Rib Shack, was the owner of Glynn Carriages.

But this was no carriage she'd ever seen him drive before. He wore a solemn expression along with a crisp, dark suit, cravat, and top hat.

"Milady." His gaze twinkled down on her as he tipped the brim of his hat.

Susanna sat back, smiling. Nathaniel was winning her all over again, shining his light of love in the hidden recesses of her heart, those private places she felt too guarded to reveal. Even when she was with Adam, she hid those secret rooms from his heart's eye.

But Nathaniel's efforts spoke to her, drew her out of hiding. He made her feel what she'd longed to feel since she first hid in her bedroom closet, turning it into a magical garden as her parents fought the War of the Truitts. Safe. He made her feel truly, entirely safe.

She could spread her arms wide, breathe in life, and know nothing would smash her in the gut.

At the end of Steven's Road, the carriage turned north instead of south toward Nathaniel's Ocean Boulevard cottage.

"Jonathan?" She peered up at the royal aide-turned-footman. "Where are we going?"

He ignored her, eyes fixed straight ahead.

She would see when she arrived. The clop-clop of the horses' hooves paired with the gentle sway of the carriage from side to side rocked her into a sweet peace. If one was going to be a princess, then one must learn to *enjoy* being a princess. She pictured Nathaniel, aching to be in his arms.

Burt called a gentle, deep "Whoa" to the horses as he pulled up to Christ Church.

Susanna angled forward, squinting at the massive glow dripping down from the trees, soaking the grounds in a white, cozy light. Did she hear an orchestra?

"Milady." Jonathan appeared at her side, offering his hand.

Raising her skirt, Susanna stepped over the side of the carriage, landing softly on the ground, shards of excitement fueling her pulse.

"What's going on, Jon?" She held on to his hand, refusing to let him step forward.

"You know, Suz, you ask too many questions."

She balked at his abrupt break of character. "Wouldn't you?" she said, squeezing his fingers.

"If you'll walk with me, and let go of my hand so some of the blood can flow to my heart, you'll have your answer." Jonathan twisted his hand from her grasp, making a face.

With a slight push on her elbow, he directed her toward the front door, pausing when they stepped under the garden entrance.

"I've been silent about things since you left Brighton, Susanna, because it was not my place to speak. But since I'm on American soil, I'll act the part of an American.

126

Don't be a bugger."

She bristled. "Jon, look, I —" Susanna broke off, laughing. "Okay, I won't be a bugger."

He grinned. "I know this is not all easy for you, but you need to know I've never seen Nathaniel like this. And I've known him a long time. He's turning his world upside down to please one person. You. He's crazy in love and using all of his kingly prowess to prove it to you. To prove he's worth everything he's asking you to give up. How can he compete with your family? With your American ways? How can he compete with *you*? Giving up your citizenship and what all?" He sighed as if he might regret his outburst. "Just know if you refuse what's on the other side of this entrance, you'll break his heart and I'm not sure he'll ever recover."

She drew a long breath, returning Jon's steely gaze. "You're a good friend, Jon. And I've no intention of breaking his heart."

"Because I know a good thing when I see it." He smiled. "My apologies for violating protocol and speaking out of turn."

"No apology needed when I've been acting like a fool." She kissed his cheek, then stretched to see around the square post of the portico. "Besides, friends speak the truth to friends."

"Susanna." Jonathan stepped away from her. "I'm going to leave you now. But wait here." He pointed his finger at her. "Your prince will come."

Nathaniel waited for Susanna to arrive in the so-called foyer of this outdoor sanctuary, wearing his grandfather's World War II uniform.

All afternoon, he vacillated between calm and panic, white-hot nerves assailing his confidence. He didn't fare well with his last public proclamation of love, but he knew he had to break free of his fear and shame.

And in his heart of hearts, he knew Susanna was the one to help him shed his shackles.

His heart skipped a beat as the clatter of horses rang in his ears and the black carriage flashed past the trees.

Through the shrubbery and swaying Spanish moss, he caught a glimpse of Susanna.

It had taken a Herculean effort not to ring her today. But if he heard her voice, he knew he'd want to see her. And if he saw her, he'd spoil his surprise.

So he purported to have king's business to attend. Which, in fact, he did, but really, he fussed about with busy work to keep his heart from going insane while waiting for this evening to come.

If she said yes to this wild idea, they'd be married by sunset. Man and wife.

Susanna's family, along with his staff, had worked half the night and through the day to create an outdoor cathedral for this spontaneous dream wedding.

Behind him, a hundred or so guests were seated in white wooden chairs while a sixteen-piece orchestra gathered from island residents played "Air" from Bach's Suite no.3.

Nathaniel's heart swelled with each stroke of the violin's bow.

The moment Susanna crested the portico, he had nearly buckled with the power of her beauty. It caused his heart to stumble in ways he never thought possible. Susanna was more than a vision standing there in a pale mauve gown; she was the essence of his soul.

Beautiful, yes, but she was also wise and kind, loving, considerate, devoted, and loyal. The kind of woman a king needed beside him.

His breathing shallowed as Jonathan headed down the brick path to his station by the wedding altar, smiling at Nathaniel and offering him a salute.

That was Nathaniel's cue to move forward to his bride.

The Bach piece peaked on a high note, then gently swooned toward Pachelbel's Canon in D, Susanna's favorite wedding music.

Nathaniel smiled, making his way to her. Her posture and presence, paired with the blue intensity of her eyes and the way her lips parted when she saw him, nearly brought him to his knees. Heaven help him, he was trapped with no way out.

"Hello, love," he said, taking her hands into his.

"Hey, yourself." Low, sweet, an inviting warmth in every syllable.

"A surprise." He gestured toward the outdoor sanctuary. "Your dream wedding. If you'll have me."

"Oh Nathaniel, you didn't —" Susanna's voice quivered and her eyes misted. "You didn't have to do this."

"Susanna Jean Truitt . . ." Nathaniel drew her close. "Will you marry me tonight? I realize the past few months in Brighton have been trying. You've done more than your fair share of changing and coming to my side. I stand here now at your side. I love you for who and what you are. Your American heart is more precious to me than anything else. I need you to know I see your heart."

"I know you do. I do . . . Nathaniel, I can't believe you did this." Tears pooled in her eyes. Her glistening, pink lower lip trembled in' time with the hovering note of the strings. "Of course I'll marry you. But I didn't need all of this to know you are by my side. I was just clinging to my old self, my old *plan*." She made a face and he laughed.

"Then this is for me. To prove to you that I adore you, love you, and am devoted to you above my crown and kingdom. You are my heart. I've a duty to my family, to my country, but even more, I have a duty to my God to love you as I love myself. This is for me." He grinned. "I want to marry the American woman who bewitched me under Lovers' Oak the moment I laid eyes on her." He squeezed her hands. "This is our day. Just you and me, with our friends and families. Let our Brighton wedding be about the crown and the kingdom, but this, love, is all about us." He reached for one of her curls, brushing his fingers lightly over her neck. "You take my breath away."

She fell into him, raising her eyes to his. "I'll marry you, Nathaniel, tonight, here in Brighton, anywhere, anytime." He brushed away her tears with a light touch of his fingertips. "God's got this, doesn't He? How can I be so narrow to always want things my way?"

"I'll help you overcome your fears if you help me overcome mine." He tipped his head toward the waiting guests. "Let's dry your tears." He reached in his breast pocket for a handkerchief and handed it to her.

She laughed through another surge of tears. "My other grandma's wedding handkerchief." She pressed it to her nose. "I can still smell her perfume."

"Your daddy gave it to me so she could be with us in spirit." He kissed her forehead while drawing a gift from his jacket. A gift he'd moved heaven and earth to have finished and shipped in time for tonight.

"What's this you're wearing?" She brushed her hand over his grandfather's white, fine wool naval jacket and medals.

"Grandfather's World War II uniform. Mum's dad. He was a naval commander and wore this very uniform at his wedding." Nathaniel drew a heart-shaped diamond pendant from his pocket. The flawless stones absorbed the white glow of the lights draped through the shadows of the trees, creating pale orbs against his skin. "I was going to give this to you on our wedding day in Brighton, but it's fitting now. Ameri-

132

can or not, Susanna, you are my wife, my princess, and . . ." He motioned to the intricate design inside the heart-shaped pendant. "Your cipher. See?" He paused, clearing his throat.

"Nathaniel, it's exquisite." Susanna trembled with her fingers over her lips.

"Your official title is engraved here." Nathaniel turned the piece over. "HRH Crown Princess Susanna of Brighton Kingdom."

"Princess. Wow, there it is." She laughed softly through her tears. "And what's this?" she whispered, touching the delicate key ornament attached to the chain.

"The key to my heart." The full force of his feelings for her burst to the surface and threatened to overpower him. "A sign of my promise to put you first, before the kingdom, before my duties as king, to the best of my weak, human ability. Only the Lord will come before you. It's the only way I can be any kind of good husband and decent king." He steadied his heart and slowly moved to clasp the piece around her neck. It couldn't have a more beautiful home.

The sparkle in her eyes rivaled the brilliance of the diamond necklace.

When he stood before her again, she hooked her hands over his arms. "I give you everything, babe. My heart, body, soul, *and* citizenship. When I get afraid that life is beyond my control, I will remember this moment and say, 'See what God can do.' "

"Let's not keep the guests waiting any longer." He offered her his arm.

"Not another moment." Her smile beamed light across the entire church grounds.

Nathaniel signaled to Jonathan, who then cued the orchestra to play Pachelbel's Canon again. Gracie and Avery rose from their front row seats and stood on the bride's side of the altar wearing pink dresses of some kind.

On the groom's side, Stephen wore his Royal Air Force uniform while Colin sported an Armani suit sent along by the designer himself. With his compliments.

As the guests stood and Nathaniel started down the aisle, Susanna drew back. "Wait, wait, wait . . ."

His beating heart screeched to a halt.

"Is this legal? Babe, we don't have a license for Georgia."

"See the man on the front row?" Nathaniel's heart started beating again. "He's from the county clerk's office. All we have to do is sign the license and we're legally married."

"Before we are officially married in Brighton?"

"That will be the case, yes."

"Nathaniel, are you sure?"

He brushed a sweet, free strand of hair from her eyes. "One hundred percent."

She tiptoed up as if she might kiss him and wrapped her arms about his neck. "I am yours forever, Nate Kenneth."

"And I am forever yours."

NINE

In all her born days, Susanna knew she never could have planned or even dreamed of such a night as this. From the moment she slipped on Granny's dress for her "evening" with Nathaniel to the ceremony at Christ Church, everything was perfect.

Maybe beyond perfect because she had expected none of it.

Granny had rejoiced to see her walk down the aisle in *her* dress. When Susanna arrived at the end of the aisle, she bent to give her a kiss.

"I knew I couldn't miss *this* wedding." Granny raised her thin, weak hand to Susanna's cheek. "You look prettier in that gown than I ever did."

"And my granddaughter will look prettier than me."

Granny kissed her cheek. "He's a good one, that king. Keep hold of him."

Now, sitting at their head table for two on

136

the ocean side of the cottage's garden, Susanna leaned against Nathaniel as Mickey, the Rib Shack's Irish singer, serenaded them from a corner spot on the white stone-and-tile veranda.

The cottage garden was ablaze with clear lights swinging from the trees along with an array of Japanese lanterns hovering above the long pink-and-burgundy-covered tables with vases of white roses and lilies.

The breeze hustled past, dancing with the lights and lanterns, leaving behind a sweet, sea foam perfume.

"Happy?" Nathaniel draped his arm around the back of her chair as he whispered in her ear.

"I don't have words," she said, cupping his face in her hands. "I feel both proud and humbled. You made me happy. Not to mention Granny and Gracie. No small feat for any man to make three women happy in one night."

He took her hand in his and brought it to his lips. "Remember when you sat on my veranda steps two years ago and stared out at this cottage's dead, dry garden? You had no idea you were really gazing into my dead, dry heart. I saw weeds, but you saw possibilities and life. Not for this garden, but for me. You reminded me of who I was and am, and who really called me to be a king. God, not men."

His sincere confession caressed her heart. "No, my heart was the dead one. Then you found me and said, 'Design a garden for me.' Sitting on those same steps, I saw possibility. For a garden, yes, but also for love." She kissed him. "We made grass angels and you helped me off the ground —"

He laughed. "How could I forget? You tripped and fell into my arms. I never wanted to let you go."

"I did that on purpose, you know." She nuzzled her face against his, butterfly kissing his cheek.

"Sure you did." He brushed his lips over hers. "I remember wanting to kiss you that day, very much."

From the veranda stage the music changed. Nathaniel shoved back his chair, taking her hand. "May I have this dance?"

Susanna rose, the silk taffeta and tulle petticoat of her dress rustling past their chairs, the heels of her golden shoes striking a solid sound on the makeshift dance floor.

The guests, sitting at surrounding tables, applauded softly.

Nathaniel drew her into his arms and began an elegant waltz as the melody of the song rose higher and Mickey began to sing.

He is now to be among you at the calling of your hearts . . .

"The Wedding Song," she whispered, a new wash of tears filling her eyes. "How did you *know*?"

"Oh, a little bird named Glo told me."

Mama, sweet Mama. "A friend of theirs sang it at Daddy and Mama's remarriage ceremony when I was twelve and so happy. My very divorced parents reconciled, remarried, and were giving me a baby sister."

For whenever two or more of you are gathered in His name, there is love . . .

Susanna closed her eyes and rested against her husband — oh, she loved the sound of the word — as Mickey's smooth melody confirmed . . . *there is love.*

When the song ended, a soft clanking arose from a table to the left, and Daddy made his way toward the dance floor, tapping his champagne glass with a fork. The sound technician passed him a microphone.

Nathaniel slipped his arms around Susanna, pressing her back to his chest.

"Well," Daddy said, his voice rattling with emotion, as he smoothed his hand over his waistcoat and lean middle. He looked good. Strong and vibrant and fit from Mama's strict diet. Susanna could almost erase her memory of him lying in the hospital bed weak from a heart attack at forty-eight. "Most of you have known Glo and me a long time. Therefore, you've known our Susanna, too. Queen Campbell and Prince Stephen, Prince Colin, Jonathan, the staff from Brighton, it's good to have y'all here for this little shindig. I'd like to thank everyone for their hard work in pulling off this surprise wedding." Daddy swerved to face the royals, sitting among the Truitt, Vogt, and Franklin clans. "If y'all wondered what kind of man and king this fella here truly was, let me tell you, you're sitting among his generous, kind heart right now. Not only was this spontaneous wedding his idea, he put boots on the ground to make it happen. Put his money where his mouth is, and y'all know how we like those who do as much as they say. And you know why he did it?" Daddy stepped toward them. "For this beautiful girl here. Our Susanna." His voice quivered, breaking down. " 'Cause he loves her that much."

Susanna trembled, feeling the love in her daddy's confession. It was watching him grow in his faith and in his love for Mama that repaired most of her childhood fears.

"Suz, you're about the best girl anyone would ever want to know. Well, you and my girl Avery. And I mean that, kitten. Y'all are probably thinking I'm saying that 'cause she's my daughter, and if so, well, you're right."

A merry laugh rippled among the guests and Nathaniel sweetened her temple with a kiss.

"But I know it because I've watched her. She's loyal, almost to a fault. She loves people. Genuinely. But watch out now, 'cause if you take advantage of her she'll give you the dickens for it. She encourages folk. But she won't tickle your ears. She'll tell you the truth in a way you can swallow it. When she was born, Glo and I felt sure God sent us an angel straight from heaven. She never cried 'cept when she was hungry. But then as a little girl, she didn't have it so good. As much as we loved her, Glo and I didn't love each other well and we fought. A lot. Couple of kids we were." Daddy wiped under his eyes with his finger. "And Susanna," — he cleared his throat with a deep cough — "would hide out in her closet, pretending it was her secret garden because she didn't know if our anger was ever going to spill over on her. So I guess it's fitting that today her wedding and reception are in a garden." Sniffles rippled up from the tables and through the air. "Suz, you found true love and I pray that your marriage will always be the safest garden you can ever find. Nate, son, see to it that my little girl is always at home in your palace and in your arms, hear me? 'Cause I think a girl's daddy trumps a king any day, and if I hear of you doing anything to hurt my girl, I'll hop on over to Brighton and take you out back for a discussion."

The men hammered the table with their fists and the women hooted. "Go, Gib!"

Nathaniel bowed toward Daddy. "I am duly warned."

"On that note, Nate, King Nathaniel II, welcome to the family, son. It's good to have another man. I've been outnumbered by girls for thirty years."

Queen Campbell rose from her seat. "Move over, Gib, it's my turn."

"Mum!"

The dowager queen stood next to Daddy, smiling, looking regal in her fitted but simple summer suit.

"When Nathaniel was seven or eight years old, one of our maids became quite ill. A chambermaid. So most of her chores had little to do with the family on a day-to-day basis, but when young Prince Nathaniel heard of her plight, he insisted on seeing her."

"You never told me this," Susanna whispered, gazing up at him.

" 'Twas nothing, really." Was he blushing? He had just purchased another piece of her heart. As if there were any pieces left.

"He slept on the floor of her room. Demanded a nurse to attend her needs full-time. We couldn't get him out of her quarters without a huge ruckus, so we let him stay, not really sure if she was contagious or not." Campbell's glassy gaze bore down on her son. "I knew then, son, you were born to be a king. Susanna, he's loved you from the start and I believe you are exactly what he needs. Welcome to *our* family, to the House of Stratton." She raised her champagne glass. "To King Nathaniel II and his bride, Princess Susanna. Long may they live."

The guests responded in robust chorus. "To King Nathaniel II and Princess Susanna! Long may they live."

The music changed and "Celebrate" hit the airwaves. Susanna boogied over to her college friends, all seven of whom had made it to the wedding, and sang at the top of her lungs, "Celebrate good times, come on." She glanced back at Nathaniel, who urged her on with a smile and a wink.

She'd once heard a profound statement, "There's no force more powerful than a loved woman," and tonight, right now, she knew it to be true.

TEN

A little after eleven thirty, Susanna collapsed onto the white leather sofa curving in front of the veranda fireplace. She was exhausted, but her happiness ran so deep her bones buzzed.

Nathaniel sat next to her, his face glistening, his WWII jacket removed and his shirt collar open, his dark hair loose and free. "I think I've danced half the night with your loony college mates."

Susanna laughed. "I know. Aren't they great?" She wove her fingers with his, loving the reflection of the hearth's flickering flames in the ocean of his eyes. "I miss them. I forgot how knitted our hearts were."

"We'll have them all to Brighton sometime soon."

"Can you see them hobnobbing with Nigel, Blythe, and Morton, or Lord and Lady Dean?"

"We'll make popcorn and sit back and

145

watch the show."

She leaned in and kissed him. "How'd I get so lucky as to find you?"

"Don't know, but I'm going to count my blessings and believe there's more where they came from. In the meantime, take a look here." Nathaniel tugged Susanna forward so she could see the dance floor where Avery and Colin were entwined.

"You think they're truly falling for each other?" Susanna shivered as midnight drew near with a chilly nip in the March air.

"I've asked him straight out, but his answers are vague."

"She's going to college next year on a volleyball scholarship."

"And he has two more years of university. But —" Nathaniel reached behind Susanna for the lap blanket, wrapping it around her shoulders. "Perhaps we started a lovely trend. Truitts and Strattons falling in love."

"Of American girls marrying European princes?" She made a face, laughing. "Good grief, if it were a book, no one would believe it."

"Susanna Jean." Mama's voice boomed around the wide stone porch post as she made her way up the steps, her strappy sandals swinging from her fingertips. "Daddy and I are leaving. Got an early delivery in the morning. The out-of-town family and friends are all swinging by the Shack for lunch around one. Grandpa will be able to bring Granny out again. We'd love for y'all to come and carry on this magical wedding one more day. I even got your people coming, Nathaniel." Mama kissed him on the head.

"Well, then —" Nathaniel said, peeking at Susanna.

"Thank you for everything." Susanna reached for her mama's hand. "I know you helped him pull this off. It was beautiful, Mama."

"One of the most beautiful I've ever seen, and I'm not saying it because you're my daughter." Mama kissed Susanna, whispered, "I love you," then shuffled back down the steps, walking around the veranda to the outer gate. "Avery Mae!" she called over her shoulder. "Get the lead out. We're heading home. Prince Colin, see you tomorrow for lunch."

Susanna yawned, really feeling her exhaustion. She wanted to crawl into bed and relive tonight in her dreams. Meditate on all the special moments.

Seeing Nathaniel standing under the oaks in his grandfather's white uniform, so regal and strong.

His confession of love.

The romantic Christ Church grounds.

Wearing Granny's gown.

Their vows.

Sigh . . . It was all so very lovely.

Standing, Susanna reached for the Louboutins she'd shed twenty minutes ago. "Avery, I'm ready when you are."

Nathaniel cleared his throat. "Where are you going?"

"Home." She glanced down at him. "Avery's my ride . . ." Her heart fluttered, revelation dawning, her body responding with fiery pulses. "Oh —" A deep blush crested her cheeks. "I hadn't even thought . . ."

"I surprised you. I understand." He stood, reaching for her. "But this is our wedding night."

"I-I guess so." She laughed low, shoving the lap blanket from her shoulders. Did someone turn up the heat in that fireplace? "I was all mentally geared for our wedding on the twenty-first. It didn't register that, you know, tonight is —"

"We have the whole cottage to ourselves. No Jon, no servants or staff. Not even Liam." He swept her into his arms and held her against him. "Come with me."

He led her into the house, through the

kitchen where the staff, the locals, and the Stratton Palace team talked and laughed, cleaning up.

Walking hand-in-hand up the broad, winding staircase, Susanna made the last mental adjustment she needed to realize that *this* was her wedding night.

Oh, she was staying. She could finally let her heart and desires go. She'd not deny this man. Not deny herself. She'd waited ten long months for this night, and she wanted to be with him every bit as much as he wanted to be with her. Plans and schedules be darned.

At the top of the staircase, a soft light glowed from the master suite at the end of the hall.

Nathaniel had turned his bedroom into a bridal chamber with dozens of candles, fresh white linens, and a fire flickering in the old stone fireplace. A small bowed gift and a bouquet of roses awaited her on the dressing table.

"Nathaniel, oh my . . . will your surprises never end?" She laughed and shoved him out the door. "Now, get rid of our last guest and the cleanup crew. Give a girl a chance to prepare. Got a dress shirt I can borrow?"

His eyes glinted with passion. "In the closet."

She rose up on her toes and kissed him. "My heart is beating so fast I can't breathe." She pressed his hand over her heart. "Give me a few minutes, and then the rest of the night, I am 100 percent yours."

As Susanna closed the suite door, Nathaniel raced down the hall and shook the entire cottage. "Everyone out! Out! Good night and good 'morrow."

Sunlight filled the room when Nathaniel woke up, reaching for his bride. Her side of the bed was warm but empty.

"Suz?" He sat up, listening for the sounds of life.

She popped out of the bathroom. "Morning, sleepy head."

He grinned. Seeing her wrapped in a towel, her wet hair combed back, his desire for her stirred. "You going somewhere?" He patted the bed next to him. Nothing had prepared his heart for what he'd feel for this woman once she was completely his and he was hers.

"It's twelve thirty. We all leave tomorrow, so I thought it would be fun to go to the Shack for lunch and hang out with the friends and fam."

He crawled out of bed. "I thought it would be fun to *hang* with my wife."

"You have the rest of your life to *hang* with me." She kissed him, teasing and slow. Then she turned him toward the shower. "Get ready. Let's go see everyone and continue the celebration."

"Married not even twenty-four hours and my wife is bossing me around already." He reached for another kiss, letting her love awaken his sleepy heart.

After his shower, Nathaniel headed downstairs, snatching up the SUV keys from the dining room table. "Suz, love, let's go. I'm dialing Liam. Making sure he's at the Shack with everyone. I'd like him there so he can have fun *and* we have security."

He'd kept this wedding private, away from the watchful eyes of the media, but he didn't want to venture far without Liam. Word was bound to spread over St. Simons sooner or later that a royal wedding had occurred.

Though he felt sure they were safe for one more day, he didn't want to risk it. Two Royal Air Force planes had crossed the Atlantic in less than a week. Surely they'd alerted someone, somewhere.

"Liam, we're on our way to the Shack. Yes, see you there." Nathaniel tucked his phone in his jeans pocket. "Suz, love, you ready?"

She bounded into the room glowing and beautiful, free and sweet. He hooked her with one arm and kissed her. "Want to walk on the beach later?"

"Whatever you desire, Your Majesty."

"Whatever I desire?" He nuzzled her neck. "You . . ."

Susanna laughed softly and leaned into him for another kiss as he fumbled for the doorknob. As he swung it open wide, a gush of cool, fresh air swirled around them, along with the battering sound of a dozen camera shutters.

Photographers flooded the front veranda, the lawn, and down the driveway.

"King Nathaniel, is it true you were married last night?"

"Your Majesty, if Susanna is still an American citizen, how does this impact your monarchy?"

"Susanna, King Nathaniel, look this way, this way . . ."

Nathaniel slammed the door shut, grimacing at Susanna, anger boiling in his bones. "I'm sorry, love, but our honeymoon is over."

ELEVEN

KING NATHANIEL II IN BREACH OF MARRIAGE
ACT; PARLIAMENT TO TAKE ACTION

THE KING'S POLITICAL OPPONENTS HEAT
UP: "HIS MARRIAGE TO THE AMERICAN DE-
FIES OUR LAWS"

BRIGHTON WEDDING NOT GOOD ENOUGH
FOR OUR KING? PEOPLE OUTRAGED AT
AMERICAN WEDDING

In the Parliament Debate Box, a window-
less anterior room outside the Senate and
Commons joint chambers, King Nathaniel
faced off with Prime Minister Brock Bishop,
Susanna standing beside him. "You can't be
serious."

"Most serious." Brock crossed his arms
with a smug glance at his vice minister.
"You knew what you were doing, Your
Majesty. Why are you surprised Parliament

is outraged? Not to mention, you robbed your people of seeing their first reigning king marry in three hundred years."

"So you're demanding my throne?" After the paparazzi surprise on St. Simons Island — Nathaniel had yet to discover who leaked the wedding — the Brightonian media exploded with stories, opinions, documentaries, online polls about the American ceremony.

Days and days of unrelenting coverage.

"Mr. Bishop." Susanna spoke with reverence and honor. "I was very reluctant to give up my American citizenship, but I've come to realize it's not what defines me. Nor does a Brighton citizenship. Sure, it's hard to give up something that's been a part of me before I was born, but I am taking the Brighton Oath of Allegiance tomorrow morning and renouncing my American ties. So what's the harm here?"

"Harm? That our king went behind our back, defied the law, and married a foreigner without her having taken the oath of citizenship. Never mind the renunciation of your civil ties to America." Brock motioned for his aide to hand him a document. "Many already see this as a compromise with another nation. The influence has started. The Liberal-Labor Party in the House of

Senators is demanding you step down from the throne."

"Pardon? *Demanding?*" Nathaniel snatched the document, his blood boiling as he read the word TREASON scrawled across the top of the page. "You are out of your mind, Brock." He tossed the paper to the floor. "You cannot charge me with treason for defying a writ. Especially when the Marriage Act states I'm allowed to marry whomever I wish."

"As long as His Majesty's government approves."

"Which it did. Last May."

"Well, your new government placed conditions which you blatantly ignored. Naturally, you'll remain a member of the royal family after you abdicate, but we are asking you to vacate your throne immediately."

"Brock, you blasted idiot! How does this accomplish your goals to be rid of a monarchy? Stephen will just take my place." Nathaniel had had enough of the politicking, the media, the naysayers, and his government using Susanna to get to him. "My marriage to Susanna on Friday was our business. Between us. When we wed here, in Brighton, we will be within the law."

"I fear it's too little, too late." Brock retrieved the petition for abdication. "We are moving forward with this action. As for your brother, we have plans there as well."

"So you're accomplishing your mission. To rid Brighton of a royal throne."

"I've never denied my sentiments toward the monarchy." He shifted his shoulders, adjusting the set of his jacket on his shoulders. "It's archaic. From another century. It's time has come to an end."

Nathaniel met the prime minister's gaze with his own rock-hard resolve. "Then shall we adjourn to Parliament?"

The morning session was just beginning. By next week, final government business was to be concluded before Parliament's spring recess. Just in time for the wedding.

Brock hesitated with a slight hint of surprise. As if he weren't expecting Nathaniel to take action. "Certainly, Your Majesty."

"You bring the petition and I'll address the assembly." Nathaniel reached around for Susanna. "Care to join us?"

Brock cast a shadow over them through the dark aura of his heart, then left the chamber.

Susanna shuddered. "Oh Nathaniel, how did he ever get to be prime minister?"

"He's head of the Labor Party. They formed a coalition with the Liberal Party for the elections. They secured the most seats in the House of Senators and thus Brock became prime minister."

"Does he hate you?"

"In his way, yes. But you know, Susanna, I've come to learn as king that whenever I meet someone I don't like or understand, I put a big X on them and remind myself, 'There's treasure buried here.' "

"Nathaniel, that's brilliant."

"So while Brock puzzles me and feels like my enemy, I remind myself that somewhere in all the supposed venom, there's treasure."

Lord, help me find the treasure . . .

Nathaniel led the way out of the room, reaching back for Susanna's hand, and took the stairs toward the grand central chamber, bypassing his robing room because he wanted to keep the Houses off-kilter for this debate.

At the mezzanine level, he entered through the King's Door and sat on his red velvet and teak throne overseeing the bright, round room with its atrium ceiling and gleaming paneled walls.

He motioned for Susanna to sit in the seat on his left. The Parliament thrones. Hand-crafted from Brighton oak three hundred years ago and covered with thick red velvet.

"Here?" She pointed to the Queen's Seat.

He chuckled at Susanna's very over-whelmed expression. "Yes, and don't worry, love. All is well."

"Too late," she whispered. "I am worried. What are you going to say?"

"The truth. Remind them of a few things." He wiggled his eyebrows. "I come with a few punches of my own."

Brock had slipped on his speaker robe and white wig and was now taking the podium. "We've before this Parliament a decree of treason against King Nathaniel II of Brigh-ton."

He recounted the issue and Nathaniel held himself in check, trying not to shake his head in disgust or scoff at the ridiculous-ness of it all. He would act like a king. Impartial. Even in cases against him.

When Brock finished his diatribe, Na-thaniel stood, bareheaded without his crown or his robes. He needed no symbol on his head other than God's delight and the love of his wife.

"Members of this esteemed parliament, I concede I married Susanna while she was an American. Out of love and deference to her. To prove my love was unconditional. She, in return, has offered all we and our law demand. She is ready to surrender her American citizenship and become a Brightonian. With no conditions. But knowing this, what do you do, slap me with a charge of treason? That is a serious charge and, according to our law, one not to be uttered lightly, as I believe it has been done here today." He paused to survey the room and many heads bobbing in agreement. "Let me remind you that if I am deposed for no other reason than that I married an American on American soil, our government will be dissolved. A new one will have to be formed. Your seats, earned by hard work and campaigning, will be gone. You'll have to begin again. In fact, our entire political existence will have to begin again. Because our prime minister has informed me he plans to rid Brighton of its monarchy."

The room rumbled. Men and women shifting in their seats. Leaning toward one another with bold whispers.

Nathaniel went on. "I remind you that our trade and peace accords will be dissolved. Not by my choosing, but by our own laws, if the monarchy is removed. All will be wrestled over and reestablished. Brighton will go on, but who will be our leader? Who will establish a new constitution? Brock Bishop? The man leading us toward chaos?

"Brighton Kingdom, which has found economic stability in the past year, will have our front door, back door, and every window in the house open to our enemies, known and unknown while you scramble to reform a government." He tapped the podium. "So as you debate this issue and cast your vote, keep those details in mind. And know that the House of Stratton will continue to stand. With or without me as King of Brighton.

"Meanwhile, Susanna will be at the Justice House swearing in as a full, complete, and proud Brightonian citizen. Good day to you all."

As he departed, trembling beneath his suit, Susanna slipped her hand into his. "Brilliant, babe. My heart is swelling with pride."

Then he heard the rumbling and shaking of the assembly floor by shouts and stomping feet.

Then at last, the one-chorus royal approval, "Hurrah!"

Twelve

WEDDING DAY!

A ROYAL WEDDING IN BRIGHTON: KING NA-
THANIEL MARRIES THE LOVE OF HIS LIFE

BRIGHTON WARMING UP TO SUSANNA TRU-
ITT: "SHE'S OUR PRINCESS; SHE MAKES THE
KING HAPPY"

Watchman Abbey
March 21
Susanna stood at the palace window, gazing
down onto the street, overflowing with
Brighton citizens who were waiting for a
glimpse of the bride. Of her.

Butterflies and bees battled in her belly.
Joy wrestled with anxiety.

Her swearing in as a Brighton citizen was
heralded on the front page of the *Liberty
Press* with the headline "America's Loss Is
Our Gain. Welcome, Princess Susanna." She

161

clipped that headline and tucked it into her Bible to read on the hard days, in the moments of doubt. Though she'd always be an American at heart, born and bred, she felt a certain newness in her soul about being a Brightonian.

At the light knock on the door, she turned back into the room. Her lady's maid stepped aside for Daddy to enter, looking dapper and smart in his tuxedo with a white cravat and waistcoat.

"Don't you look handsome." He'd even slicked back his hair.

"You're even more beautiful the second time around, kitten." Daddy joined her at the window. "You nervous?"

"A little." They leaned in unison to peer outside. For as far as the eye could see, people filled the streets, gathering under the Brighton banners snapping from every lamppost. A barricade of dark-uniformed police officers held them all in check.

"Shee doggies, that's a lot of people, Suz."

"And we have to drive through *that* to get to the abbey."

"Speaking of, it's time to go. Avery and your mama just left for the church. They'll meet us there." Daddy squeezed her hand. "Come on, this is a piece of cake. You're an old married lady of two weeks now."

She exhaled and made her way toward the door, picking up her bouquet of white roses.

"I'm not sure being married for a hundred years could prepare me for that crowd out there."

"Remember this, Susanna. They are all for you. Cheering you on. Did you see the headlines this week? Seems the press is coming over to your side."

"They've been kind this week." She smiled and took his hand. "Let's get this show on the road."

With Daddy, Susanna maneuvered down the palace steps, her ivory organza and tulle skirt taking up nearly half the width of the staircase. The fitted bodice with the Cinderella neckline was made of organza and handcrafted lace. And she wore the Princess Crown, designed by Cartier in 1860 for the royal family.

Today, all the world would judge her beauty and her fashion sense. Was she ready? She quelled a blip of nerves by calling up a memory from her garden wedding at Christ Church. Then she remembered Gracie and Ethan, Granny and Grandpa, along with parishioners, family, and friends who were gathering on the grounds right now to watch her wedding. Again.

Then she remembered the man waiting

for her at the abbey.

He was so worth it all.

In the palace drive, just beyond the doors, a white carriage with red and gold wheels stood waiting. Four footmen dressed in breeches and buckle shoes helped her ascend the carriage steps and settle in beside her father. The moment the carriage left the palace with security officers riding beside the coach on dark, curried mounts, the abbey bells began to ring through the crisp air, pealing a wedding sound through all of Brighton.

The noise of the crowd rose to a fevered pitch.

Susanna waved and smiled, a peace beyond understanding rising in her heart. This was her destiny. What God created her to do and be. And at the end of this life journey with Nathaniel, she'd meet another amazing King face-to-face: Jesus.

Daddy leaned toward her, laughing, shouting, "I think they like you, Suz."

"And I'm starting to love them."

Once they arrived at Abbey Road, she stepped out of the coach with Daddy's aid, pausing for the photographers. She'd given permission to each approved media outlet to send one photographer to walk with her, at a distance, as she made her way down a carpeted path to the abbey's entrance. It was tradition for the bride to walk from the road to the church on a red velvet runner.

Besides, this was Brighton's day as much as hers and Nathaniel's. *Their* day, their *first* wedding, would always be a private, special memory.

Avery met Susanna at the beginning of the walk and helped her lower her veil. When Daddy offered his arm, Avery picked up Susanna's long train and they commenced the slow processional. As they made their way toward the ancient church down the path lined with hornbeam trees and potted hyacinth and hydrangea, the people cheered.

We love you, Susanna.

The walk stopped at the abbey's ivy-covered walls where the archbishop met them, looking regal in his intricately embroidered robes. The Royal Brighton Orchestra began to play, filling the abbey with the notes of their own unique wedding song.

"Ready?" Daddy said, holding on to Susanna as much as she was holding on to him.

"Yes, I am. Very much."

Together they followed the archbishop down the long, red-carpeted nave.

Susanna's heart fluttered at the first sight

of Nathaniel waiting for her on the altar steps, amazing-looking in his own dark blue naval uniform replete with ribbons and medals, his silky hair clipped and trimmed, shining in the soft light.

When she arrived before him, he bowed ever so slightly and reached for her hand. "You are stunning."

With all the warm confidence of love, she held his hand and followed him up the steps, never looking back, never feeling so comfortable and safe as she did right now. In the garden of her husband's heart.

DISCUSSION QUESTIONS

1. Susanna has given up everything to marry King Nathaniel. But when he tells her that she has to give up her American citizenship, it pushes her over the edge. Some of my missionary friends feel very proud and possessive of the American heritage and citizenship. Giving it up would be letting go of their last hold on home. How do you feel about this? Would you hesitate to give up your citizenship — your last piece of "you"?

2. The reverend reminds Susanna that her citizenship is really in heaven. Not Brighton or America. This revelation is something I try to meditate on. I'm of the kingdom of our Lord and His Christ. What about you? Has this reality impacted you? How does it change the way

you live?

3. Nathaniel has a romantic wound. The public rejection of Lady Adel. It causes him to hesitate with Susanna. But he faces his fear when he sets up the surprise wedding. Is there a wound in your past that causes you to be afraid of something or someone? Even the Lord?

4. Love and marriage require a lot of giving, a lot of commitment. Susanna surrendered everything for love. Love is worth our all. Don't we see this in Jesus's birth, death, and resurrection? How He became His own creation because of love. How can we be more like Him? He's worth giving up everything for love.

5. The Bible tells us that love covers a multitude of sin. It also enables us to trust and give, allows us not to cling to our own ways. We see this in the blending of low-country Georgia culture and European royal culture at the wedding reception. How can growing confident in His love for you enable you to love others more?

ACKNOWLEDGMENTS

Thank you to the HarperCollins Christian Fiction team for inviting me into the Year of Weddings novella collection. I had great fun writing Susanna and King Nathaniel's wedding.

I appreciate the efforts of my editor, Becky Philpott, whose taste in story mirrors my own.

Thank you to Sandy Moffett for information on private jets. Any mistakes are mine.

A shout-out to Susan May Warren and Beth Vogt for sounding out my crazy story ideas. You keep me grounded with your friendship.

Much love to my husband who allows me all kinds of space to be who God's called me to be. And who found a video game to play while I write on deadline. Way to take one for the team, babe!

To all the readers who take the time to

read my stories. I really, really appreciate you all! Thank you!

ABOUT THE AUTHOR

Rachel Hauck is an award winning, best-selling author. Her book, *The Wedding Dress*, was named Inspirational Novel of the Year by *Romantic Times*, and *Once Upon A Prince* was a Christy Award finalist. Rachel lives in central Florida with her husband and two pets and writes from her ivory tower.

An April Bride

LENORA WORTH

To Shiny. You know who you are!
I love you. :)

ONE

"April showers bring May flowers."

That old saying might hold true, but in this particular garden spring had already arrived. And just in time for the big event. A wedding. Her wedding to the man she'd loved since she was five years old. She and Marshall had met in kindergarten and gone all the way through school together and attended the same church. They'd been high school sweethearts who'd always planned to be married someday. So why was she so afraid today?

Stella Carson loved April. It was the one month when the Louisiana heat and humidity seemed bearable, the one month when the whole landscape turned into a blaze of riotous color that rivaled any Monet painting. She loved spring and the scent of the jasmine blossoms that covered the pergola her daddy had built in the backyard when she was only three years old. She loved the

177

dazzle of the hot pink hibiscus bushes on her mother's back porch, and she especially loved the sassy salmon-colored azaleas that lined the white picket fence between the horse pasture and the front drive.

Right now, she stood admiring her mother's prize hydrangeas. The big, blue clustered blossoms would soon spill out of the old, hardy bushes that ran across the front porch line. She planned to have those colors in her wedding — blues and mauves, lavenders and delicate pinks, just like the colors in this yard each spring. And hopefully, some hydrangeas sprinkled here and there, even if they had to be ordered from a nursery.

Across the old country road, the Mississippi River gurgled and whirled as it flowed out to the Gulf of Mexico. Wishing her worries could flow away with the river, Stella leaned over the second-floor railing of Flower Bend — the house she'd grown up in — and marveled at God's beauty. The old moss-draped live oaks swayed and creaked in the late afternoon wind. She could hear the squirrels quarreling and playing as they rushed over the gray, wrinkled bark, could hear the blue jays fussing at each other as they fluttered from tree to tree.

Stella allowed the beauty of this old place

to soothe her while she said yet another prayer, asking God to help her through the next month. She planned to get married at the church and have the reception here in the garden. She'd dreamed of this for most of her life.

But this spring was both special and confusing. Her fiancé, Marshall, was coming home today, and Stella was so thankful. Her soldier boy was returning from the Middle East to marry her in four weeks. He'd been back stateside for a while now, and she'd only seen him once. He'd been in the hospital in Germany for a month, then in Maryland for over two months, recovering from injuries he'd received when an IED — a bomb — exploded near his Humvee.

Stella thought back on that awful time, remembering how worried she'd been after Marshall's parents had called her with the bad news. She'd immediately wanted to go to him, but his parents had asked her to wait. They'd rushed to his side in Germany and called Stella to let her know the extent of his injuries. Marshall had been in a coma when he'd arrived at the hospital in Germany. When he arrived back in the United States, she'd visited him but he'd been so groggy and disoriented, things didn't go very well. He didn't seem to know anyone, which only agitated him. So she'd come back home to wait and pray. When she'd finally been able to talk to him on the phone, he'd asked that she stay away. Asked that she give him time to heal and adjust. They'd talked on the phone once or twice a week, but something about those conversations bothered Stella. Marsh, as she'd always called him, just didn't sound the same. When she'd asked him about the wedding, he'd been vague.

"Should we postpone the wedding, Marsh? If you're not well enough . . ."

"Keep the date, Stella," he'd said. "I'll be better by April. I promise."

She'd waited. She'd prayed. She'd planned.

Now he was coming home.

And she was terrified.

"Stella, where are you?"

Stella whirled at the sound of her mother's singsong voice. "Coming, Mama." Her wedge sandals tapped their way back into her bedroom. "I'm almost ready."

Checking her reflection once more, she nervously smoothed her blue sundress and touched a hand to her dark blonde hair. What would he think when he saw her?

Her mother, Joyce, stood at the open door and grinned, her hands on her hips. "Are you excited?"

"I'm about to burst with pure joy," Stella admitted. "But I'm a little worried too."

"Worried? About what?" Her mother had dressed in her usual conservative manner in a white short-sleeved blouse and crisp, beige linen pants.

Stella finished checking her hair and makeup in the mirror of the antique vanity that had belonged to her maternal grandmother. "What if . . . what if Marsh doesn't feel the same about me anymore, about this marriage?"

Joyce shook her head and tugged Stella down on the puffy floral comforter covering the tester bed. "Honey, Marshall Henderson gave his heart to you twenty years ago when you hit him with a water balloon at the annual church picnic. Being gone for a year isn't going to change that one little bit."

"I love him too," Stella replied, doubt clouding her joy. "But . . . he's been to a place we can't even imagine. He's a hero, Mama. But he's also seen and done things that . . ."

Her mother frowned. "You're afraid serving his country might have changed him? Or that he's changed because of his injury?"

Stella nodded. "Yes. He seems so disoriented over the phone and . . . him not wanting me there with him really hurt me, but I had to do what was best for him. He used to be so strong and sure, but . . . he was wounded. I know his physical wounds will heal, but what about how he feels? What if his feelings for me have changed? I've researched post-traumatic stress disorder and head injuries enough to know that they can both be tough on relationships. He could suffer from bouts of depression and anger and possibly memory loss."

She'd practically memorized each Internet article and book chapter she'd found in spare moments at work. After all, running a bookstore with Internet access did have its perks.

She got up and went over to the mahogany armoire where her wedding dress had pride of place and unzipped the white protective garment bag. Then she touched one of the shimmering seed pearls scattered down the gathered satin skirt. "Even after he returned from Germany, he didn't want me to come up to Maryland to see him, so I honored that request. He just seems so distant on the phone, not like himself. I worry that he's not telling me everything." She pulled at her clothes. "I'm beginning to wonder if his mom and dad have been keeping something from me, maybe to honor his wishes."

Her mother got up and came to stand by her. "I'm sure he's gone through all kinds of emotions, darling. From what I've heard, too, head wounds can be mighty tricky. But he's much better now. Gerald and Kitten wouldn't keep anything bad from you unless Marshall requested it. His parents love you as much as they love him. He's healing now, and he's coming home to marry you."

Stella stared at the white satin wedding dress, her dreams caught in a net of doubt. "If he still loves me, he should have let me come to visit him in Maryland, Mama."

The New Orleans sun shot a golden path across the tarmac. Stella stood at the airport escalator waiting for Marshall to come down to the baggage claim area. Her heart roared a beat that rivaled the loud engines on the plane.

What would Marsh say? How would he act? Had he had second thoughts about marrying her? Did he want to stay single? Or did he just want to be away from her?

He told you he loved you.

Well, when she'd told him on the phone how much she loved him, he'd been silent for a moment, and then he'd replied, "Me too. I mean, I love you."

Why did he seem to think about that a

moment too long?

"Stop fidgeting, honey."

Stella pivoted to see her daddy, Ralph, smiling down at her. "Sorry. I'm nervous. We haven't seen each other in almost a year, and when I'm on the phone with him, I do most of the talking. Things change, Daddy. People can change too."

He patted her on the arm. "Have faith, suga'. A soldier's life is always hard, but you know Marshall and you know his heart. He loves you. That won't change."

She smiled up at her daddy, but Stella had to wonder about his reassuring words. Love could change in a heartbeat. She'd never worried about that before. Her life along the Old River Road had been happy and idyllic, to say the least. She had good friends, a loving family, and a strong faith community. And she'd always had Marshall. He was more than the boy next door. He was the love of her life. But if he didn't feel the same way, she'd be destroyed. She'd have to cancel the wedding.

She looked up to find Marshall's mother staring at her. Was that a look of pity or compassion? Kitten came over and took Stella's hands in hers. "It's gonna be all right, Stella. He loves you. Remember that, okay?"

Sure now that something was wrong, Stella held tight to her future mother-in-law's hands. "What's wrong, Miss Kitten?"

"Here they come," her mother called, motioning Stella toward the group of passengers coming toward them. "C'mon, Stella. You need to be the first person Marshall sees."

Stella glanced between her mother and Kitten Henderson, wishing she could be more confident. But right now, the tension moving through her made her want to run to the nearest exit. Kitten turned and pushed Stella toward the rush of people coming off the plane. And then Stella saw Marshall — tall, strong, his dark hair longer now. He was wearing civilian clothes but he looked gaunt and tired, and he had a scar near his left temple.

She had to wonder what other kinds of scars he might be hiding.

Then Marsh searched the area and his eyes met hers.

Stella started toward him, ready to rush into his arms.

But for some reason she stopped short and stood staring up at him, her heart racing with love — and panic. "Marsh?" she said, fear filling her heart. "Marsh, are you all right?"

185

He stood a foot away, his blue eyes as bright as ever. But something was missing. He almost didn't seem to know her.

"Marsh?"

"Stella?" It was more of a question than a statement.

Stella moved a step closer. "It's me. In the flesh."

Then, because she was so afraid, so concerned, she made the move toward him and lifted her arms to hug him close. "You're home. At last. I missed you so much. I was so worried."

He folded her into his arms and, after a moment, held tight. "I missed you too. We have a lot to talk about."

Relief poured through Stella. "We sure do. Just a month until our wedding."

He pulled back and gave her a long, confused stare. "The wedding. We . . . uh . . . we need to talk about that too."

Then Kitten was there, tugging him into her arms. Wiping at tears, she sent a helpless look toward her husband, Gerald. "We all want to catch up, but you're tired. Better get you home and all settled in."

Marsh hugged his mother but then slipped away from her. "I want to talk to Stella. Alone."

Stella's whole system went cold. "I

brought my car. Mama and Daddy rode with your parents." She whirled to find Kitten and her mother staring at them. "Is that okay?"

Kitten looked up at Marshall. "Will you be all right?"

"I'm fine," he said, his voice threaded with fatigue. "I promise we'll be home soon." Then he grinned, and for a minute he looked like the old Marsh. "I can't wait to eat some gumbo."

"We'll have it ready," Gerald said, his tone cautious.

As they all walked out of the airport together and found their cars, Stella kept glancing at Marshall's parents then back to him. Something was wrong, so wrong.

This man wasn't the Marshall she'd always loved. Despite his hug, he was like a stranger. His words and actions seemed stilted and unsure, as if he'd rehearsed them over and over.

When they reached her red Miata convertible, he stopped and looked surprised. "I don't know if I can fit in that little thing."

She laughed at that. "You were with me the day I bought it. You got in on the passenger side and your knees went up against the dashboard. Remember?"

He turned to her then, and she saw it in

his sweet eyes before he stated the obvious. "No, honestly, Stella, I don't remember."

Two

"What do you mean?" Stella maneuvered the little two-seater through the airport traffic. "You don't remember this car? Me?" She swallowed hard. "Or us?" If he was suffering from memory problems, that would explain how confused and abrupt he'd sounded in some of their phone calls. Yet he'd never let on in any other way.

Marsh gave her a quick glance, then stared down at his hands. "This is so hard. Harder than I ever imagined. I don't remember a lot of things. Remembering comes and goes. It's mostly from the concussion, but the PTSD only makes things worse."

She looked at his scar. It moved from his left temple up to his forehead with a jagged zigzag. "You were hurt worse than you told me," she said, her mind moving in the same kind of zigzag pattern. "Is that why you didn't want to see me?"

His sheepish expression told her there was

more. "Let's stop somewhere so we can talk. Mom and Dad won't mind waiting awhile."

She nodded, too numb to do anything but drive. When she saw a little roadside park just outside of the city, she exited the highway and pulled up underneath the thick umbrella of an old live oak. Putting the car in park, she turned in the seat. "You need to tell me everything, Marsh."

He nodded and seemed to search for the right words. "Yes, I do. I wanted to wait until we were face-to-face. This is why I didn't want you to fly to Germany or come up to Maryland. So let me explain, okay?"

Stella swallowed back a retort, the tone of his voice warning her away from any protests or questions. "I'm listening."

Marsh took a deep breath. "Our Humvee got hit when that IED exploded and we all went every which way. A piece of shrapnel hit me right in the head." He pointed to his scar. "Hit me there, and I was bleeding everywhere, but the driver took the worst of the explosion. He didn't make it. Several of us were ejected when we crashed, and I hit my head on a rock."

"So you had two head wounds." She reached up to touch his face, her fingers moving lightly over the scar. She should have been there at the hospital, she kept thinking. She should have known what was going on. His parents had kept her up-to-date, but when they'd returned home, they'd only told her about the gash and that he had a concussion and that he was healing and going through therapy.

Why hadn't anyone told her the truth? All these months of worry and an aching heart and . . . he'd been hiding the worst of it from her. How could they build a marriage on that?

"Yes, two wounds," he said, taking her hand away from his face but holding it close. "The scar you can see and another one."

"The one that's causing you to have memory problems."

Again, he nodded. "It's also causing post-traumatic stress. For a while, I couldn't remember anything."

"But you're better, right?"

She prayed he would tell her that he was much better, that he remembered her and their engagement. And their wedding plans.

"I'm getting better every day. I didn't remember my parents until a few days after I woke up."

Stella got out of the car and paced underneath the tree, memories of his confusion and agitation when she'd visited him sharply in focus now. When he walked toward her, she stopped to gaze up at him. "Marsh, do you remember me? I mean, really remember me?"

He looked away, giving her the answer. When he turned back, she could see the fear and dread in his blue eyes. "I . . . I've had a hard time remembering anything. Mom and Dad were great, even when I didn't recognize them. I was kind of out of it, and I didn't handle things very well at first, especially seeing you. I didn't want anyone to know. But the doctors had to prepare my parents for their first visit with me. They brought photo albums and . . . cards I'd sent them, stuff from high school. Things like that. When they mentioned you and the wedding, I . . . I drew a blank."

Stella gasped and held a hand to her mouth. "Are you telling me that you really don't remember anything at all about me or asking me to marry you?"

He took her hands in his. "I'm sorry, I don't. Not yet anyway."

Stella tried to find a way to breathe. "Our wedding is at the end of the month —"

"I know," he said, his tone low and gravelly. "Mom kept me posted."

Anger overtook Stella's fear. "But I talked to you on the phone about the wedding. I went on and on. You should have told me right away. We could have changed the date. We can postpone it if you think —"

"I don't know what to think," he said, his eyes full of a quiet despair. "I have these shards of memory, but the doctor said I might not ever get everything back."

"Meaning me? Meaning us and our love and our wedding?"

She didn't need him to give her an answer. She understood now why he'd asked her to stay away. Why he'd sounded so distant and stilted on the phone and why he'd acted so strange when he arrived. "Your parents knew and they never said a word to me or my family."

"Don't be mad at them. I begged them to wait. I didn't want to hurt you. I kept thinking I'd get better."

"And all this time, you . . . you didn't trust me enough to tell me this?"

"I don't know who to trust," he said, his frustration visible in his flushed face. "I'm lost, Stella. Lost in a cloud of partial memories. I want to remember. I've seen pictures of us together, and I want to remember so much."

"What if you never do?" she asked, her heart cracking with a piercing pain. "We can't get married like this."

193

"That's what I wanted to talk to you about," he replied as he pulled her down onto a bench. "I'm not sure I can go through with this wedding."

Marshall stared at the pretty woman sitting at his side and wished he could take away her pain. She'd grown so shocked and silent when he'd told her the truth, that he thought they might need to cancel the wedding.

"Maybe," he finally said there underneath the great oak, "maybe we can go on as planned." Then he suggested something he knew was crazy. Taking her hand, he traced a finger over her palm. At least that gesture seemed familiar. "Can you give me a few weeks? The doctor said I might get my memory back in pieces or all at once. I'd like to try."

Stella didn't respond at first. But after a couple of minutes she nodded and wiped at her eyes. Finally her expression changed from confused and hurt to strong and resolved. "I'd like to try too. Three weeks? Is that enough time?"

They'd never have enough time. But he didn't voice that thought. "It's a good start. But if you think we should go ahead and cancel the wedding —"

"I don't. I mean, we'd have to pay for everything anyway. That doesn't matter right now. I believe with all my heart that you love me and that you know me in your heart. I'm willing to go on faith that you'll remember me before the wedding."

He smiled over at her. "Mom and Dad told me you'd be stubborn about this. They also told me that you were the woman God had picked to be my wife. I've held on to that, Stella. I need you to keep fighting. I need you to believe in us too."

"Your parents are right," she said through a sniff. "I won't give up easily. You and I were meant to be together. This is just a setback, nothing more. A test of our endurance, of our love."

He took her hands in his and felt a stirring in his soul. "I'll pray for that too. And I'll do my best to make that happen."

"It's all we can ask for," she said. "You're the only man I've ever loved and . . . I won't take that lightly." She stared down at their hands. "Before, you moved your finger across my palm. Marsh, you've always done that. Since . . . forever. It was your little way of telling me you loved me."

She turned his hand over and touched her fingers to his palm. "Remember this, okay?"

Marshall gained a strong respect for his

fiancée. And somewhere inside his buried memories, he saw a shard of light piercing through. He'd heard her tell him that before.

Please, Lord, help me to remember this sweet woman. Help me to see her with new eyes, but also bring back my memories of her.

He'd seen pictures of them together and wished with all his heart that he could remember being with her. He'd dreamed about this same woman when he was in and out of consciousness. He did remember that. But the dream had been vague and just out of reach, and it had happened after his parents told him about Stella and shown him her picture.

He turned to her now, hoping to take away some of her shock and grief. "I did have this dream about you, about us. You were laughing. I think we'd gone on a walk."

She gasped, then nodded. "We like to take long walks along the river. On the levee." Excitement colored her words. "You proposed to me there, right near the gate to Flower Bend — my parents' house."

She lifted her left hand and held it out to him. "See. You gave me this ring. It belonged to your grandmother."

Marshall stared down at the solitaire diamond set against an intricate filigree gold band. Something flashed through his mind.

The face of another woman.

"I . . . I remember Granny. I do. She had dark hair and she was petite." He smiled, glad to have something to hang on to. "She's dead, isn't she?"

Stella nodded again, her eyes misty but hopeful. "Yes. She passed away two years ago. I went to the funeral with you, right before you left for your first deployment."

He remembered a beautiful hymn. " 'Love Lifted Me.' "

"They played that during the service."

He gave Stella a reassuring smile. "See, being with you has already brought back some memories."

"I intend to bring all of them back," she said, wiping at her eyes again. Then she glanced over at him. "What . . . what should we tell everyone?"

"I don't know," he said. "Mom told me we're having a big party this weekend. I don't know if I'll remember anyone." And he hoped he wouldn't have one of his flash-backs.

Stella put a hand to her mouth. "Oh, I'd forgotten about your homecoming party. We've been planning that for months too. Your friends want to see you. Your best man —" She stopped, dropped her hand back onto her lap. "Do you remember Nick

197

Prescott? You and he are best friends. You played football together."

"Mom showed me his picture," Marshall replied. "I think I remember a little bit. Did he and I get in trouble once for taking the four-wheeler and getting it stuck in the swamp?"

"Yes, when you were fifteen. Yes." Her smile rivaled the sunshine piercing through the trees. "That's good that you remember that. He's your best man."

"Okay. I think I can recognize him from the pictures."

"I'll show you our high school yearbook. That should help."

He nodded. "Stella, I want you to show me everything about our wedding too, okay?"

She sent him a perplexed glance. "What do you mean?"

"I want to know the details. Mom said you wrote to me in Afghanistan every week, and I have the letters in my duffel bag. But I was afraid to reread them. I wanted to wait and see —"

"If you could remember me when you saw me?"

"Yeah."

"I'll include you in everything about the wedding. I did tell you all about planning it in my letters, but showing you might shake out some more memories."

"Or create new ones," he said, his heart warming to her enthusiasm and hope.

They talked a few more minutes. He listened while she gave him details of living in rural Louisiana, then they got in the little car and headed home. Marshall decided even if he couldn't remember Stella, he certainly could enjoy getting to know her again. She was a sweetheart — charming, polite, and smart.

What more could a man ask for?

She pulled the little car into the driveway of a two-story brick house. "This is where you grew up, Marsh. You're finally home."

He glanced at the neat yard and the long front porch. Why couldn't the memories come back?

"I won't be home until I remember this place . . . and you."

Then he got out of the car and stood staring at the past he'd lost.

THREE

Two days later, Stella watched as Marshall strolled around his parents' backyard and stopped to talk to friends who'd dropped by to welcome him home. She'd gone over names and matched them with pictures of friends who would be there today, as well as everyone in the wedding party. His best man and two other attendants, her maid of honor and two more bridesmaids, the flower girl, the ring bearer, and several other wedding helpers were all here. She'd even shown him pictures of their caterer, her best friend Rhonda Guthrie, some old friends of her parents, and anyone else she could think of.

Had she helped him or confused him?

"How you holding up?" Rhonda asked, handing Stella a fresh cup of tea punch. After dropping Marshall off at his home, Stella had immediately called her close confidante, asking for advice.

"I'm better," Stella admitted. "It was so

hard, realizing that he didn't remember me. But he's trying. He's a fast learner, that's for sure. His mind is still almost photographic when presented with something new. He can remember the names that go with the faces, thanks to our flashcard game the other night."

Rhonda touched a hand to her short, white-blonde hair. "According to Miss Kitten, you're doing exactly what needs to be done to help him. You're being very brave and strong."

"I'm not so strong, and I'm certainly not brave," Stella replied. She watched the man she loved and prayed the same prayer she'd been reciting for days now. "I hope he'll find his way back to me. I've asked God to please help Marsh." She glanced over at her friend.

"What if God doesn't answer that prayer? Am I to assume he doesn't want me to be with Marsh?"

Rhonda touched her hand to Stella's shoulder. "I believe everything will turn out all right, no matter what happens."

Stella tried to find comfort in that. "I want to marry him. I want to have the life we've planned together. I love him, and I'm determined to make him love me again."

Rhonda gave her a quick hug. "That's

exactly what I'm praying for too."

Stella decided she would keep praying. Right now, just being near Marsh made her happy. *He's alive,* she told herself. *He's home and safe. We will have the life we've planned.*

She closed her eyes in a silent prayer, and when she opened them Marsh was looking at her from across the lawn. Stella smiled and waved. He excused himself from the people he was with and came toward her.

"Hi," he said, grinning down at her.

"Hello." She'd never felt awkward around Marsh before, but knowing he might not want to marry her had put a whole new spin on her actions and reactions. The awkwardness they'd felt at first, however, was slowly changing to a kind of shyness that, while still different, was much more bearable.

"How's it going?"

The light in his eyes dimmed. "It's weird, hard to deal with, but I've managed to slip inside and get myself together when I start to panic. I hope I haven't insulted anyone by not remembering them." He shrugged. "Mom and Dad have kind of prepared everyone now that you know. I . . . I didn't want you to hear it from anyone else."

"I appreciate that. The small-town grapevine can be cruel sometimes."

"I'd never be cruel to you," he said.

She accepted this because even without his memories he was a gentleman. Was that why he hadn't stopped the wedding? Did he feel a duty even if he didn't feel any love for her?

"Your new memories seem to be sticking with you," she said to encourage him and calm her own fears. "You know, I always envied you and your amazing memory when we were in school. You'd get a whole history lesson without taking a note. And I'd have to study every night just to get by, even in college." She stopped, images of them studying together clouding her mind with a sweetness that hurt. They'd decided to wait and get married after he'd been in the Army for a year or so. Now she wished they'd gotten married between his deployments. "You helped me study, and that's why I passed."

"But you're a smart woman," he pointed out. "Without your help, I wouldn't know any of these people."

Stella studied the people mingling around the pretty backyard where she'd spent so much time. The Henderson home wasn't as historical or spacious as Flower Bend, but she'd always loved the square backyard with the comfortable swing underneath an old oak. "Everyone here loves you, Marsh. The minister, the church choir, your old baseball and football buddies. Even ornery old Mr. Turner from the grocery store — you worked there part-time almost all the way through high school."

He looked toward the elderly gentleman sitting in one of his mother's white rocking chairs. "He is a character. He's a veteran. Served in World War II. I had a good talk with him, but I had to speak in a loud voice so he could hear me."

"Yes. He's lost his hearing, but that's no surprise since he's turning ninety at the end of the year."

"I hope I live that long." He gazed over at her. "I've been given a second chance, so I hope I can make the most of it."

Stella nudged him with her elbow. "Hey, you were a good man before you left to serve our country, and I believe you're still a good man. No matter what happens with us, that will never change."

"Thanks," he said, his grin back. "My dad told me another thing about you."

"What's that?"

"He told me you were a good woman." He chuckled. "He said, 'Son, even if you can't remember her, Stella is the girl for you. You couldn't ask for a sweeter, prettier, kinder woman to spend your life with.' "

Stella met his gaze and felt a soothing warmth move through her like a glowing beacon. Marsh's eyes flared with that same warmth. Did he feel it too?

She had to swallow to keep from bursting into tears. "That's so sweet of your daddy. I think he embellished my credentials, though. I've been known to throw a hissy fit now and then."

"I'd like to see that, but not directed at me, of course." He leaned down and whispered in her ear. "But I believe my dad was telling the truth."

She couldn't speak, so she just nodded and blinked back the tears that had seemed ever present the past couple of days. "I want to make you a good wife," she finally said.

"Are we getting married in the church?" he asked, the shyness chasing away that sweet moment they'd just shared.

She squelched her disappointment and nodded again. "Yes, we'll have the formal ceremony there, then we'll go back to my parents' house for the reception." She pointed to a couple visiting with her parents. "Mike and Jackie Tatum own a tent company. They're in charge of all the decorations for the reception at Flower Bend."

"Flower Bend?"

Another arrow of agony pierced her heart.

"My home. I mean, the place where I grew up."

"Where is that?"

Stella reminded herself to be patient. "A few miles from here. On the river road. It's a big Victorian house, and it's been in my family for over a hundred years."

An awareness lit his eyes. "Mom showed me pictures of that house, but she never told me it had a name. She kept saying, 'This is where Stella lives.' "

"I'm living there until we get married," Stella said, her tone gentle in spite of the frustration coloring her heart. "I didn't renew the lease on my apartment over the bookstore in town where I work."

He looked confused and . . . almost afraid. "Where are we going to live?"

Stella inhaled a breath. "In the house we bought before you left last year. It's a little cottage near a park up the road from Flower Bend."

"In Renaissance?"

"Yes. Did you just remember that?"

He laughed. "I guess I did. Or maybe Mom mentioned that too. That's the town here, right? Our town."

"Right." Stella's heart surged. "We went to Renaissance High. I manage The Book House on Fifth Street."

"You always did love books."

Their eyes met at that declaration.

"Yes. You gave me a new book every year on my birthday. I've read all of them twice over."

"That's why you're so smart and wise . . . and adorable."

Stella wanted to jump up and down and kiss him, but that would bring back the awkward discomfort that volleyed between them. Instead, she took his hand and tugged him toward the table full of food up on the open patio.

"I was so nervous when we first got here, I couldn't eat. Now I'm starving."

"Me too," he said. "But you might have to remind me what some of this food is."

"Surely you remember crawfish?" she said with a chuckle.

"Spicy, hard-to-peel little critters — and good. So good. Louisiana lobster."

She laughed again and thanked God for tiny blessings. "That's right, soldier. And I think I can out-peel and out-eat you by at least a pound."

"You're on," he said, smiling over at her.

Stella gestured toward the long table covered with white plastic where mounds of the strange little crustaceans lay piled up with spicy boiled corn and potatoes. They did look like tiny lobsters, but they were called mudbugs around here.

"Do you remember how to peel 'em and eat 'em?"

He picked one up, pulled off the tail, then discarded the rest of the body — mostly legs. Then he put the tail to his mouth and slipped out the tender, spicy white meat. "I think I do remember that. Amazing."

Stella thought he was amazing. She'd be terrified if she couldn't remember anything. He'd told her that at first he didn't recognize his parents, but after a few days with them, the memories started returning. Now, being home, he recalled familiar things — places, faces, scenes in his head.

Stella wished with all her heart he could remember her, but one step at a time. That's all she could hope for right now.

The afternoon wore on, and everyone gathered in the backyard for cake and lemonade. When Marshall's parents asked for everyone's attention, Marshall took Stella by the hand and moved close.

"I want to thank all of you for coming today to welcome my son home," Mr. Henderson said, his voice lifting out over the yard. "Kitten and I are blessed and thrilled to have Marshall safe and well. You've all heard by now that he's had some struggles, some wounds that have healed and some wounds that will take time to mend. We ask for your patience and understanding and your prayers during this time of transition."

He looked at Marshall and Stella. "These two are determined to have that wedding they've talked about since high school. We need your prayers to make that happen."

Everyone stood silent until a few people shouted, "Amen!"

Stella glanced up at Marshall, her heart stammering and stalling. "You do want to marry me, don't you, Marshall?"

His eyes held a troubled glint. "I promised you I would," he said. "I just need you to be patient with me too."

"I'm trying," she said. "But if you have any doubts —"

"I have a lot of doubts," he replied. "And this head wound stuff makes me cranky sometimes."

"Of course. You must be exhausted."

He took a long glance around. "I don't remember some of these people. I'm trying to fill in the blanks, but it's hard. I don't want to let anyone down."

"You only have to worry about yourself and being well again," she said. "If the wedding is too much pressure —"

"It's okay. I've decided I'm marrying you,"

he said, his tone curt now. "If I promised you that, then it will happen."

Surprised at that determined declaration, Stella nodded. "Not if you don't want to marry me," she said, her throat raw with unshed tears. "I won't force you to do that."

He tugged her away from the crowd. "I have to do this, Stella. Don't you see? If I don't have this wedding to look forward to, to get through, then what's left for me? I need something solid and sure in my life and . . . you seem to be so strong and so full of faith that I know God will see us through."

"I don't know what to say," she admitted, her heart torn with agony and empathy for him.

He put his hands under her elbows and gazed into her eyes. "I need someone to be honest with me. And . . . I want that someone to be you. I need you, Stella."

Stella fell into his arms. "I need you too, Marsh. We'll figure this out."

"Thank you," he said. "And you did promise to include me in all the details of the wedding."

"I will, starting tomorrow at church," she said. "I'll show you the altar where we'll say our vows."

He held her away and gave her a hopeful

look. "Maybe being back in church will trigger a memory for me."

"If nothing else, you'll find some peace there. You still have your faith."

"Yes." He closed his eyes for a moment. "I had to keep the faith over there. That foundation held me together."

Stella thought of all the moments they'd shared in the old church building. She'd relive all of them with him if she had to, because in her heart she'd already promised to stand by him through sickness and health. And now, through the final plans for their wedding.

FOUR

The next morning, Stella waited for Marshall on the church steps. It was a glorious spring day. She could smell the beginnings of the wisteria blossoms that curled around a massive pine tree in the churchyard. A few more weeks and the ancient magnolia trees would be blooming. She loved the lemony-vanilla scent of magnolias. She kept her mind on her surroundings to keep from fretting about Marshall. Would he come to church today?

When she saw his daddy's white SUV, she breathed a sigh of relief. Marshall was in the backseat.

"Hi," he said when they reached her. "Thanks for waiting for me."

Stella greeted his parents and allowed them to go ahead of her and Marshall. "How are you doing today?"

"Okay," he said. "I slept better. I've been having nightmares about the blast. Doc told me that will take time and more therapy."

"Does it help to talk about it? Or would you rather keep what happened over there to yourself?"

"I don't mind talking about things I remember, but I guess I've repressed the worst of it. My therapist thinks I've repressed the best of my memories too. Maybe because I thought I was going to die."

They were inside the narthex now. People would start greeting them soon. "Marsh, you didn't die. You're here with me and your family. You're safe."

"I keep telling myself that, but it's not me I worry about. It's . . . remembering my friends dying over there. I can't forget that, no matter how much I talk about it or try to put it out of my mind."

Stella wanted to reassure him, but some old friends saw them and hurried over to welcome Marsh back. They'd have to save that talk for another time. And she'd need to remember that he'd been through something she couldn't even comprehend.

Had his suffering triggered some sort of protection mechanism so he could store away the memories of her and the life they'd planned? It broke Stella's heart to think of such a strong, dependable man being so traumatized that he'd tried to forget both the worst and the best of his life.

She prayed he'd find her constant reassurances comforting. And that her fortitude and determination would be enough for both of them — enough to bring him all the way home.

Marshall saw flashes of memories. Each time that happened he got even more frustrated. His past life seemed there, just out of his reach, but he couldn't bring many memories to the surface. He didn't like feeling this helpless.

"Trust in the Lord."

His mother's whispered words came floating to the surface. When had she said that to him? When he'd been lying in that hospital in Germany, wondering where he was and even who he was? Had he been trusting in the Lord? Or had he been trying to fix this because he felt he had a duty to Stella and his family to do so? Maybe he did need the Lord instead of trying to do it on his own.

Why couldn't he remember the woman he was supposed to love?

Was his therapist right? Had he buried the memories of Stella to protect himself and her? While his therapist had gently cautioned Marsh against marrying a woman he couldn't remember, Marshall had stubbornly refused to cancel the wedding.

In his mind, he knew he was supposed to marry Stella.

The mind could certainly play tricks on a person.

After the service, he waited with Stella to talk to the minister. Reverend Howell had been right there praying for him when he'd first been wounded. He'd offered to come to Maryland with Marshall's parents when Marshall had been moved to the hospital there, but Marshall hadn't wanted anyone but family with him during those days.

Not even his fiancée. Because he couldn't bear the emptiness of lost memories. Because somehow in his heart, he knew he'd hurt this kind, beautiful woman if he told her he couldn't remember her.

Now he wanted the opposite. He wanted to soak up everyone in Renaissance and absorb their memories so he could bring back his own. So he could bring a real smile back to Stella's face.

"Hello, you two," Reverend Howell said. He pushed his glasses up on his nose and hugged Stella before shaking Marshall's hand. "So good to see you two together again."

Stella shot the minister a tentative smile. They'd explained Marshall's issues to the minister yesterday before the party got started. "I thought maybe if we talked about the wedding, it would help Marsh to feel . . . more comfortable."

"Let's go into my study," Reverend Howell said. "I have coffee and cookies. A gift from a member. And since my wife is always fussing about eating healthy, I certainly can't take the whole tin home with me."

"I know I've never turned down a cookie," Marshall said, grinning because he remembered his mom baking a lot.

Once they were settled with the coffee and cookies, Reverend Howell wiped crumbs off his fingers with a napkin and plunged right in. "Marshall, I can't imagine how you must be feeling these days. You're all in one piece physically. But your head is still confused, right?"

"Very confused," Marshall admitted. "But each day brings new revelations. I recognized some of the hymns we sang today."

"That's good," Stella said, her smile fresh and encouraging. "Do you remember the sanctuary?"

He nodded. "I had this image of you and me with a big group. But we were young."

"Probably Vacation Bible School or maybe

with the youth group," the reverend offered. "For as long as I've been pastor of this church, you two have always been together."

"So I hear," Marshall said. When he glanced over at Stella, he saw the trace of disappointment in her eyes. "I'm glad those times seem to be resurfacing."

Reverend Howell's brown eyes moved from Marshall to Stella. "And how are you handling this new normal, young lady?"

Marshall wondered that too. He gave her the same encouraging look she'd given him so many times. "Be honest, Stella. I want to know the truth."

She glanced down at her hands and then started twisting her engagement ring. "It's been hard," she said, an apologetic expression on her face. "I've dreamed of being Marshall's wife for as long as I can remember. I always felt so secure in our love and in the life we'd planned."

"And now?" Reverend Howell nodded for her to answer.

"Now, I'm not so sure. Is this a test? Is God testing us to see if we can hold up? I don't understand."

Marshall's heart went out to her. He'd put her through so much by not allowing her to visit him in the hospital and by keeping her in the dark about what was really wrong with him. "I'm so sorry," he said, taking her hand.

Reverend Howell offered her a tissue. "You have a right to question this situation, Stella. This was a big blow — and right before your wedding too. Sometimes we don't know the answers to the why and how, but we do know the Lord is in control. Do you still believe that?"

She lowered her head and wiped at her eyes. "I tell myself not to worry, but . . . my whole life has changed overnight. I don't feel so secure and confident in anything these days."

Marshall tugged at her hand so she'd look at him. "You can be sure about me, Stella. I don't back down on a pledge. And if I pledged myself to you, then that's how it's gonna be. I won't desert you."

"But what if you don't love me anymore, Marsh?"

Marshall couldn't take the hurt on her pretty face. "I believe I do still love you, deep down inside. I just have to find a way to bring all those feelings to the surface." He got up and bent down in front of her. "Don't give up on me, okay? Stella? Okay?"

"I'm sorry," she said, embarrassed now. "I didn't mean to cry. Really, I didn't."

"Hey, it's okay," Marshall said. "This was

a good idea. This discussion has shown me that I need to be careful of your feelings too. It's not all about me, you know. It's about us."

She nodded and smiled. "And God's plans for us."

Trust in the Lord.

"Yes." Marshall pulled her to her feet. "I'm so sorry to put you through this."

Reverend Howell stood and came around the desk. "You two love each other. That we all know. Marshall, you're admirable to go through with the wedding while you're still not one hundred percent, but be very sure you both can handle this hurdle. Weddings are stressful even when everything is hunky-dory. So pace yourselves and remember you have the rest of your lives to get through this."

"But we only have the rest of this month until the wedding," Stella said. "I don't want any regrets."

Marshall understood what she was saying. "I don't think any man would regret being your husband."

"I don't want just any man. I want you," she said. "All of you." Then she thanked the reverend and left the room.

Reverend Howell gave Marshall a solemn stare. "I think you and I need to say a prayer, son."

Marshall nodded in agreement and closed his eyes.

Stella waited by her convertible, her prayers centered on trusting in God. Her faith had always been her stronghold. She wouldn't waver now. She found comfort in knowing that even if the worst happened, she'd get through it. She had the best parents in the world, and she had a solid faith community to see her through.

But what if I don't have Marsh?

She couldn't think beyond the here and now. She had to take baby steps right along with Marshall. When she saw him coming out of the church, she took a steadying breath and waved.

"Sorry," he said. "The reverend gave me a little advice."

"What did he say?" she blurted. Then she held up her hand. "I mean, you don't have to tell me. That's private."

"It's okay." He opened her door to let her into the driver's seat, then he came around and folded himself into the passenger's side. "We prayed together."

Stella felt a rush of tears again, but she pushed them away. She'd never been such a crybaby. But knowing Marshall was also relying on the Lord made her feel so much better.

"We have to keep the faith," she said as she shifted the little car into reverse.

Marshall looked straight ahead. "Yes. I guess having faith is a lot like not remembering. The unseen things are right there out of your reach and you have to trust that everything will make sense one day."

Stella shot him a smile. The old Marsh was still here. She could cling to that. "I thought we'd take a drive around the lake. Pelican Lake. Do you remember it?"

He took in the countryside. "Church picnics, camp meetings, after-school swimming. Yeah, I . . . I can see it in my mind."

She wanted to ask if he could see her in his memories, but Stella was learning to be patient. "It's not a big lake, but it's pretty. Remember Old Jake?"

He squinted and frowned. "No."

"He's a big alligator. We used to sing 'Hey, Jake from Pelican Lake.' He travels back and forth from the bayou stream between the river and the lake. I used to be scared to swim there because of Old Jake sightings. I guess he's still there somewhere."

"Just like my memories," Marshall said, his tone full of frustration.

Stella refrained from agreeing with him.

"Let's grab some burgers and have a picnic. We used to spend a lot of time out there."

"That sounds great," he said before changing the subject. "So we're getting married at the church. I like that."

"Good. We agreed on that a year ago. Right before you left." Her voice drifted off as memories flashed through her mind like a river flood. "Then we decided to go ahead and find a house. Our own house. Your dad helped my dad fix it up. Our moms helped me decorate it."

"Let's go to the house," he said, his eyes lighting up. "If I'm gonna live there, I probably should see the place, right?"

Stella wasn't sure. She'd wanted to show him the house right away. But that had been before . . . before the new Marshall had walked into her life. "Are you up to this?"

"Why wouldn't I be? I told you, I need details. I'd say the house I obviously now own is one mighty big detail."

When she didn't respond to his rough tone, he touched her hand. "I'm sorry. This . . . isn't easy. I can't remember and I get aggravated. I didn't mean to snap."

Stella held on to the gear stick and shifted. "The house it is, then. I hope you like it. I sent you pictures."

He gave her a frustrated stare. "Mom kept

telling me about your letters and pictures. They must be in the bundle of my personal belongings that got shipped here."

Stella mirrored his frustration. "You really haven't read any of my letters?"

"I was so out of it in Germany, I didn't want to read them. Mom decided to ship my belongings home so they wouldn't get lost," he said, his tone softening. "I'll get them out and read them again. I promise. Everything's been kind of mixed up."

Stella's hope warred with her agony. If he didn't care enough to read the letters she'd sent to him on a regular basis, why should he care about anything?

She whirled the car into the drive-through and ordered their burgers, then she took a turn on the street where they were supposed to live. She spun the tiny car up onto the driveway of the Craftsman-style house they'd picked out all those months ago, her pain and anger simmering beneath a smile.

But when she turned to look at Marshall, her heart melted for him all over again. He had such a look of awe on his face that she couldn't be mad at him.

"This is our house?" he asked in a low whisper, glancing from the house to her and then back again.

"Yours, mine, and the bank's," she replied.

"C'mon. I'll give you the grand tour."

When they got to the front door, Marshall turned to her. "About the letters. I . . . I was afraid to read them, Stella. I was afraid I wouldn't remember, so Mom sent them home to keep me from getting all frazzled and upset. You have to understand, I was wounded, bitter, and scared. I haven't admitted that to anyone, not the doctors and not even my parents." He took the bag of food from her and looked down, his gaze locked on her. "I'm going to read your letters now. I want to know everything, okay?"

"Okay," she said, her heart so full of love she thought it would fill this whole house. "Okay, Marshall. Every little thing will bring you back to me, one memory at a time."

"Starting with these burgers," he said, a teasing light in his eyes.

"Starting now," she replied. Then she unlocked the door to their home.

FIVE

Marshall took a step into the little cottage, trying to picture living here with Stella. "I like the built-ins and the fireplace," he said.

"You zoomed right in on that when we first looked at the house," she explained. "It was a mess back then, empty and sad and in need of some tender loving care."

That described him too, but he had to quit comparing all her happy memories with his empty ones. He took in the new floral sofa across from the double windows and the cozy leather chair and ottoman tucked in one perfect corner. "I guess you went furniture shopping."

She moved toward the shiny white built-in shelves, then asked as if she knew what he was thinking, "Do you remember any of this?"

He glanced around. The house smelled of new paint and freshly polished wood. A picture of a garden scene hung over the sofa. A sweet-smelling round yellow candle was centered on the trunk that served as a coffee table. Already she'd worked to make it homey and comfortable.

Marshall closed his eyes and let his mind wander. "I remember a song playing on the radio."

He heard her intake of breath and opened his eyes.

She nodded. "It was the Realtor's cell phone. He kept getting calls and we giggled about it. It was a rendition of 'When the Saints Go Marching In.' "

Marshall snapped his fingers. "Yes, I remember that song, and I can see the house — this room — in my mind."

She rushed toward him. "Do you see me there in your mind?"

He couldn't lie to her. He'd already done enough to hurt her. "I just hear the song and I see this room, empty."

"Oh." She looked so deflated he wished he had told her she was in that particular scene. But that wouldn't help the situation. At least she was here now.

"I'm sorry," he said, taking her hand. "Show me the kitchen."

She forced a smile. "You know how I love to bake. This is the perfect kitchen for that."

He didn't correct her slip-up. So she loved

to bake. That made sense. She was almost too good to be true. In spite of jumbled memories, he felt a tug toward her. She was pretty, smart, and capable. All the things any man would want in a soul mate. But Stella had another quality that seemed to draw Marshall like the pull of the river. She had an exuberant, unshakable outlook on life, coupled with a strong faith. How could he not smile when she was in the room?

She tugged him through an archway. "This is the dining room. I sent you pictures of the antique table and chairs Mama and I found at a flea market. We're restoring the set, so it's back at Flower Bend in my daddy's workshop."

"He restores things," Marshall said without preamble.

Her smile lit up again. "Yes, he does. He owned a furniture store, but he sold that a couple of years ago, and now he likes to fiddle around in his shop and restore old furniture. He's making a nice little income thanks to a lot of our friends."

"He restored an old chest for my mother."

"Yes, he did. You remembered!" She pointed to the polished trunk. "He buffed this and brought it back to life. You should have seen it before. It looked like it had traveled the world, all battered and scratched."

"I'll have to tell my mom I remembered that about him." He shrugged, then looked out the big bay window. "This has been hard on her too."

"I'm sure it has," Stella said, some of the pain leaving her eyes. "I need to remember this isn't about me. You've been through so much —"

"And now I'm home and building new memories."

"But still searching for the old ones."

"Yes. It's a challenge but . . . life with you certainly isn't dull."

She laughed at that. "I'll take that as a compliment. Look at this kitchen. I can just picture us here with friends. You'll grill burgers and I'll make potato salad. I might even bake an apple pie." She pushed him through the bright, sunny kitchen to the large window. "See that old live oak out there in the backyard? Don't you think it begs for a tire swing?"

"It does," he said, imagining a little girl just like her out there calling to him. His heart swelled with a sensation that he'd tried so hard to control.

"Marsh, are you all right?"

Marshall's pulse accelerated. His breathing became erratic. He turned to find Stella staring at him. "Yes. I mean, I'm okay. This is just so overwhelming at times."

"So do you want to go? We haven't eaten our food, but you can take it home with you."

"No." He decided he wouldn't ruin this time with her. Maybe if he pushed through that wall that blocked his past, their past, maybe he'd be able to overcome his fears. He took a deep breath and silently counted to ten. "I think we should have a picnic right there under that old tree."

"Really?"

He loved the excitement in her eyes. "Really."

"I left some old blankets in the hall closet," she said. "Let me get one and we'll spread it out and . . . eat our lunch. What a great idea!"

Marshall watched her hurrying down the short hallway, her cute flowery sandals clicking on the polished hardwood floor. How could any man not fall head over heels in love with Stella?

Dear God, bring back that feeling for me. Help me to show this woman that I can honor our promise to each other. Help me to find those precious memories that I've hidden away.

He finished his prayer and followed Stella. "I want to see the rest of our house."

She met him in the hallway with a big faded blue blanket. "You said 'our.' Our house."

"I guess I did."

She looked as if she wanted to say more, but she dropped her head and started again. "Okay. A nice master bedroom on the right with a bath — our dads remodeled that for us. They teased me about making the closet bigger — all those shoes, you know." She moved across the hall. "And two smaller bedrooms on the left. I haven't finished those yet. I was waiting for you —"

"To come back to you," he finished. He took the blanket from her. "Let's eat, and then you can tell me everything. I want to hear how I fell in love with you the first time."

"The first time?" Her question was shy, but her eyes held a deep, abiding hope.

"Yes, so I can enjoy it all over again when I fall in love with you for the second time."

Stella's heart was full of joy.

She and Marshall had a wonderful day. Showing him the house had helped to unlock something deep inside that he'd held away. She could see the difference in him with each story she told him. They'd talked about the house, and she'd explained how they'd made a bid but the seller had counter-offered with a price over their budget. So they'd looked at their finances again and made another offer. Finally the seller had agreed to sell it to them.

"We celebrated that night, right here underneath this tree," she told him while they ate their food. "I didn't want to mention it since you seem to get frustrated if I throw too much at you."

"Tell me now," he said, giving her an encouraging nod.

"The house had been empty for a while, and the yard was a mess, so you carried me through the tall grass and . . . well, you know."

"Know what? Tell me what I can't remember, Stella."

She'd blushed at that request. "You kissed me, right here, and told me that one day our children would have a swing underneath this old oak."

"You didn't mention that part before."

"No. I . . . I was afraid you wouldn't want to hear that."

"You're right. I don't want to talk about kissing you. I want to *try* kissing you."

Instead of getting angry or aggravated, he'd leaned over and, well, he'd kissed her. Right there in broad daylight.

Now Stella was home and dusk was falling over Flower Bend, and she stood in her favorite spot on the upper porch and closed her eyes. She thanked God for that gentle kiss. It had been a soft, sweet touch of his lips to hers, but she'd felt its power. She was pretty sure he had too.

Marshall was coming back to her. Everything would be all right. She'd taken him all over town, showing him the places they'd been together, showing him the parks and the stores and the high school and the spot on the river where he'd proposed to her. During their afternoon together, something had changed between them.

He had hinted at falling for her all over again, and she was surely falling for him in a new way. She still loved him, no matter what.

Now she was tired, but elated too.

"Tomorrow will bring more memories," she said to herself. "He'll come back to me. I just have to hold on and keep praying."

Marshall woke up that night in a cold sweat.

He'd had the dream again, the dream he never shared with anyone except his therapists. In the dream, he could see himself from above. He was lying on a dusty, rocky road, reaching out a hand to someone in the distance. His buddies were lying all around him, some moaning for help and some silent and still.

He couldn't reach his weapon. He couldn't move.

In the gray mist of that scene, he could see a smiling woman walking toward him. She was wearing a brilliant white wedding gown and holding out her hand.

He sat up in bed, gulped in air, and ran a hand over his damp hair. Then he rubbed his eyes. The dream had changed. Now he knew the woman in the dream was Stella.

It had always been Stella. She'd been on his mind, even when he was unconscious and unable to put a name to her face.

In the dream, he screamed for her to run, to go away. But the explosion always hit before she could understand.

And he always woke up before he could save her.

Six

"Want some more coffee, honey?"

Marshall glanced up at his mother. She meant well, but she'd been hovering ever since he returned home.

Home. He was slowly starting to remember more. His doctors had told him it might take time. But he didn't have enough time to recover a lifetime of memories. He wanted to remember everything before he married Stella. Seeing the house on Sunday had added to his anxiety. The dreams were coming almost every night now.

"Marshall?"

"Oh, sorry, Mom." He lifted his cup. "I could use a top off."

Marshall stared down at the morning paper. He didn't want his mother to see the fatigue in his face. "Where's Dad?"

She poured the dark brew into his cup before refilling her own. "Your daddy went over to visit Ralph. They're working on the dining room table."

"For the house, the one Stella showed me yesterday."

Kitten handed him another apple muffin. "Yes, that's right. I didn't want to ask how your day went last night, but you had a smile on your face when you got home."

He smiled now. His mother had the patience of Job. And the heart of Mary. She'd been so good to him, allowing him space, never pestering him about his dark moods. Everyone was tiptoeing around him these days. Everyone except Stella.

She read him like a book. But then, she did love books and she was an avid reader. Maybe that gave her an edge on people's emotions. Or maybe he had a big crush on his bride already.

His forgotten bride.

He glanced at his mother's expectant face. "So you want to know about how it went yesterday?"

Kitten wiped the counter for the third time. "If you want to talk about it."

He broke off a piece of the moist muffin and chewed it. "Stella is amazing. She's so full of life, so positive. I mean, I walk back into her life, half the man I used to be, and she still believes in me, still seems to love me —"

He stopped, took a sip of coffee. "I guess you want to hear about the house, huh?"

Kitten wiped at her eyes. "No, no. I love hearing about you and Stella. I was so afraid —"

"That I'd refuse to go through with the wedding?"

His mother bobbed her head and grabbed a paper towel to wipe her eyes. "You two belong together, Marshall. I know it's so hard, but you and Stella were . . . are . . . the real deal."

"I'm beginning to see that," he admitted. "And Mom, the house is nice. It looks like a home. I want it to be our home, but I also want to remember the house before it becomes our home."

"Are you regaining some of your memory?" She sank down on the stool next to him and put her elbows on the big counter. "Did you remember anything more yesterday?"

"I did," he said. "I remembered that her daddy refurbished that old chest you had out in the garage."

"Yes, he sure did," Kitten said, clasping her hands together. "He's so good at that, and your daddy's taken a liking to helping him. The dining room set is going to be gorgeous."

"Maybe I'll ride over there to see it," Marshall said. He was pretty sure he could remember how to get to Flower Bend.

"I could drive you," his mother offered.

"No, Mom. You showed me the house the other day, and I memorized the way. It's not that far."

"Okay." She patted him on the hand. "I guess I'd better get ready for my committee meeting at the church."

Sorry that he'd been short with her, Marshall swirled on his stool. "Oh, Mom, where are the letters you found with my personal belongings?"

She put her hands on her hips, but Marsh saw the sympathy in her eyes. "You mean the letters from Stella and us? You told us to ship them home." Stepping back toward him, she asked, "So you want to see them?"

"Yes."

"Your father put your duffel bag in the attic. Until you were ready to go through all of that."

"I'm ready now," he said. "I think I'll sort through my things and then maybe go see Dad and Mr. Carson later."

"That sounds like a busy day," his mother replied. "Oh, and don't forget, you have an appointment with your therapist tomorrow."

"I've got it on my phone," he said, tapping his pocket.

"I read that these fancy new phones can be such a boon to amnesia victims. Like a little electronic cheat sheet."

"I have to agree with that," he said. "I have lots of notes in here, trust me."

After his mother left, Marshall went upstairs to open the drop-down stairs to the attic. But his phone buzzed before he'd even tugged on the cord.

"Marshall, it's Nick."

Nick? His best friend growing up and his best man for the wedding. He waited for an image of Nick's face to pop into his brain. "Hi. What's up?"

"Just didn't get to talk to you much at your homecoming party the other night. Thought we might get a bite of lunch and catch up."

He could tell Nick was trying to choose his words carefully. "Sure. I'd like that. Name the time and place."

Nick suggested a country-style diner. "Do you remember the Roxie Diner?"

"No," Marshall said with a chuckle. "I'm teasing. I have an image in my head. Tell me the address and I'll find it. I'll meet you there around noon."

After they'd firmed up the plans, Marshall opened the folding stairs and climbed up to the hot attic. Old toys, Christmas decorations, and several large boxes greeted him. Wishing he had time to go through everything up here, he looked around. He saw his heavy green duffel bag sitting in the corner, *Henderson* letter-blocked on it. A flash of memory drifted by. Soldiers talking and laughing. A pickup football game in the hot desert air. A mess hall full of voices, laughing, talking, eating. Then a blast going off, people running, commands shouted over the many voices. He could see himself and several other soldiers getting in the Humvee and driving away. Away toward the danger.

His whole system screaming, Marshall climbed down and pushed the attic stairs back into their slot in the ceiling before shutting the door. He sat down on the stair landing, took in great breaths of air, and willed his heart to stop racing. Maybe he wasn't ready to go through his things after all. Especially letters from home.

"What's it like being home?"

Marshall stared over at the man who apparently was the best man in the wedding. Nick Prescott was blond and big-boned, with an easygoing smile that seemed laid back. But Nick was a successful businessman. As with all the people he'd been reintroduced to, Marshall had shadowy, almost-there memories of him.

"It's different," he said. "I mean, my mind's still befuddled and scrambled. I feel like an old computer trying to race to catch up with modern technology."

"You need a reboot, man," Nick replied with that sappy smile. "After we eat, I'll show you some of the places where we used to hang out."

"My mom says we stayed in trouble."

"Yep. We weren't exactly choirboys, but hey, we made it this far."

"Yeah, I guess so." They sat in silence until the waitress brought their blue-plate specials.

"What'll you do now?" Nick asked. "Any plans for a job?"

Marshall laughed at that one. "I've been told I had planned to take a long honeymoon with my bride, then come home to settle down to a career in real estate."

"Is that what you want to do, or what everyone else has told you that you should do?"

"I honestly don't know," Marshall said, glad to have someone to be honest with. "It's a mess. Stella is wonderful and beautiful and . . . what else could a man want?"

"But if you can't remember her or any of the plans you made with her, that's kind of tough, huh?"

"Worse than tough. I don't want to hurt her."

"Do you still love her?"

He stared over at his friend and felt a connection that gave him hope. Nick might seem like a big puppy dog, but Marshall had a feeling he could trust him. And that he *had* trusted him, many times over. "I love what I know of her right now. She's adorable and smart and hardworking and so full of this light that seems to shine through. Stella has enough faith for both of us."

Nick nodded then crunched on an ice cube. "She might at that, but . . . you need that kind of faith too. You need to consider that before you go ahead with this marriage."

Marshall stared across at Nick. "Are you happy in your marriage?"

"Marriage has its ups and downs," Nick said with a shrug. "But I'm happier married than I'd be single. I'm better with her than I'd be without her. I love my wife."

While the two men enjoyed their meal and caught up on everything from football to the weather, Marshall wondered if being with someone he cared about was the key.

Having someone to share life with you would surely make it all better. He'd cling to that and hope the rest would work out.

"Thanks, Nick, for listening," he said after a while.

Nick grinned, then tore into the coconut pie the waitress had just brought. "Hey, that's what friends you can't remember are for, right?"

Marshall laughed and dug into his own dessert. "That, and for paying the tab."

SEVEN

The next morning, Stella hummed a happy tune while she inventoried a new shipment of the latest fiction. Mornings were usually slow at The Book House, but today she planned to keep busy so she wouldn't think about the next few weeks. A couple of customers were sampling the paperbacks on the remainder rack, and over in the corner café the smell of Mr. Denham's freshly brewed coffee mingled with the scent of just-out-of-the-oven cookies and breads. On most days, she considered this the ideal job — books to read, coffee to drink, and tempting desserts to consider. She was glad she'd convinced Mr. Denham to start his café inside The Book House.

Patty Parker, her right-hand sales associate and all-around confidante next to Stella's best friend, Rhonda, walked up and propped herself against the big counter behind the cash register. "So, are you getting excited about the wedding?"

Stella lifted her head and pushed at her always-wavy hair. "Yes and no." She glanced around to make sure the two Tuesday-morning customers were still browsing on the other side of the long narrow store. "I'm worried about Marshall."

Patty lowered her head. "Is he still having trouble?"

"Yes, but he's getting better every day. I read up on head trauma and amnesia, and one of the things I've tried to do is show him the people and places he can't remember. That's supposed to help in retaining new memories."

"So that's working, then?" Patty's short red hair stood in little spikes and twirls around her head. Her bifocals were hot pink to match her sensible but sequined pink tennis shoes.

"I think maybe it is making a difference since he's able to retain most of what we tell him and show him," Stella replied. "We had a good weekend." She smiled and held a book with a beautiful historical cover in her hands. "We went to the house after church Sunday."

"Oh, your precious little house. What did he think?"

"He seemed to like it and he . . . sounded

as if he'd like to live there."

"But?"

"But . . . I want the old Marshall back. He would have been moving from room to room, making suggestions, fussing because he didn't get to help with the remodeling. He would have shown more excitement and . . . he would have grabbed me up in a bear hug. This Marshall is more reserved and . . . almost afraid. He didn't even remember the old oak tree. That tree is one of the main features of the yard. We both loved it."

"So what happened?" Patty asked, all ears.

"He made up for not remembering," Stella said. "He insisted we have a picnic right there underneath the tree. Thankfully, Daddy had mowed the yard just last week."

"So . . . how did the picnic go?"

"Nice," she said. When she saw a customer approaching the cash register, she whispered, "He kissed me."

Patty's little squeal of delight caused the stoic woman with several paperbacks in her arms to turn and stare.

"Sorry," Patty said with a shrug. "We were talking weddings and . . . love."

The woman made a face and handed her book choices to Stella. "Hmph. I don't believe in all that stuff."

"Have you ever been married?" Patty, ever so blunt, asked.

"Once, and that was enough for me."

The woman paid Stella, took the bright yellow paper bag with the bold emblem of a house made from books, and turned to leave. But when she reached the door, she pivoted back. "Whichever one of you is getting married, I wish you the best. I'm just a bitter old woman who lost her husband to a war."

"Oh." Stella came around the counter and rushed to the woman. "I'm so sorry. My . . . my fiancé just came home from the Middle East. He's in the Army — a staff sergeant. He was wounded right before Christmas."

The woman's stern expression softened. "I heard some people talking at a dinner last night about a soldier from here who'd been wounded. He's lost his memory?"

"Yes, but we're working on helping him to remember things," Stella said, not knowing what else she could say. Did the whole town know of their dilemma? Even a stranger in her bookstore?

"You have my prayers," the woman replied.

"Thank you," Stella said. "When you said once was enough — about being married — what did you mean exactly?"

The woman shifted her bag full of books. "Don't listen to me, honey. I didn't want him to join the Army, but he insisted. He wanted to serve his country. And he did for ten years. But then he got wounded and . . . I lost him. That was over forty years ago. Vietnam." She let out a wobbly breath. "What I mean is, I only had one love in my life and . . . I never found anyone else to match him." She patted Stella on the arm. "You and your fellow are blessed. He made it home."

"Thank you," Stella said, "for shopping at The Book House and for . . . sharing your story with me. It means a lot. And so do your prayers."

"I'm on it," the woman said with a sad smile. "I can't bring back my soldier, but I can certainly pray for you and yours."

After she left, Patty said, "I don't think I've ever seen her in here before."

"Me either," Stella replied. "Maybe she's new in town."

"Maybe so. A bit opinionated, huh?"

"Yes, but she's still grieving." Stella stared out the window, her thoughts churning with worry. "I prayed the whole time Marsh was gone that he'd come home safe. And that prayer was answered. I shouldn't ask for anything more."

Patty gazed over at Stella with solemn brown eyes. "But you didn't expect him to come home without the memory of you, right?"

Stella shook her head. "Never in a million years. It's like talking to a stranger, but he's still the only man for me." She lifted her chin toward the door. "I don't want to wind up like that woman, old and alone. I want Marshall to want this too. What if he doesn't?"

"I could tell you it will be okay," Patty began, "but we both know I can't predict the future. That's in God's hands." She took Stella by the wrists. "But I will tell you that your faith is solid. Lean on that. Be patient and stay hopeful."

"I will," Stella said. "Each new day brings another challenge, and we're making progress. But we're also running out of time."

"Why is that?"

"Patty, I'm beginning to think if Marsh doesn't have his memory back by our wedding date, there might not be a wedding."

Patty stood speechless for a minute. Then they heard the bell jingling on one of the double front doors of the old building. Patty turned around to see who it was, then whirled back to Stella.

"It's my lunchtime," she said, then made a beeline to the café.

Stella found the strength to put on a smile for their next customer and turned toward the front of the store.

Marshall stood just inside the door, his gaze roaming over the wooden bookshelves and the open café area. "So this is where you work?"

"Yes." Stella was glad to see him but still unsure of how to handle him. "Do you remember any of this?"

He took another long look around. "I don't know. It feels familiar."

"I've been working here off and on since high school," she explained. "I started part-time after school and on weekends, then full-time during summers home from college. Now that my aunt Glenda has retired, I'm the manager."

Stepping closer, she said, "You used to meet me here and we'd go get a burger or take in a movie after work."

"And I worked at my dad's law office."

Stella nodded. "Yes, you did. You were a runner."

His grin reminded her of the old Marshall. "I do remember being tired after football practice and then making deliveries for my dad."

Stella thought about those years now. "We used to sit inside the screened porch at Flower Bend — on that old glider my mom won't give away —"

"And we'd fall asleep," he added, moving toward her. "I remember that, Stella."

Stella went still. "You remembered me, just a little bit?"

"I did." He gazed down at her, his eyes full of hope. "I can see you there on the glider. In my arms." The look of hope turned to something else. Confusion? Anxiety? Regret?

"Marsh—"

"Hey, Marshall, come on over here and get a free lunch on me!"

Stella stepped back and thanked God for that one small memory. Then she put aside her doubts and found her manners. "Do you recall Mr. Denham? Doug Denham. He was our Sunday school teacher for years."

"His voice sounds familiar," Marshall said. "Probably used to get onto me a lot for disrupting his lessons."

"He did," she agreed, giggling. "He got onto both of us."

Marshall laughed too. "So what does he have over there to eat?"

Stella guided him through the archway between the bookstore and the café. "Treats of all kinds that he and Mrs. Denham bake, and sandwiches and salads."

Before Marshall could say anything, Doug Denham came around the long wooden counter and reached out a hand. "I'm sure glad to see you, son. We always have a special deal here for our returning soldiers. Anything you want, on the house."

"Thanks, Mr. Denham," Marshall said before giving Stella a helpless glance. "Seems like everyone wants to make sure I eat a good meal." He turned back to Stella. "I had lunch with Nick yesterday. Guess I'm making the rounds." He grinned at her. "Will you have lunch with me?"

Stella was about to say she couldn't when Patty came breezing up. "I just finished, so you go ahead. I'll watch the store."

"Are you sure?" Stella asked. "You still have nearly all your lunch hour left."

"Which I'll use to take an afternoon coffee break," Patty said, her expressive eyes sending Stella a message. "Go ahead. Enjoy being with your fiancé."

Marshall looked straight into Stella's eyes. "First time I've heard it put that way. I guess I am your fiancé."

Stella's heart fluttered and crashed. Why did he look like a deer caught in the headlights? "That's entirely up to you," she

251

replied. "You don't have to be my anything if you're not ready."

"Let's get some food." He walked past her and started talking to Mr. Denham.

Stella had no choice but to follow, but she turned and shot Patty a confused look, then in desperation straightened the sugar and cream bar. Her friend motioned for her to go ahead.

Swallowing her qualms, Stella said a quick prayer for discernment and plastered a smile on her face. "I'm starving," she said as she waved to the other lunch customers and chatted with them to steady her nerves. When she reached Marshall, she asked, "What are we having today?"

Marshall followed her to a table in the corner. "Mr. Doug says I used to love the chili. Did I?"

Stella couldn't stay hurt when he appealed to her in such a sweet way. "You sure did. At least two bowls every time we came in here."

"Chili it is," he said. After he'd given a waitress their order, including a salad for Stella, Marsh leaned over the table. "Mr. Doug said you're the one who convinced him and his wife to manage this place a few years ago. Is that true?"

This was hard. He'd been so proud of her

for trying to help the lonely couple. "It was selfish on my part," she said, telling her hurting heart to straighten up. "I loved all the good food he and Miss Anne brought to the church dinners. So I asked my aunt Glenda — she owns the bookstore and this building — if we could open up this wall and put in a little café." She shrugged. "When I told her I thought the Denhams would be great at running it, she agreed. And here we are."

Marshall put his hand up to his mouth to hide his next words. "Don't be so modest," he whispered. "He told me you saved both of them by creating a new purpose for them after their only son died in a car accident."

Stella was surprised, and a little gasp escaped before she could control herself. "He said that?"

Marshall nodded. "Just a minute ago when you were still standing over there and I was already over here. I think it might have been during that minute when you were wondering what you'd gotten yourself into, sticking with a man who can't even remember who you are. Am I right?"

Stella looked everywhere but into his eyes. She didn't want to hurt his feelings, so she went back to the subject of the Denhams. "They were depressed and lonely, and I hated seeing the hurt in their eyes, so yes, I might have had ulterior motives but . . . we've all benefited from it. They're here most days, and when they want to travel or take a few days off, they have a well-trained staff to help, including my mother at times and even my aunt."

He grabbed her hand. Stella finally scanned his face, thinking he was upset with her. "What?"

Marshall's smile was indulgent and real. A real smile, just for her. "You're amazing, you know that?"

Stella waited to respond until the waitress placed their food on the table. "What . . . what do you mean?"

"You're a kind, considerate person, Stella. Anyone can see that, even old amnesiac me. You go out of your way to make me comfortable and to spare my feelings." He held her hand. "But don't think you're fooling me one bit. I've seen how this situation has hurt you."

"I'm fine," she said while she blinked back tears. "Really, I'll be okay." *If you still want to marry me.*

"Will you?" he asked, his eyes full of questions and his words reflecting her feelings. "Do you still want to marry me, Stella? Or

254

are you just going along with this because it's too late to turn back?"

EIGHT

Marshall saw the pain in Stella's pretty face. This was a woman who always had a positive outlook on life. But having him back in her life had shaken her to the core. How could it not?

He stared across the little round table, the steaming bowl of chili forgotten in front of him. "We don't have to do this, you know. We can postpone the wedding or . . . not get married at all."

"You don't want to marry me, do you?"

The hurt and shock in her eyes made Marshall feel like a first-class loser. "I don't know what I want right now. It's hard to piece together so many shredded memories. My therapist thinks I have what they call hysterical amnesia."

Stella gave him a sympathetic look. "I read up on that and every other kind of amnesia. I'm trying to do what I can to help jar your memories. Am I pushing too hard, too fast?"

"No," he replied. "You've been great. Everything you've done, all the places you've shown me, that's helped put some of the pieces in place." He shrugged and finally starting eating. "I've always liked things in order. I like control and a plan. I get that in the Army. I can remember football games where I'd study the plays over and over so I'd have a certain picture in my mind. I can't do that now. Now it's just a blank page. Nothing."

She toyed with her salad and then finally put down her fork. "I'm trying to help you fill in those pages," she said, her head down, her fingers clutching a cracker. "But if you don't want to go back to . . . us . . . I can understand. You've been through so much."

"I want to go through something good, something solid and sure," he retorted. "I made a promise to you before I left, and I intend to carry through on that promise."

The cracker fell to her plate. "Because you love me and want to be with me? Or because you're an honorable man who always keeps his promises, no matter what?"

How could he explain this to her without breaking her heart? "I've enjoyed getting to know you again. I like being with you. Can't that be enough for now?"

"It could be," she said, her voice low. "But

is that any way to start a marriage, to plan a life together?"

"There are worse ways to spend your life," he replied.

"That's not a very reassuring answer." She stared down at her salad. "I think I'll have Mr. Denham wrap this up for later. I'm not that hungry after all."

She started to get up, but Marshall pulled her back down by the hand. "Stella, I'm saying this all wrong, but I'm not ready to give up on us just yet. We agreed on a few weeks. We've got less than three weeks until the wedding. And you still have to show me the cake and the color theme and . . . all of our shower gifts."

Her expression had gone from forlorn and defeated to surprised and intrigued. "How do you know about all that?"

"Oh, you're not the only one who's been trying to fill in the blanks in my brain. My mother has been chattering almost nonstop about all of the above."

"It's still hard on her. She's been so excited about this wedding."

"Very hard." He swallowed, ran a finger across Stella's palm. "I hear her crying sometimes, but she never lets me see. She's strong and good, and my dad — well, he just walks around in his own quiet way. But he's always willing to listen when I get frustrated."

"You have good parents, Marsh," she said, her tone more relaxed now. "We both do." She put her other hand in his. "But none of them expect us to go into something we're not sure about."

"You were sure." He squeezed her hand. "I have that to go on and . . . I'm trusting in God. He brought me home, Stella. He brought me home to you. I don't take that lightly."

She let out a little sigh. "That's one of the things I've always loved about you. You always do the right thing." She let go of his hands, got up, and gave him a soft smile. "Even if it's for the wrong reasons."

"Hey, this isn't wrong," he replied, trying to keep her from walking away. "Give me time and . . . show me all the things that go into a wedding."

She nodded and gave him another wobbly smile. "The first thing is love." Then she hurried to the counter and asked for a to-go box for her salad.

That night Stella opened the front door of Flower Bend and let Marshall inside.

"Welcome," she said, still reeling from their lunch conversation. "This is where I grew up." She motioned him into the open foyer with the sweeping, freestanding curved staircase. "You used to spend a lot of time here."

Marshall let out a whistle. "Impressive. And old, from what my mom tells me."

"It's close to one hundred and forty years old," she explained, trying to imagine her home through his eyes. "Flower Bend was built in the late 1800s, a few years after the Civil War was over."

He pointed out a window toward the front yard. "And on the river, at that."

"Yes, right across the road. You can see it from the second-floor porch. This place has seen storms and floods and a lot of good and bad times."

Their eyes met over that statement. Marsh didn't waver. Stella felt a current of understanding pass between them.

"Show me the rest," he said. "And show me our shower gifts. I hear that's a really big deal with women."

She had to laugh at that. After their lunch, he'd followed her back into the bookstore and insisted on coming to visit Flower Bend tonight. And here she'd thought he wanted to end things with her. But no. Marshall was determined to see this through to the bitter end. And that end could be bitter and

260

tragic for both of them if they weren't careful.

She'd had to do some hard praying to allow this to continue. But both Stella's friend Rhonda and her mother agreed that if they ended things now, it wouldn't help either of them. In fact, it might put Marshall into an even deeper tailspin. He'd feel as if he'd let her down.

And she'd feel as if her heart would never heal.

"You love him, Stella," Rhonda had told her this afternoon on the phone, the baby wailing in the background while she tried to calm Stella's nerves. "I'm your matron of honor, so listen to me. Give him time. If you have to postpone the wedding, do it in a kind and loving way or you'll spook him." Then she'd added, "But he'll fall for you all over again, so quit worrying."

But she did worry. How could she and Marsh build a marriage on so many swirling doubts and emotions? Where was the love in that?

Dear God, I hope I made the right decision today at lunch. She'd come close to calling off the wedding, but something in his passionate plea to make this work had touched her.

"C'mon in," she said, guiding him down

261

the central hallway into a cozy paneled den in the back of the house. Just off the den, the deep wraparound porch offered rocking chairs and a view of the backyard. Magnolia trees and crepe myrtles vied for attention along the paths and walkways, and colorful orange and white daylilies and azalea bushes with hot pink blooms shined in the growing dusk. The hydrangeas her mother so loved carried into the backyard too, with several massive bushes in sunny areas.

She waited while Marshall took it all in.

"Beautiful."

She turned to agree and found his eyes on her instead of the yard. Did he like her floral sundress? She'd worn it a dozen times before and he'd seen her in it. Did it bring back memories?

"Uh, do you want a glass of mint tea?"

He nodded. "That'd be great."

She moved through the den and into the big country kitchen across the way. "Mama and Daddy are out in the garden, picking a bushel of cucumbers and peppers for your mom."

"She'll enjoy that." He lifted his nose and sniffed. "Something sure smells good."

Stella turned to where he stood between the den and the kitchen. "We're having pot roast for dinner."

"I love pot roast."

"My mother knows that," she said, hoping to lighten the situation. "We're all conspiring to smother you with good food and a lot of hugs and memories." She handed him a crystal goblet full of rich, sweet tea with lemon and a sprig of mint. "We're determined to bring out all the memories you're holding dear."

He stopped and gave her a look full of awareness. "I do hold them dear. I do."

Stella could see something different in his expression. "I didn't mean to tease you. I'm sorry."

"No, no." He set his tea down on the big butcher-block counter where her mother had placed crackers and cheese and pickled peppers and peaches. "You've hit on the very thing that makes me want to keep going, Stella."

Walking around the counter, he touched a finger to her loose ponytail. "I'm holding something dear, or as the therapist thinks, I'm holding back these memories because I think I have to protect them. I just never understood until this minute that it's not so much repressed memories as it is cherished memories."

Stella's confused heart raced to keep up with him. "So . . . you think you . . .

cherished me?"

"I must have." His eyes held hers with that promise he refused to break. "If I didn't believe that, I wouldn't be standing here now."

Stella smiled up at him. "Want to see our shower gifts before we eat dinner?"

"I'd like that."

"They're mostly in the dining room right now. We passed it, but the doors are closed."

"I can't wait to dig right in. I mean, most men just love to shop for china and to gloat over household goods, right?"

She had to giggle at that. "Yes, of course."

He took her hand and followed her to the front of the house. And for just a minute, everything seemed right in Stella's world.

She had some memories she planned to cherish too. And this would be one of them.

NINE

"That is a really big mixer," Marshall said. "It looks like it could mow the lawn too."

Stella touched a dainty hand to the bright red monstrosity. "Oh no, buddy. This stays in my kitchen, right there on what I call the baking counter."

"You did mention you like to cook."

"Doesn't every Southern woman?"

"I guess so. Y'all sure do know the way to a man's heart."

Her smile was as brilliant as the big mixer's shine. "So we're getting to you, right?"

He rubbed his stomach. "That pot roast is calling my name."

She ran her hand over the shimmering silver bowl that went with the mixer. "We also have banana pudding. And not from a box. My mama makes her pudding from scratch. Cooks it on the stove and adds fresh bananas and crisp vanilla wafers."

"You are seriously killing me."

He grinned at her and was rewarded with that cute smile again. Her green eyes were the color of fresh grass.

"So, a mixer, a food processor, a fancy cookware set, plus several dish towels too pretty to actually use. And all these other gadgets. That's called a kitchen shower."

"Yes." She moved on to comforters and blankets, cushions and pillows, or "linens," as she called them. "I've had five showers so far, each with a different theme — kitchen, garden, linens, recipes and cookbooks, and china and everyday dishes. According to proper etiquette they have to all be done and finished several weeks before the wedding so I won't be distracted, but who's counting?"

"I think you have more than enough distraction," he said on a soft note.

She didn't miss a beat. "Moving on. You have to see the fine china."

He followed her to a long buffet cabinet where the "fine" china was being displayed. He listened while she discussed the pros and cons of Lenox versus Wedgwood or Waterford.

"So finally, I went with a Wedgwood pattern." She pointed to the butterfly floral design. "It made me think of the gardens here at Flower Bend. And Wedgwood is traditional in my family, so I would have caused a scandal if I'd picked something else."

The china was beautiful, delicate, and dainty, just like her. He didn't really understand, but if this stuff made her happy then he'd go with it. "So I missed out on all that."

She gave him an indulgent smile. "Most men would be more than glad to miss out on a bunch of chattering women admiring all these beautiful gifts. The whole trousseau part involves registering for what you'd like and then allowing your friends and family to throw showers and buy you gifts. Then it's all about lime green sherbet punch and lots of delicate finger sandwiches and a themed cake. The one for the kitchen shower had the cutest design on it — forks and spoons and spatulas in all colors and all edible."

He snapped his fingers. "I really hate I missed that one." Then he laughed. "But you were holding out about the punch and cake. I don't think I've ever turned down either."

"Don't worry. We'll have that at the wedding. We haven't had a couples' shower, where there would be plenty of food. But that's okay. We don't need to face another crowd."

She stopped, put a hand on a fluffy, embroidered white bath towel, her eyes on the big *H* monogram scrolled in black. She lifted her gaze to him, her eyes doing that misty thing. "It's amazing how much I took all this for granted. How much I took you for granted."

"You didn't do that," he said, coming around the big table to take her hands in his. "You were planning our wedding just as you should have been doing. I'm the one who messed up."

"Going to war and then being wounded isn't messing up, Marshall. I'm so glad you made it home." She shrugged and then lifted an unopened package wrapped with an elaborate white bow. "This morning a customer at the store told me she had given up on love, and when I asked her what she meant by that, she explained that her husband died in Vietnam. She never remarried."

Stella gazed up at him with those big eyes, her expression full of thankfulness. "I thought about how that could be me. All alone and bitter. I shouldn't whine about anything when I have you standing right here in front of me."

She placed the gift box on the side table with several other unopened packages. "Looking back, I can see I've been so caught up in the wedding, I forgot to plan for the marriage. I need to consider that our lives are about to change. Even more than they already have."

Marshall once again marveled at this woman's strong faith and practical logic. The way she looked at him told him how much she loved him. His heart did a little shifting thing, like a flower breaking through dry, cracked dirt. The stirring in his soul made him reach for her and tug her close.

"We can make this work," he said, wanting it. "Changes happen in life, right? We can make this work."

"My mama always says marriage is hard work," she replied. "I just never knew it would be this hard."

"We can have some good parts," he said, hoping she'd be able to enjoy being with him. "Like this." He lifted her chin and gave her a tentative kiss. Then he leaned back and stared down at her, marveling at her grace and determination. "See, that wasn't so hard, was it?"

She smiled, but he saw a hint of that mist in her eyes. "I remember your kisses," she said in a soft whisper. "I missed you so much, Marsh."

He should tell her that he missed her too. That her kisses seemed familiar and wonderful. He should tell her that he loved her, that he knew in his heart he'd always loved her.

But that old cold dread held him back.

"I've missed out on much more than towels and cookware, haven't I?"

"Yes," she said, her head down. "I wish I could make it all right again, but . . . that's in God's hands."

"Do you believe God will give me back my memories?"

She gazed up at him, her face mirroring his doubts. "I believe God has allowed you to store your memories in a safe place, but maybe you're not so sure. Maybe you're afraid to bring them back out."

He almost told her about the dream, about seeing her walking toward him with her hand outstretched. But as with all the other times he'd thought of the dream, his heart started racing and he broke out in a cold sweat, the fear that gripped him cutting at his breath.

"Marsh, are you all right?"

Dazed, he blinked and nodded. "I . . . I think I need some air. Just . . . can we go outside?"

"C'mon," she replied, fear clouding her eyes. "I'm sorry for dragging you in here."

"It's okay. I'm okay. Just . . . need some air."

She hurried him down the hallway and out onto the back porch. Marshall grabbed one of the sturdy posts and held on, his head down, his mind whirling with dark images. Why couldn't he get past this? When would it end?

Would he be forced to walk away from Stella so he could heal himself? His gut told him if he walked away now, he'd never be able to come back to her.

Trust in the Lord.

The words shattered the dark walls around his soul.

He had to trust that he was doing the right thing and for all the right reasons. He had to trust in the plan God had for his life.

And the only way to do that was to march forward toward the light of Stella's undying love so he could emerge a new and better man than the one she thought she'd lost.

He took another deep breath and then turned to Stella. "I'm sorry. It's the PTSD. It comes and goes. I'll be okay."

"Is there anything I can do?"

"No. I have images of war inside my head. They come at odd times and . . . sometimes

271

I still have nightmares." He didn't go into detail or tell her that she was in his dreams. "The doctors say it'll get better as long as I keep going to therapy."

"I hope so."

She looked so scared. Was she afraid of him?

"I didn't mean to upset you," he said.

"Oh no, I mean, I understand. I thought I was the one who'd upset you. All that stuff for a house you don't really remember —"

He realized she thought he'd become stifled by the wedding and shower gifts. No wonder she looked so lost and embarrassed.

"Stella, it's not that. Really, it's not."

She looked doubtful, but before she could say anything else, her parents walked up.

Her dad grunted. "Look at this, Marshall. We have enough vegetables here to last your mama a month of Sundays."

Marshall tore his gaze away from Stella. "Wow, she'll sure appreciate that."

Stella's mother took one look at them and went into overdrive. "Where are my manners? You're probably starving, and here I am all hot and a mess from picking vegetables."

"It's okay, Mama," Stella said, her tone flat. "We . . . came out to enjoy the night air."

"Let's get y'all inside, and Stella, if you don't mind helping me to warm up the dinner rolls, we'll get on with our meal."

"Sure." Stella shot Marshall a questioning look. "I'll see you inside."

He wished they could sit down alone and away from all the well-meaning people who kept interrupting them. As he watched Stella walk away, Marshall decided to take matters into his own hands.

Come this weekend, he intended to kidnap his bride and take her away from all this. Just for a few precious hours. And after seeing all that he'd missed, he came up with an idea that might surprise her too.

TEN

The first week of waiting for Marsh to remember her had gone by.

Stella went over her planner notes to make sure she'd covered everything for the wedding. She'd already had formal photographs taken of her in her wedding dress. Those would go to the local newspaper to run the week after the wedding.

She stopped, held a hand to her heart, and stared out her bedroom window. She could see the Mississippi River flowing and gurgling, as old as time and such a constant in her life. She'd been so happy the day the photographer had come out to Flower Bend to take those pictures. The whole garden had awakened in a riot of color that made her shimmering white dress stand out like a single magnolia blossom caught in a bunch of azaleas.

She'd been excited and happy after she'd seen the photos. Her hair had been curled in a loose chignon with her grandmother's lace veil caught in a crystal tiara, and her dress — the portrait neckline a clear satin white that showed off her mother's pearls, the long flowing skirt accented with seed pearls and embroidered flowers.

She couldn't show those pictures to Marshall. Not now, since he wasn't supposed to see her in the dress before the wedding. Maybe not ever. But she'd described her dream wedding to him in detail in her letters.

Letters that, as far as she knew, he still had not read. But why? What was holding him back?

Three more weeks, Lord. What should I do?

A soft knock at her door brought Stella's head up. "Come in."

Her mother opened the door and peeked inside. "What are you up to so early in the morning?"

Stella lifted the thick wedding journal. "Double-checking."

Her mother came in and sat down on a seafoam-green slipper chair next to the white desk. "How you doing, honey?"

"I'm okay," Stella said. "Marsh has called me every day this week. He told me he helped his dad with some yard work and that he's beginning to consider what he'll do now that he's home. He's still interested in real estate." Her wry smile hid her concerns. "He has a business degree, if he can remember what he learned in college."

"That sounds positive. He's planning for the future, so I'm sure he's beginning to remember a lot."

"Yes, he is making plans," Stella said. She shut the journal. "I just don't know if I'll be in that future. I think the whole town is holding its breath on this wedding."

"No, the whole town is praying toward this wedding," her mother said on a soft, sure note.

Stella thought her mother was incredible, so calm and confident, so positive and encouraging. She'd be lost without the love of her parents.

"I should have stopped it the day he came home, but I was so in shock, and I kept hoping."

"Honey, he didn't want to hurt you. Kitten said that's why he wouldn't let them tell anyone. He wanted to be the one to tell you, so you could work through this together. That indicates he cares a lot about your feelings. He loves you."

"He's being a gentleman, Mama. Marsh has always done the right thing. He's that kind of man."

"Well, my heart assures me he'll be the man who promised to marry you, because somewhere in his scarred heart, he still loves you."

"Do you think he's afraid to show that love?"

Her mother got up and ran a hand over the wedding dress hanging in the protective garment bag on the old armoire. "War does strange things to a person. We can't know what he went through, but . . . he lost some of his best friends in that awful explosion. He survived, but he might feel guilty for that, and yes, he might be afraid now. Afraid to love again, to show his true feelings. A brave, strong man like that can hide a multitude of repressed emotions. You just need to be patient, no matter what happens."

Stella got up and gave her mother a hug. "I love you, Mama. You always say exactly what I need to hear."

"That's part of my job, suga'." Her mother fluffed her short brown hair. "Now I'm off to get my hair done. Do you have any plans other than work for the weekend?"

"I don't know," Stella admitted. "I'm kind of in limbo about everything." She touched a hand to the journal. "Mama, I told Marshall something the other night, something

I can see now."

"What, honey?"

"I've been so involved in planning this wedding. I poured myself into this the minute he went back over there. For the last ten months, I've focused on the ceremony, the reception venue, the food, the invitations, my dress, my attendants — everything to do with this wedding. It's all in here."

"That's part of being a bride."

"But . . . somewhere in there, I forgot about the groom."

"Honey, you wrote him almost every day, and you told him all about the plans."

"I did, that's true. I tried to include him, to keep him up-to-date."

"So what's bothering you?"

"I managed to forget what he was going through. I think I subconsciously forgot he was in danger, and I used our wedding as my shield. I got so wrapped up in getting married, I forgot about being married. I forgot about my groom and his feelings."

Her mother smiled over at her. "You'll learn that as you go into this marriage. You have to consider each other always. You just need to keep God at the center of all your decisions and he will help you."

Stella took a glance at her dress. "It's not

a fairy tale, is it?"

"No, I'm afraid it's not," Mama replied. "But . . . being married to someone you love and respect is better than a fairy tale. It's the truth and happiness, tears, love, and sometimes conflict and trouble. But it's worth it. You know that, right? You aren't having second thoughts, are you?"

Stella shook her head. "No. I still love him. I'm willing to fight for him. But I need him to fight for me too."

"He has, darling. And he still is — fighting for you and for the life God has planned for both of you." She tapped a hand on the full-skirted dress. "You've never been the patient type, but this is certainly a lesson for you to learn and then grow. Sometimes all you can do is wait and pray."

After her mother left, Stella finished her checklist and put her wedding journal back on her desk. She had a full day at the bookstore with enough work to keep her mind off her troubles.

"I have no troubles," she repeated to herself as she finished getting dressed. "I just need to be patient."

Her cell buzzed as she was about to walk out of her room.

Marshall!

"Hi," he said, his tone tentative. She

prayed each day to hear the old Marshall's confident voice.

"Hi. How are you?"

"I'm good. Dad and I went fishing yesterday. I remembered how to bait a hook, at least."

"That's great." She didn't know what else to say.

"Hey, I was thinking, how about you and I go someplace private tomorrow? Somewhere away from here and different."

"You mean, like a date?"

"Yes, like a date. I actually think I remember how to go on a date."

"That would be nice," she said, her heart doing a tug-of-war. "What time?"

"How about all day?"

"All day? Are you sure you're up to that?"

"Yes. I need to get away for a while. With you."

So he needed some space. Understandable. "Do you need me with you? Or would it be better if you took some time to be alone?"

"I want to be with you," he said. "If you want to be with me, I mean."

"I do," she said, unable to say no to him. "I'll have to make sure my aunt can cover for me at the bookstore since it's a Saturday. I'll call you and let you know, and if I can go, I'll be ready bright and early."

"Okay. Good. Are you off to work?"

"Yes. Busy day. We got in another new shipment. I have to shelve all the books."

"Okay. I'll call you later."

She put away her phone and hurried out the door. A whole day with Marshall. The man was trying, she'd give him that.

"But I need you back," she said as she cranked her car and headed into town. "I need you back, Marshall."

"So, I thought we'd go to the zoo in New Orleans."

Stella's surprise must have shown on her face.

"Is that okay?"

"Yes." She grinned. "You took me there years ago, when we officially started dating in high school. You'd just gotten your driver's license and wanted to take a short road trip. Did you remember that?"

"Yes. And no one told me about it. Mom and I were talking about how you love animals and I remembered being with you at the zoo. I guess it's in there somewhere." He tapped his temple and winked at her. "Maybe my brain is beginning to work again."

Stella sent up a silent prayer to that end.

■ ■ ■ ■

Marshall maneuvered his dad's car through the interstate traffic. "I can't remember the last time I came into the city," he said. Then, realizing his slip, he started laughing. "I can't remember much of anything."

Stella's expression changed from cautious to smiling. "You know, laughter is good for the soul. I'm glad you can laugh at yourself."

"Me too. Some days are better than others."

"How's your therapy going?"

He changed lanes and glanced over at her. "Pretty good. I'm blessed to find a good therapist close to home. And I've been talking to Reverend Howell a lot. He comes by the house to check on me."

"Really? That's good. He's so easy to talk to."

"Have you talked to him — about us?"

Stella shifted in her seat. "I did when you were gone, of course. And . . . after I found out what had happened to you. He's been wonderful. He's a good listener."

"He suggested we come back together to give him an update."

"We could do that. Maybe tomorrow afternoon, if he's free."

Marshall checked the speedometer. "All we talk about is me and my lack of a memory," he said. "I know it's there between us, but for today can we pretend everything's okay? I need a normal day."

"A normal day?" She wagged a finger at him. "You make me sound so boring."

"No, not boring. Just a day that's quiet and fun and . . . with no pressure."

"I can do that." She sat still, her hands in her lap. Then she lifted her head and closed her eyes.

Marshall watched her, thinking she looked so pretty with the sunlight moving over her as the car sped along the road.

"What are you thinking over there?"

"I'm thinking I'm with the man I love and it's only three weeks until we can begin our life together. And that today will be a carefree, relaxing day without wedding worries or anyone asking imposing questions."

Marshall didn't respond, but he wanted a day with no worries too. He could only think of the here and now, today.

"What are *you* thinking?" she asked, her eyes on him now.

He hesitated, but then decided he had to be honest. "I'm thinking I'm with an amazing woman who takes my breath away, and that no matter what happens down the road, today will always be special to me."

Stella's expression changed from one of expectancy to disappointment to acceptance. "Are you taking me away from everything and everyone so you can break up with me, Marshall?"

ELEVEN

Marshall's frown filled with confusion. "What do you mean?"

Stella pivoted on the seat and leaned against the door. "You're making such a production about this, I figured you wanted to get me away from everyone to save me a lot of embarrassment. I know I can be a drama queen, but if you're expecting theatrics, you can rest assured I'm stronger than I look."

His frown intensified with each word. "You think I went to all this trouble just so I could break up with you?"

"Isn't that what this is about?"

"No," he said, now with a scowl showing his disappointment and anger. "Why would I be so cruel?"

"Because you don't want to hurt me or embarrass me. But if we call off the wedding, everyone will know anyway. I'll have to return all the gifts and call the caterer.

I'll have to . . . sell my dress or at least pack it away. The whole town will know, Marsh. So just tell me now and get it over with. I can handle all that as long as you're honest with me."

Marshall pulled the car off at the next exit and found an empty parking lot by a little roadside park. He sat still for a few moments before he shut down the engine and opened his door, and then he came around and opened her door.

"Marsh?"

"Stella, get out of the car, please."

Was he really going to let her down easy right here in this deserted parking lot?

She swallowed the growing lump in her throat and slowly slid out of her seat. Wiping her sweating hands on her jeans, she leaned back on the car, her knees turning to noodles.

"Go ahead. I'm ready."

She held her head down, prepared to take her lumps and then start to pick up the pieces of her life.

Marsh lifted her head with a finger underneath her chin. "You look like you're walking to your execution."

"Aren't I? The jilted bride who goes on to be an old maid with too many cats? Maybe I won't be executed, but that will be my

286

sentence."

"Aren't you being rather dramatic about this?"

She glanced up to find him smiling. "Are you laughing at me?"

He nodded. "I am, but not for the reasons you think. I'm laughing because you are so incredibly cute when you have a major pout going on."

"This is more than a pout —"

He didn't let her finish. Instead, he pulled her into his arms and hugged her close. "Stella, I know this has been awful for you, like a bride's worst nightmare. But I'm here to tell you that you need to trust me and know that I'm not going anywhere."

"But —"

"But I'm here," he repeated. "I wanted to spend today with you so we could maybe reconnect. I remembered taking you to the zoo. I did, really, with no help from anyone. But today I want to make new memories with you. New memories with my new girl."

She sniffed and pulled away. "So I'm your new girl now?"

"You're my only girl now. You are the reason I get up every day. This is like a new adventure, and believe me, while my mind is in constant turmoil and I have nightmares to no end, the thought of talking to you or seeing you each day keeps me going. So please, stop worrying, and let's do what we set out to do. Let's just have fun together, okay? Can you do that for a wounded soldier?"

She nodded, a mortified blush heating her skin. "Now I really feel embarrassed. I told you I could be a drama queen."

"You're a cute drama queen."

She hugged him close again and savored the spicy clean smell of his hair and clothes. But she thanked God for once again showing her that she wasn't the only victim here. Marsh was the one who had to suffer through this.

And she had to be the one who pulled him through.

So she lifted up on her toes and kissed him on the cheek. "Never mind," she said with a wry grin. "Just never mind me. Can we start over?"

"Isn't that what this is all about?"

"Yes. Yes, that's exactly what this is all about."

"Good." He opened her door for her so she could get back in the car. Then he leaned down and grinned at her. "We're going to the zoo, okay? But no more monkey business from you."

"Okay." She felt small and petty, but she

288

couldn't hide the sigh of relief that rushed through her system. While he ran around the car to get in, she whispered, "Okay, Lord. I'll try to be patient."

The hour drive into New Orleans seemed like only minutes to Stella after that uncomfortable confrontation. For a while, it seemed like nothing had changed between them. They laughed at old jokes, and she filled him in on things he tried to piece together.

Soon enough, they were in the city and walking through the gates of Audubon Zoo. The day was warm and a bit humid, but a nice breeze played through the old live oaks and danced over the gray Spanish moss that clung to the trees like tattered lace threads. The sound of children laughing and playing reminded Stella of all the times her parents brought her here.

She thought about her first date with Marshall and how they'd admired the exotic cats and the tall giraffes. She'd loved the monkeys and the orangutans, but Marshall had most enjoyed the bird aviaries and the alligator exhibit.

That much hadn't changed either. She longed to ask him what exactly he remembered about their first date, but they were sticking to the rule of being in the moment. They had a lunch of hot dogs, popcorn, and funnel cakes.

"I ate too much," she said later as they strolled toward the gate. "But that was so much fun."

"I had fun too," he said. Then he rubbed his stomach. "But I'm pretty sure I could eat some cotton candy."

Stella laughed and moved ahead. "I'm getting you out of here before you get a stomachache."

Reluctantly chasing after her, he said, "We could take a stroll on the Moonwalk. Are you up to that?"

She wanted to tell him she was up to anything that would keep them together. "That sounds nice."

They left the zoo and drove up St. Charles, passing old wedding cake mansions and quaint cottages until they reached Canal and then turned onto Decatur. Marshall found a spot in the public parking area by the river.

"Not too crowded today," he said. "This city is a constant paradox. A beautiful place with a lot of lost souls."

Stella looked up at him. "You said that so naturally . . . as if you knew that already."

"I do know that," he said. "I mean, I find

lost thoughts and connect them, but I remember the broad pictures at times. It's frustrating and scary and I feel completely helpless about it, but I'm learning to take each memory as a gift."

They'd reached the boardwalk along the river, called the Moonwalk. It was a good place to see the moon over the Mississippi, but right now late afternoon sunshine dappled the brick path with changing shadows. The smell of beignets and chicory coffee coming from the Café du Monde made Stella wish she hadn't eaten that funnel cake.

"Do you want some coffee?" Marshall asked as they strolled toward the Audubon Aquarium. He pointed to the ticket line. "Or do you want to see some underwater creatures now?"

She thought about her choices. "No to the coffee right now." Glancing up toward the aquarium entrance, she shook her head. "No, as much as I love sharks and eels, I'm good for now."

"You're terrified of sharks and eels," he said, his laughter floating out over the river.

Stella stopped walking and gave him a questioning glance. "How did you know that?"

He shrugged and grinned as he pointed to

his head. "I told you, it's all in here. I just need to keep digging to get it out."

They laughed together, and Stella held this moment in her heart, storing it up with all the other precious moments.

"Let's find a bench and sit," she suggested, hoping a few more memories might surface.

They hurried toward a spot underneath the shade of some nearby tall bushes. Stella sat down and waited for Marshall, but before he could join her a loud pop echoed through the air.

Marsh jumped, and then he grabbed her and shoved her down on the bench, covering her with his upper body.

Marshall heard the voice from his nightmares. Stella's voice.

Surrounded by fire and smoke, he tried to call out to her. "No, go back. Go back."

"Marshall?"

He blinked and the smoke disappeared. Glancing down, he saw the horror in Stella's eyes. He held her close in a tight, protective embrace. "What happened?"

Stella lifted up and straightened her hair. "I think a car backfired. Or maybe a gun went off. I'm not sure."

Marshall sank onto the bench. "I'm so

sorry. I thought — I don't know what I thought. I'm sorry." He stood, ready to get her home where she'd be safe.

But Stella kept sitting. "Marshall, we need to talk."

"No," he said, pacing around in a circle. "No. Not about this. I've talked to my doctors and my therapists and I'm tired of talking. It won't bring any of my buddies back. It won't protect you."

Stella stood then and took his hand. "Marshall, look at me. You're not over in Afghanistan anymore. You're home and you're safe."

"I'm not worried about me. It's about my buddies," he said, brushing his hair off his forehead. "I . . . I think we need to go home."

Marshall realized Stella didn't understand the overpowering anxiety he felt. How could he explain without hurting her or scaring her?

She gave him a hopeful glance, but when he didn't say anything she got up and started walking. "Okay. I'll drive."

"No, wait." He hurried after her, his legs trembling like swamp mud. "Stella, please."

She turned, the compassion on her face tearing at him. "You won't talk to me about the one thing you seem to remember. You won't talk to me about what you went through over there." Her heart in her eyes, she said, "I wish there was something I could do to help you. To take on some of your pain."

He let out a settling breath and willed his body to calm down. "Come back and I'll try to explain."

Stella had her hand on the strap of her tiny purse, the look of determination in her eyes breaking down some of the barriers he'd hidden behind.

"Stella?"

"Okay." She came back and sat down to stare out at the muddy waters of the Mississippi. Up the river, the commuter ferry made its way across to the other side of the river.

"You can't imagine," he said, the remembered sights and sounds around him causing him to cringe. "I have flashbacks, but my therapist keeps telling me I'll get better with time. And they have settled down to some extent, thankfully."

He couldn't tell her that he'd curled up in a ball like a frightened child when he'd first woken up at the hospital.

"I understand," she said, her hand touching his. "I wish I could erase those bad memories and replace them with the happy ones."

"You and me both." He gave her an encouraging smile. "I'm sorry I scared you, but it happens now and then. When I heard that popping sound, I went into battle mode."

"You threw yourself over me," she replied. "I appreciate that you want to protect me, but . . . I'm so afraid I might say or do the wrong thing. That's why I need to understand some of your pain and your fear."

She was right. If they were going to make a life together, he needed to be completely honest with her. But as he sat there and described his memories of the day his world exploded, he couldn't bring himself to tell her too much more about the recurring dream.

Because he was afraid if he voiced that dream, he'd have to live it over and over again. Maybe in real life. So he kept pushing that particular scene away to protect her from *his* worst fear — that he'd lose her forever.

TWELVE

"Are we wrong to continue with this?" Stella asked two weeks later.

Her mother, Aunt Glenda, Rhonda, and Kitten had assembled on the wide back porch at Flower Bend for last-minute wedding preparations, just one week away from the big day. Stella looked at the women who'd been such a constant in her life. Their support meant the world to her — especially during these last weeks as she and Marsh continued to struggle in their relationship. Marsh didn't want to see her as much as Stella would have liked, and she found the effects of his memory loss to be overwhelming at times.

Though she had the nagging suspicion these women all knew something she didn't, she'd been enjoying their talk while they labeled the words *Marshall and Stella* and the wedding date on bottles of bubbles and stuffed netting with birdseed. But then the conversation had turned to Marshall and his wounds, and Stella needed reassurance one more time.

"Miss Kitten, you'd tell me the truth, wouldn't you?" Stella went on. "Do you think Marshall can handle the wedding, handle getting married?"

Kitten Henderson laid aside the netting she'd been meticulously cutting and placed her hands in her lap. "Suga', there is no right or wrong way to answer that question. You and Marshall were so in love." She shrugged and paused. "And now —"

"And now he's being forced to honor a promise he made before he was injured," Stella replied. "He keeps telling me it will all work out, and I'm trying to trust him on that. But I don't want to force him into getting married if he's not ready."

Kitten shook her head. "What I was going to say is now that he's home again, he's much better than he was when we first flew to Germany to see him. He couldn't even remember us at first, and he had horrible flashbacks. It was so hard to bear, but we didn't give up. We started telling him about his life, and at first he got upset and frustrated." She looked up, her eyes on Stella. "He didn't want you to see him like that. He was afraid for you to come there. I think he was afraid of you, period, because he couldn't remember."

"He told me the other night that he needed to protect me," Stella said. "But I'm a big girl. I could have handled it. And if I'd known, I could have easily postponed the wedding. I can still do that."

Rhonda's blonde hair curled around her square face. She was married with two children, but she was always willing to talk to Stella on the phone, as they'd done a lot lately. "Maybe he's holding back because he does love you, Stella. He went through a lot of trauma from a head injury and this amnesia. Maybe he's not ready to face reality."

Kitten's look of sympathy just about did Stella in. "The doctors do believe part of his amnesia might be hysterical. That means he's afraid of something or he's purposely not remembering certain things."

"To protect himself or me? Or both?"

Kitten nodded. "I think maybe you, Stella. In his mind, he's protecting you from what he had to endure."

"Me? But I'm the reality he can't face," Stella said, still holding a white bottle full of bubbles, the ribbon she planned to tie around the lid forgotten. "Maybe he's not ready to face a future with me."

Her mother glanced over at Kitten and a worried look passed between them. "Honey, you can stop this at any time if you're not sure."

Stella had thought of nothing else since the day Marshall returned, but each time she came close to calling off the wedding, something inside her heart held her back. She could get past the public humiliation and the whispers of gossip. But she wouldn't get over losing Marshall — or worse, hurting him by deserting him. How could she walk away now when it seemed he needed her more than ever?

"He wants to marry me," she said. "In spite of everything, he's as committed to this marriage as I am."

Kitten got up and came over to hug her close. "Then we're all behind you, honey. You know we feel like you're family already. And I truly believe our faith and our love for you have helped calm Marshall's concerns. He's coming back to you, I just know it. I mean, he talks about you all the time. You've given him something to hope for."

Stella dabbed at her wet eyes. "I'm so sorry for getting all emotional. Jitters, I guess."

Her mother's steady gaze held hers. "You're entitled to jitters. Weddings are always stressful, even when things are going perfect."

"As are marriages," her aunt said with a grin. "But it will all be worth it."

Stella settled down to finish the tasks at hand, but later that night in her room she wrote in her wedding journal.

"Dear heavenly Father, bless this marriage with your love and grace. Help me to be a good wife and give me the wisdom to help Marshall heal, however long it takes." Then as she had each day since he'd returned, she recorded little notes of encouragement in the journal.

We had a wonderful time at the zoo. Panic attack on the Moonwalk. It must be so hard for him. Forgive me for doubting. I know you have a plan for us and I love him enough to wait for you to reveal that plan.

The next morning, Stella woke up feeling more confident, her heart so full of love and joy that she didn't have room for any worries. The beautiful Sunday morning practically sang with that same joy.

After a light breakfast, Stella got dressed for church and headed back downstairs. Her phone buzzed before she'd made it to the kitchen.

"Hello."

"Want a ride to church?"

Marshall.

"I'd love that. I was about to leave with Mama and Daddy, so I'm ready." She glanced around the foyer where her parents were usually waiting for her. "But apparently, they're running behind for some reason."

"I'll be by in ten minutes."

She put away her phone with a smile.

"Who was that?" Mama asked as she walked in from the kitchen.

"Marshall. He's picking me up for church."

Her mother shot her a knowing smile. "Good. That means he's going, and that also means he wants to spend time with you."

Stella came around the corner and nodded. "And *that's* good because we have less than a week before we tie the knot."

Marshall's mood was considerably better this morning. He'd slept like a baby last night, and he'd opened his eyes with Stella on his mind. He had a surprise for her.

But he couldn't help but go back over his time at home. Partly to remind himself that he could remember things and partly to assure himself that he was on the right track.

He'd been terrified to meet her.

Now he wanted to keep her around. He wanted to keep remembering her.

Somewhere between his disoriented mind, being home, and trying to grasp bits and pieces of his life, he'd discovered the one constant in all of this.

Stella.

She had the cutest smile. She had the purest heart. And she had the faith to move mountains. He liked being around her.

So he'd gone from despair and fear to acceptance and contentment. Would that be enough to start a life with her?

In my heart, I know her.

He had to trust in that. And he had to trust in God.

I came back here for a reason, Lord. I will do my best to honor this marriage and to make the most of what I have.

And hopefully, one day he'd truly love the woman who'd pledged her heart to him.

When he pulled up the long gravel drive to Flower Bend, he once again got that strange feeling in his stomach. He knew this place too. He could almost see the images in his head. Why did this part of his memories seem to stay just out of reach?

His therapist had suggested that he follow the shadows to find the memories, but sometimes that just gave him a headache.

Not today. Today he wanted to see what was behind that curtain that refused to open. Talking to Stella more and more had helped a lot.

She came out the back door and waved to him. Marshall took in her full-skirted green dress and cute white sandals. Her dark blonde hair was down around her shoulders. She looked young and fresh and lovely. He envisioned her in a wedding dress, coming down the aisle.

And his heart stopped and sputtered from joy to terror.

"Hi." She was in the car before he could catch his next breath.

"Hi," he said, his lungs tightening. Breaking out in a cold sweat, he willed himself to calm down.

Breathe. Breathe.

"Marshall?"

He gave her a panicked glance, then held up his right hand. "Give me a minute."

Stella stared at him, worry coloring her face a pale white. "Are you having another flashback?"

He shook his head. "I'll . . . be okay."

She didn't force him, but she did touch

her hand to his.

When Marshall finally caught his breath again and the images had receded, he glanced over at Stella. She had her eyes shut and her lips were moving in a quiet prayer.

"Hey, I'm okay now."

She opened her eyes and turned to him. "Are you up to church?"

"Yes." He tapped the steering wheel. "I can't hide away. I have to keep going, keep moving. I have to put one foot in front of the other and get on with my life."

"Is that what you're doing with our wedding? Putting one foot in front of the other so you can make it happen?"

He couldn't lie. "Some days are harder than others." Seeing the disappointment in her eyes, he said, "Hey, we had a little breakthrough after we went to the zoo. We're getting there."

Stella shook her head. "Are we? Or are you getting worse? The closer we get to the wedding, the more you seem to have these panic attacks."

"It's not about the wedding," he tried to explain. "It's about . . . everything. Just . . . don't get the wrong idea."

Stella didn't respond. But Marshall could tell her good feeling went downhill pretty fast.

■ ■ ■ ■

Marshall had things under control by the time they arrived at church. He couldn't blow this. He'd been planning the surprise for days.

"Lots of cars here for social hour," he said, smiling. "Must be the donuts."

Stella gave him a measuring glance, probably to make sure he wouldn't flip out on her again. "We don't have to do the meet and greet," she said. "We can sit here or go inside the sanctuary."

Pushing away his anxieties, he said, "No, no. I want a donut. I missed donuts so much."

They looked at each other, and he saw the relief in her eyes. "You always did love jelly donuts."

"Yes. I remembered that when Mom had a whole box waiting for me when I came home."

He got out and came around to open her door, and together they walked into the fellowship hall. Stella's eyes widened when she saw the crowd inside. Then she held a hand to her mouth.

To Stella and Marshall. Congratulations!

The big banner had been hand painted by the youth group in shades of blue and silver.

"What's all this?" she asked, her eyes bright with questions.

"You mentioned that we never had a proper couples' shower," Marsh said. "So some of your friends got together to give us one right here at church."

Rhonda came rushing up to hug her. "I worked all week on this, but we had to keep it quiet. That's one reason Marshall took you to New Orleans a couple of weeks ago. We had a quick meeting while you were away."

"That and . . . I really did want to be alone with you," he carefully amended. He indicated the table full of finger foods and donuts. "We eat and greet and . . . I guess we get more loot."

Stella's gaze moved over the tables and then back to him. "You helped plan this?"

"I asked my mom about it and she called Rhonda — just to make sure about the protocol, of course. They decided to have it here and invite all our friends who still live in the area."

He didn't add that his mother had been concerned about him being with so many people, but this would be quick and contained, so he could duck out at any time if things got to be too much.

Stella stood still, taking it all in. "That's why they were acting so weird the other day. I can't believe you did all of this . . . for us."

He took her by the hand. "Well, I wanted you to show me off to all our friends. You remember them, I hope."

She laughed at that. "I sure do. And I hope you will too."

Marshall breathed a sigh of relief and tugged her forward. "Well then, let's get this shindig going. We don't want to be late for the church service."

Stella gave him a grateful smile before she started hugging and greeting people. Seeing her so happy helped Marshall to calm down and focus on what he knew to be true.

Stella would make the perfect bride.

Which meant he had to be the perfect groom.

Fifteen minutes later, he was caught in a corner with several people he couldn't remember. Somebody mentioned he sure did have a beautiful bride. Marshall nodded, ready to agree. But already his heart started pumping too fast and his breathing became shallow.

"Excuse me," he said as he pushed past an older couple. He had to get outside. He had to find some air.

He saw the image again, the one in his dreams.

Stella was walking in the smoke, her white dress growing gray with dirt and soot. He could hear engines roaring, could hear the explosion of gunfire and the sound of people screaming.

"Go back," he tried to call. "Go away. Stella, go away."

He turned and saw her standing right behind him, shock turning her pale.

Then she spun on her heels and hurried back inside.

THIRTEEN

Marshall stared up at the attic door, his hands in the pockets of his jeans.

"Looking for a particular spot on the ceiling, son?" His dad stood a few steps away, down on the staircase.

Marshall turned and sat down on the landing. "I need to read those letters, Dad."

"Sure you're ready for that?" Gerald asked, his expression laced with worry. "You sure got upset back at the hospital when you tried that."

"I wasn't ready then. I was too messed up. I'm better now."

"We're all glad for that," Gerald replied. "You made Stella happy by getting everyone together for that surprise shower yesterday." His dad looked down at the stair tread. "But you left kind of early. Didn't even stay for church."

He couldn't tell his dad that they'd had a little spat after Stella had overheard him telling her to go back. He'd tried to explain, but her hurt expression told him to give her some time.

Now he searched for the right words. "I got a little overwhelmed and had to leave. But I'm glad about the shower. I missed all the other wedding festivities, so I wanted to do something for her that would include both of us. Mom said a couples' shower would work. And it did until . . . until I started feeling kind of funny. Too many people asking too many questions."

"Your mom is a very wise woman, but maybe we shouldn't have pushed this on you. None of this."

Marshall couldn't argue with the notion of too much, too soon. "I'm blessed to have both of you, and you didn't do anything wrong. The shower was my idea, but then I messed things up and now Stella's more confused than ever."

Gerald marched up the remaining steps and sat down beside Marshall. "I can't imagine what you've been through, but I'm thankful you came home in one piece. You and Stella might need more time to adjust though."

Marshall put a hand against his forehead. "Still a little fuzzy in here, but . . . I do like being with Stella. I just have to convince

310

her of that. I wish I could remember more about her."

"But you remembered your mom and me right away after we began telling you about your life. Why do you think it's so hard to remember one of the best parts of your life?"

"You mean Stella and the wedding?"

"Yep. That's the topic of the day around here."

Marshall slanted an appreciative gaze toward his strong, usually silent father. "I guess I haven't been the best patient, huh?"

"It's okay, son," his dad said. "We're so glad you're alive, we figure we'll work on the rest. That's what family is all about."

Marshall accepted his father's words. "And about Stella? I can't explain it." He took a deep breath. "I keep having this dream about her." He shrugged, wringing his hands together. "Lately, the dream has become more frequent. I have this scene in my head, of Stella walking right into the war zone. I'm trying to tell her to go away."

"Dreaming about Stella might be a sign that your memory is finally coming back, even if it's uncomfortable."

"Except in the dream, she's there with me in the fray. The bomb blast pushes me through the air, through a heavy smoke, and I hit the dirt and I can't breathe. Stella's walking toward me, but I'm yelling for her to go back, to run away." He shrugged. "She never hears me. She just keeps on coming toward me." He gave his father a helpless glance. "She heard me talking to myself yesterday when I was having a panic attack and took what I said the wrong way. Now she thinks I don't want her around."

His dad patted him on the knee. "Maybe she heard you, but she doesn't want to run away. Stella is fighting her own battle, son. Think about that."

Marshall nodded in agreement. "And I keep hurting her over and over. I think it's time I read the letters. We've only got a few days before the wedding. Maybe the letters will fill in the spots that are still blank."

"Do you love Stella?" his dad asked.

Marshall looked down at his hands. "I want to. She's so easy to love."

"You did love her, you know. You two made the cutest couple, always cuddling and cooing, laughing and having fun. Reminded me of your mom and me when we were dating."

"I have fun with her now and I like being with her, but why can't I just let go and get *that* feeling back?" Marshall asked, wishing it with all his might.

"You were very ill, son. You've still got

312

some healing to do." His dad pointed to his chest. "In here. It might take time, so don't rush it. If you love Stella, you can make this work, one way or another. But if you're not sure, you owe it to her to be completely honest. You two can work through this without the stress of a big wedding and worrying about the intimacy of marriage."

Marshall swiped at his hair, his hand touching on the scar left from his injury. "I'm not sure about anything. Each time I think about stopping the wedding, I see her face and I see the disappointment in her eyes. Then I remember the dream and something holds me back. I can't stop her in the dream. But I could end all of this in reality." He shrugged. "Only I don't want to end it. In spite of all my doubts, marrying Stella seems like what I need to do."

His dad tented his hands across his knees. "What is your heart telling you?"

"To do the thing I promised to do. To marry the woman I love." He shifted, held on to one of the old oak railing spindles. "Or at least I want to love her again."

His father sat still for a minute or two. Then he stood up and glanced at the attic door. "You do need to read those letters. They'll tell you the story you can't seem to get right in your head."

Marshall watched his father walk back down the stairs. Maybe Dad was right. Maybe he needed to take his cue from Stella and quit running.

He got up and tugged at the drop-down door, unfolding the rickety stairs and locking them in place. Then he slowly made his way up.

Two days later, Stella's heels hit the slick wooden stairs in a tap-tap of urgency. A rainstorm had hit the minute she'd shut down the bookstore for the day, and now she was soaking wet and so tired. But the caterer had called with a major problem. Two of her workers had a spat and they'd both walked off the job for good.

She hadn't heard from Marshall since Sunday night. He'd called her, apologizing for not staying for the church service. But he'd left her there alone with all their friends and all the gifts they'd received. The whole town was probably buzzing with the magnitude of that embarrassing incident. And what she'd heard him say . . .

He's trying, she reminded herself. *We're both trying.*

He'd sounded contrite and sincere in his apology, but now her doubts had doubled. Maybe this problem with the caterer was a solid sign to call it quits.

Myrtle Palmer was waiting for her at the top of the stairs right by the "Myrtle's Fine Food and Catering" sign. "I'm so sorry, Stella. But with just days until the wedding, I thought I should let you know right away."

Stella hugged the curvy older woman, the scent of cinnamon and freshly baked wedding cake surrounding them. "Can't you hire new people?" she asked, her mind whirling with last-minute jitters.

Myrtle brushed drops of rain off Stella's jacket and guided her into the office above the catering kitchen. "I could," she said as she sank down in her leather chair and dabbed at her brow with a wrinkled white handkerchief. "But that takes vetting and checking and getting references. You know, I only hire the best, but these two had been at it for way too long. Good at their jobs, bad at getting along. I gave them every chance, and then they went at it again. I had told them last week, either shape up or there's the door. Today they chose the door."

Stella wondered why Myrtle had given the two workers the ultimatum just days before her wedding, but she could see the stress lines all over Myrtle's plump face. "I understand," she said, not really understanding at all.

But they were down to crunch time. The wedding was this Saturday. She tried to breathe, tried to calm herself, tried to convince herself that what she'd heard when she'd found Marshall outside the church doors had only been part of his anxiety.

"Stella, go away."

Should she do just that?

Except for that one phone call to apologize and explain, she hadn't heard from Marshall at all. Why was he avoiding her now, this close to the wedding? All sorts of scenarios played in her head, and none of them were good. Each time they took a step forward, things seemed to slide two steps backward.

"Honey, I'm so sorry," Myrtle said again. "I might be able to pull it off, but I'm gonna need some help. Planning ahead for two hundred and fifty people involves a lot of crab legs and marinated shrimp."

Stella pulled out the wedding journal she'd taken to work with her and studied the remaining days, hoping some comforting words would pop up on the page. Finally, she gulped back the need to have a good cry and smiled at Myrtle. "You know what? We don't have to have a lot of fancy food. We can cut back on some of the appetizers and focus on what you can get done. Whatever you serve at the wedding will be wonderful. And we can get volunteers from church to fill in as helpers. They do weddings and showers all the time."

Myrtle's surprise moved down her ruddy face like candy sprinkles until her mouth dropped open. "I declare, I've never had a bride say that to me in all my twenty-eight years of catering events. Usually by this point, I'm either refunding money, asking for more money, or they're standing there calling me names I can't even begin to repeat."

She sank back in her chair. "I'm gonna make you the prettiest wedding cake this town has ever seen."

That brought the tears. Stella turned into a blubbering, sobbing bundle of waterworks.

Myrtle's expression went from surprised to horrified. "Oh, honey, I didn't mean to make you cry. I'll get you some appetizers going too. I promise. If I have to do beanie-weenies, you'll have appetizers."

"It's not that," Stella said through her sobs. "It's just everything."

Myrtle got up and came around the desk. "C'mon into the kitchen with me, little lady. I just made a batch of my marshmallow brownies. I'm gonna cut you a big slab or two and you're gonna tell me every little thing."

Stella obediently followed Myrtle down to the big kitchen where workers scurried around doing their duties. Taking in all the wonderful smells, she said, "You're too busy to bother with me."

Myrtle shook her head and wagged a finger at Stella. "I am making an exception. Remember, I taught you in Sunday school, and you were always the most precious thing. I tried to guide you in the right direction back then and, suga', I'm sure gonna do that with this wedding. I know your man's a bit befuddled, but . . . honey, you look confused yourself." She pulled Stella close in another bear hug. "Now come on and let's find a nice cool spot to have us a little brownie break."

Soon Stella was sitting in a quiet corner, eventually working on her second brownie and her third cup of coffee. By the time she finished her tale of woe, her stomach groaned with chocolate contentment and she practically glowed with caffeinated energy.

"So now I'm wondering what to do. I had to have my dress altered because I've lost weight from worrying. And then this problem with your staff . . . The groom might not even show up."

Myrtle chuckled. "Those brownies should

help with all that."

But Stella wasn't done. "The flowers I wanted for the altar had to be changed from hydrangeas and baby's breath to lilies because of an error on the shipping date, and while I love lilies, I really love hydrangeas." She sighed and put her head in her hand. "I think I'm asking too much, wanting the perfect wedding."

Myrtle patted Stella's hand and gave her another tissue. "What you need to aim for isn't perfect, baby doll. You need to aim for the best you can do. Because that's all you can do, any day of the week. You just do the best you can do and let the rest work itself out."

Stella nodded and wiped her nose. "But am I doing my best? Or should I just give up and let Marshall go? I mean, every time I think he's making progress and he truly wants to marry me, he backs away and becomes even more distant. I've prayed and I've tried to be patient. And now days before the wedding, everything's just falling apart. Is that a sign I should just give up?"

Myrtle pursed her lips and got up, her hands on her hips. "You are not giving up, no ma'am." She pulled Stella toward the front door and then out onto the sidewalk. "Look up there," she said with a smile of assurance.

Stella looked up at the sky. "A rainbow. How did you know?"

Myrtle's chuckle echoed down the street. "The whole time you were pouring your heart out to me, I could see out the window. When it stopped raining, I saw part of this rainbow shooting through the sky."

Stella lifted her gaze to the heavens. The rainbow spread across the clouds into a multicolored arc that sparkled between the clouds and the sun like ribbons trailing after a gift box.

"God never gives up, so why should you?" Myrtle asked. She pointed to the rainbow. "The sun was behind you, but the rain was all you could see in front of you. You know, the rainbow is formed when the light hits millions of water droplets and bends into an arc. Then it changes into those brilliant colors. It's the same light you saw before, sweetie. It's just shifted into something else. Something that holds the promise of God's love."

Myrtle stared up at the rainbow. "I learn a lot, watching the Weather Channel." Her eyes sparkled. "Your Marshall is the same man you fell in love with. He's just been through something that bent him and he's changed color a little bit." She patted Stella on the back. "But he ain't broken yet, no sir. Together, you and that man can still have something beautiful."

Stella smiled and started crying all over again. This time her tears were resolved and determined. But her resolve and determination had shifted to something more than her wedding.

"I never knew you were such a romantic philosopher, Miss Myrtle," she said. "But . . . you make perfect sense."

Myrtle clapped her hands together. "Not perfect now. But I do the best I can with what I've got."

Stella decided that was exactly what she would do too. She wasn't giving up, but she had to let go.

FOURTEEN

Marshall sat in his bedroom. This upstairs room at the back of the house held pieces of his memories like the lace of a spider-web. Football and prom pictures, spring break and youth trips.

Stella was in just about every picture. His mom had left it all right here even though he'd been away at college and serving in the Army for years now. Why?

Was it hard for her to let go of her only child?

Glad now that his mom had kept his room pretty much intact, he sat back on the bed and stared at the bundle of letters he'd saved. Letters from home.

Letters from Stella.

She'd written detailed accounts of her days at the bookstore and her nights with friends, painting and polishing the little house they'd both fallen in love with in the months before he'd left for his second deployment.

Marshall closed his eyes, his thoughts jumbled and tossed. He'd always wanted to serve his country, even after getting a business degree in college. He'd gone over and over his choice with his parents, and finally, after a lot of prayer, they'd given him their blessing.

Stella had agreed, reluctantly but proudly, as she'd put it in one of the letters, to let him go too.

"I'll be fine right here in Renaissance, Marsh," she'd said. "Because I know you'll come home to me and then we can begin our life together."

Her resolve and devotion had been sprinkled throughout her colorful letters. In one of them she had told him a funny story about a church committee.

Mrs. Mims came to a meeting with a granddaddy long-leg spider in her hair. You should have heard all of us screaming. But she thumped him off and then picked him up and let him go outside. I would have stomped him, but I guess she has a kinder heart toward creepy creatures than I do.

"You have a kind heart," he said now, smiling.

He picked up the phone, dialed her number, and waited to hear her voice.

"Marsh, how are you?"

She sounded breathless, her voice husky and hopeful.

"I'm okay. Sorry I haven't called in a while. I've been sorting through some things."

"I understand. You needed some time to think."

"I don't want you to take it the wrong way. I've been talking to my parents a lot, trying to put each memory in its proper place."

"I didn't want to pester you," she said, "so I've tried to give you some space." She went silent and then added, "But we do need to talk. I've reached a decision . . . about our wedding."

Marshall stood on the riverbank, staring out at the churning Mississippi River. The undercurrents running through his mind matched the gliding water that swirled and twisted down below the levee.

Stella had asked to meet him here, and he thought he knew the reason. He'd proposed to her here, according to his mother's telling. Stella had only mentioned it once in passing, probably so as not to disturb him.

He didn't want this walking-on-eggshells kind of life. He was pretty sure Stella didn't want it either. He turned and stared across the highway to the big white house sitting like a wedding cake on the other side. Stella's home was beautiful and strong, steeped in tradition. She wanted that kind of wedding. She expected that kind of life. The life where the china pattern was as old as the family tree. The life where traditions and customs and manners counted. A beautiful, gossamer life that spoke of faith, hope, and love.

He'd wanted that life too, hadn't he?

Why can't I remember?

He'd tried to pray, had tried to read the letters. But with each new letter, with each word leading up to this wedding, he became more and more agitated. He'd stopped reading when he reached the letters he'd received the week he'd been injured.

Too close. Too painful.

Why can't I get past my pain and this tremendous fear?

"Marshall?"

He saw her now. She'd parked her little car at the end of the long drive, and now she was walking toward him.

Marshall waved and waited, his heart crushing into his rib cage, every muscle in him tightening with a strange hurt that far outweighed any injuries he'd suffered. This beautiful woman deserved better than the likes of him.

She made her way up onto the levee and stopped to stare at the river. "It never stops moving," she said by way of a greeting. "It changes and makes new paths, but this river just never gives up."

"But you have, right?"

Stella turned to him then, her nod so quick he almost missed it. "I . . . I haven't given up, but I'm giving in."

"What does that mean?"

She pushed at her hair, blinked back tears. "I just can't do it, Marsh. I can't railroad you into a marriage that you're not ready to be a part of."

"Stella —"

"No, don't." She put her hands together, held them against her midsection like a shield. "I've thought long and hard about this, and I've talked to the caterer and the church and I've got people on standby to call everyone who might be traveling too far to turn back."

She inhaled a great breath. "I've decided to call off the wedding, Marsh. It's the best thing for everyone." She finally looked at him, her eyes clear and bright and full of resolve. "I wanted a big, beautiful wedding, but what I want more than that is a good, strong marriage. With a man who can love me the way I love him." She stared off at the river, then brought her gaze back to him. "You used to be that man."

Marshall's heart cracked. He rushed to her and put his hands on her cheeks. "I'm so sorry. I . . . I wanted to make it right, Stella."

"I know you did," she said, tears streaming down her face. "I know, and I love you all the more for it, but we can't force something that's not the same."

She was right and he knew it, but something inside him seemed to shatter and crash. "One day —"

"One day we might be able to start all over, but not now. Not too soon." She handed him the ring that had belonged to his grandmother. "When you're ready, you meet me right back here and . . . if you truly love me, I'll be here. But . . . I want you to get well and . . . I'll love you no matter what. Always. If you never get your memory back, I'll be okay. I know I will. It won't be easy, but I'll be fine. And so will you."

She placed her hands up on his shoulders.

"Your health is more important than . . . anything."

Then she turned and walked back down the levee.

While the sun set over the river behind his back.

The house was silent.

Marshall's parents had gone to a Wednesday night supper meeting at church.

He had to do something. He had to decide if he wanted to stay here in Renaissance or maybe move away so he could start fresh somewhere else.

But . . . he didn't want to move away. He didn't want to give up on Stella either. He'd stay and fight somehow. He'd discovered that this battle wasn't about sending her away. This battle was about pushing through his pain to make her stay with him. He had to show Stella that somewhere in the deepest places in his heart, he loved her.

So he went into his room and pulled out the last packet of letters.

Dear Marshall, just a few more months until our wedding. I have my dress! I picked it out the other day. Mama and I drove to New Orleans and had a nice lunch, then we went to the bridal salon and

I tried it on again. It's so beautiful. I hope you'll like it. I can't send you a picture since tradition dictates that the groom can't see me in the gown until the wedding. So I'm not even going to describe it because I want you to be surprised when you see me walking down the aisle toward you.

Marshall stopped, the image he now dreaded rising up in his mind. He remembered reading this letter before. He remembered picturing Stella in a beautiful white dress walking toward him.

Walking toward him.

He'd been reading this letter right before their convoy had headed out and been hit by that IED. The image of Stella in a wedding dress had been on his mind all day that day. *All day long.*

Marshall sat there on the bed, staring at the graceful words as memories tore through his system like rushing water.

He'd just tucked the letter into his locker with the rest, smiling as he thought about Stella walking toward him in a white dress. That image had been in his thoughts when he'd rushed out the door . . . and then moments later his world had gone black.

He'd woken up in a hospital, in pain and

without any memories.

He read the letter again, his breath hitching, sweat popping up along his spine, and with each word, memories poured through his mind, filling his heart with a piercing, breathtaking love. A love that quieted his fears and opened his heart.

"Stella," he whispered as tears fell down his face. "Stella, I was trying to protect you. I did tell you to go away, to turn back, but I was trying to warn you."

He could see it all now. The letter, the image of the dress, the vision of Stella coming toward him, smiling, laughing.

And then the horror of a searing pain and screams and sand and smoke surrounding him. Fire and heat and rage. The fear of being helpless, of not knowing what was happening. And then, with one last image of the woman he loved in his mind, darkness and blessed sleep.

Marshall sat there, clutching his fists against the palms of his hands until he had fingernail marks indenting his skin. He cried out to God to help him heal, to help him get past the pain of guilt and the grief of losing his buddies. But he especially prayed with a thankful heart that he'd finally remembered everything about the woman he loved.

Now he understood why he'd pushed Stella away, why he'd blocked out the sweet memories of being with her again, of marrying her and never letting her go.

He'd been so afraid of putting her through the danger of battle. Then of having her all dressed in white, waiting for him forever when he thought he was never coming home. In his mind, he'd somehow believed that Stella would be standing over his grave instead of meeting him at the altar.

"I was trying to protect you," he whispered. "From all of it."

He had to find her, to tell her the truth, to hold her in his arms and tell her he loved her more than life.

But what if it was too late?

FIFTEEN

Stella stared at the dress she'd dreamed of wearing at her wedding. Two days from now, she was supposed to have married Marshall. But now, that dream was over. Myrtle had cried almost as hard as Stella when Stella had given her the news.

"The wedding is off, Miss Myrtle. So you don't have to worry about having help to finish the menu. But . . . we do want you to do something special with the food you've already prepared."

Myrtle blinked back tears, then grabbed her ever-present white handkerchief. "I'll save it, just in case."

"No. Take it all to the soup kitchen downtown. You know our church supports that and the homeless shelter too. Let them heat it up and enjoy it."

"Even the cake?"

"Is it finished?"

"No, but . . . all I had to do was thaw the

layers and add the icing."

"Do what you have to do to make it special for them," Stella had replied, her words husky with unshed tears.

She'd also talked to the rental company and told Mr. Tatum to cancel setting up the tent and tables.

"But we found hydrangeas for the tables," his wife, Jackie, had said, her own voice raw with emotion. "Your mother and several of her friends are cutting them fresh from their gardens."

Stella had been so overwhelmed by that, she couldn't respond. That had brought her another motherly hug and a promise from Miss Jackie. "You call us if you change your mind. We'll be there."

Canceling a wedding halted a lot of work for a lot of people, but at least they'd get to keep most of their fees.

Thankfully, Stella and her helpers had kept things pretty simple. She'd only had a couple of bridesmaids and they all lived nearby, but instead of having a last get-together with them tomorrow night, she'd be home alone in her old pj's, crying her heart out.

Fingering the dress that still hung on the door of the armoire, Stella smiled one last time. "It's not about wearing a beautiful dress. It's about . . . doing the right thing."

That's what Marshall had tried so hard to do.

She loved him even more for that, at least.

A knock at her door caused Stella to drop her hand away from the dress and wipe at her eyes. "Come in."

Her mother peeked in, then walked a couple of steps toward the window. "Honey, I think you need to look outside."

"What is it, Mama?"

"Just . . . take a look," her mother said, her eyes watery too.

Stella wanted to curl up in her bed and never leave the house, but the insistent look her mother gave her made her wonder what was going on.

She went to the French doors and opened them wide to the late afternoon wind. Her mother followed and pulled her to the railing. "Look, out on the levee."

Stella stared into the sunset and let out a gasp.

"Is that Marshall?"

"I do believe so," her mother said, touching her shoulder. "Don't you think you should go out there and see what he's doing?"

Stella stood there, her hands on the wooden railing, disbelief battling with her weary heart. "I . . . I don't know."

Marshall stood on the levee wearing a white shirt and khaki pants, holding a bouquet of exquisite blue- and lavender-colored hydrangeas, his gaze on the house.

On her.

"He called me," her mother explained. "He wants you to go down there."

"What?" Stella blinked. "What is he doing?"

"Honey, I think you should go and ask him," her mother urged.

Stella washed her face and hurried down the stairs and out the door. She walked at first, trying to maintain a polite decorum, but when she reached the old white gate and opened it, her gaze met Marshall's and . . . she started running.

By the time she saw the expression on his face, she realized the truth. "Marshall! You've finally remembered me!"

Marshall stared at the woman he'd loved for most of his life, tears forming in spite of his need to control them. He nodded. "I . . . I . . ." He tugged her into his arms, his gaze holding hers. "I love you so much, Stella."

Then he kissed her to prove he was back and whole and that he wanted to make a lifetime commitment to her.

When he lifted his head, he saw her tears of happiness. Wiping at her cheeks, he said, "I read the last letter, Stella. The one where you talked about your wedding dress."

She didn't speak. She just kept moving her head, tears misting in her eyes.

But he had to explain. "That was the last letter I had from you before . . . the explosion."

"Oh, Marsh."

Now she was wiping his tears away.

"That image I kept having of you in my dreams. That was the image I had in my head when the bomb exploded. So seeing you walking toward me in a wedding gown got all muddled with the images of smoke and wounded soldiers and . . . death. I didn't want you to be a widow before we were even married."

He tugged her close again. "I wanted to protect you, but really I blocked all that out to protect myself. Does that make sense?"

She nodded again. "That's why you told me to go away when you had that flashback at the couples' shower?"

"Yes, yes." He breathed a sigh of relief, his heart hammering a new beat now. "I saw it all after I found that letter. I saw you, Stella. The real you."

Stella couldn't speak. She just kept smiling through her tears.

Marshall kissed her again, then handed her the flowers. "Myrtle says you're partial to hydrangeas." He winked. "I happened to remember that myself too."

She laughed, wondering why he'd been talking to Myrtle.

Marshall smiled, reached in his pocket for his grandmother's ring, and got down on one knee. "Stella, will you marry me?"

Stella let out a little gasp. "Yes," she whispered. "Yes, a hundred times yes."

He put the ring on her finger and grinned. "Once will do just fine."

Then he stood up and pulled his bride into his arms and hugged her close, the memory of her surrounding him with ribbons of brilliant light that rivaled the rusty mauves and golden oranges of the sunset over the river.

"Oh, and one more thing," he said, smiling again. "Will you marry me this Saturday at the church, just as we'd planned?"

She almost nodded, but then stopped. "I can't. I mean, I canceled everything already."

Marshall chuckled and pushed back a strand of her wayward curls. "I went behind you and un-canceled everything," he explained. "Miss Myrtle screamed so loud on the phone, I might be deaf."

"I can't believe this," Stella said, regaining some of her practicality. "What if I'd said no?"

Marshall kissed her hand. "I had faith that you wouldn't do that," he admitted. "And I prayed toward that end."

Stella finally laughed, the relief in her eyes shining as brightly as the contented sky. "I can't believe this is really happening. And you really, really remember me?"

"Every precious part of you," he replied. "Let's go tell your parents." He took her by the hand and guided her down the levee. "They might be busy calling everyone to let them know the wedding's back on."

"You told them already?"

"I sure did. I shouted it from the rooftop to my parents, and then I came straight here and asked your dad for permission."

He walked her across the country road. "Your mom went into action, calling the church phone tree. I think by now the whole town knows we're back on."

"We might not have appetizers at the reception though."

"Miss Myrtle told me about that. She said to give you a message. Something about beanie-weenies?"

Stella laughed out loud. "Sounds wonderful to me."

Saturday afternoon.

The church shined with a festive attitude. The altar was covered in lilies and hydrangeas, baby's breath and white roses. The groom waited impatiently to finally get his first glance of his bride in the wedding dress he'd waited a lifetime to see. The music played a soft rendition of "Faith, Hope, and Love."

When "Wedding March" began, his heart seemed to lift to the sky with joy and thankfulness.

And then his bride came into full view and his breath stopped. But this time, she was the one who took his breath away, and all the fear and chaos of battle receded into a fine mist of lost memories. This was real. This was the here and now. This was the most beautiful scene he ever could have imagined.

An hour later, Stella stood in that same dress with a smile spreading across her face. "I hope this isn't a dream."

Marshall kissed the top of her head. "This is real, but a dream come true. I can't believe I almost let you go."

"I can't believe I decided to let you go,"

she countered.

"You did the right thing. It forced me to face my worst fears."

"It's over now," she said. "With time and your therapy, you should heal completely, right?"

He nodded. "With you by my side, how can I not? I always knew you in my heart, even when I couldn't remember you."

Stella looked around at all the people she loved. They'd all come together to get the wedding plans back on track. Mr. Tatum gave her a thumbs-up as he checked a tent mooring. Miss Jackie smiled and pointed to the lovely table arrangements. They'd given Stella a beautiful hydrangea to plant in her new yard. And the whole town had brought flowers and gifts, and everyone had rejoiced in this day.

"Time to cut the cake," Miss Myrtle said through a shout of glee. "It might be my best creation yet."

Stella had to laugh at that. Her colors of blue, lavender, and pink had made it to the cake too. Miss Myrtle had created a ridge of flower-encrusted edible icing around each layer.

But she'd also added a rainbow across the top, over the miniature bride and groom sitting on the topmost layer.

"Just as a reminder," she'd whispered to Stella earlier. "Remember, God is always in charge, honey."

"I will," Stella promised.

So she ate cake and danced with her new husband while lifting up a prayer to the Lord for helping her see the really important things that go into making a marriage work.

"I love spring," she whispered to Marshall. "It's all about rebirth and restoration."

"And I love you," her husband said, his gaze holding hers. "Let's go make some new memories and start our honeymoon in our new home."

Stella couldn't think of anything she wanted more.

DISCUSSION QUESTIONS

1. What is it about a spring wedding that feels so magical? Do you think having a wedding in the spring has something to do with the rebirth we witness at this time of year?
2. Stella and Marshall obviously loved each other, but do you think they rushed into their wedding? How did Stella's strong faith see them through?
3. Marshall was dealing with a lot of war wounds, on the surface and emotionally. Have you or anyone you love ever had to deal with memory loss or a head wound? If so, how did your faith help you?
4. Stella and Marshall had a strong sense of community and fellowship. Does having a church family help you during the hard times?
5. Marshall was holding back on his

most precious memories to protect himself and Stella. Do you believe this type of trauma can cause memory loss? How did his faith help him work through the worries and fears?

ACKNOWLEDGMENTS

Thank God for the opportunity to be a part of this whimsical, wonderful wedding series. Who doesn't love a wedding? I'd also like to thank Ami McConnell and Becky Philpot, two awesome editors who actually saw something in my work and encouraged me during this project. To all the other amazing authors involved — I appreciate the company and the encouragement. And to my marketing department at HarperCollins Christian Publishing — Wow! Also, to my hardworking agent Pam Hopkins, thank you so much for everything you do.

And finally, to my husband, Don. Thank you for putting up with my strange writer moods and for being a great "manager." I love you, Big D.

ABOUT THE AUTHOR

Lenora Worth has written over fifty books for three different publishers. Her first Love Inspired, *The Wedding Quilt,* won Affaire de Coeur's Best Inspirational for 1997, and *Logan's Child* won *Romantic Times*' Best Love Inspired for 1998. Three of her books have finaled in the American Christian Fiction Writers Carol Award, and her Love Inspired Suspense *Body of Evidence* made the *New York Times* bestseller list in Mass Market Paperbacks. With millions of books in print, Lenora continues to write romance and suspense for several imprints. For several years Lenora also wrote a weekly opinion column for the local newspaper and worked freelance for a local magazine. She now enjoys writing fiction full-time and going on adventures with her retired husband, Don. Married for thirty-eight years, they have two grown children. Lenora enjoys writing, reading, baking, and shopping . . . especially shoe shopping.

A MAY BRIDE

MEG MOSELEY

To Jon, my one and only.

ONE

The activity that soothed my soul wasn't quite legitimate. Some people might have called it trespassing. I called it saving my sanity.

At daybreak, in jeans and a flannel shirt against the early February chill, I knelt to weed my secret garden. It wasn't impressive now, with only pansies and camellias in bloom, but it would be gorgeous again in the spring. I'd discovered it on a sultry day several years before when I'd stolen onto church property to snap a close-up of some amazingly blue hydrangeas — and there it was, a miniature Eden in all its summer glory. Hidden in a hollow of the rolling grounds, the flower bed was set well back from a busy road that must have been unpaved and narrow before Atlanta swallowed its suburbs.

Shaking soil from the roots of each handful of weeds, I stuffed them into a plastic bag. At first I had barely enough light to work by, but broad daylight would arrive soon, along with the clergyman who often roamed the grounds. In his baggy black suit and broad-brimmed hat, he looked like an old country parson lost in the heart of the city. If he ever caught me, I wasn't sure what I would say.

Still, my peace grew deeper with every weed I pulled. Too bad it wouldn't last. Even early on a Saturday morning, I couldn't escape traffic noises. Weeding helped me de-stress, though. This was the real Ellie Martin. Dirt under my nails. No makeup. No phone. No electronic tether to my desk.

The bag was half full when a car door thudded shut in the parking lot — and then another and another. Maybe the youth group was gathering for an early-morning event. Whoever they were, they'd have no business among the flowers. I kept working.

Over the next few minutes, I heard more thuds mixed with subdued laughter. I moved to the rear of the flower bed where tall camellia bushes provided cover.

Then I heard music. A car stereo? But it sounded like a single guitar — not on a stereo, but live. Coming closer.

Before I could squeeze further into hiding, fifteen or twenty people walked over the rise, led by three young children who gamboled across the lawn like puppies. Bringing up the rear, a man in a black suit walked arm in arm with a woman in an ankle-length white dress. She held a loose sheaf of bright red roses.

A guerrilla wedding. I'd heard of such things.

They were headed straight toward me. Naturally. The camellias were a perfect backdrop, and being down in the hollow, the site wasn't visible from the street.

I should have run when I'd had a chance. I hunkered down among the bushes, wrapped my arms around my knees, and thanked God for the muted shades of my shirt and my camo baseball cap. Even my dark hair might blend in with the dark foliage of the camellias.

Now I saw where the music came from. A ponytailed man played a guitar as he strolled along, grinning at the bride and groom. Close up, I could see that she was a fresh-faced blonde — who must have been freezing in her short-sleeved gown. Her dapper groom wore a confident smile and a rosebud boutonniere. They slowed at their appointed spot with their guests making a loose semicircle behind them.

A stocky young man carrying a black book stepped forward and positioned himself not ten feet from my hiding place. He stood before the happy couple, blocking my view of their faces.

"Dearly beloved," he began quietly.

I sighed. So romantic — and sneaky. I could just hear what Mom would say.

They're trying to get out of paying a fee. That's stealing — from a church!

They might have paid the fee, though. Maybe they'd only wanted an offbeat wedding at the crack of dawn.

"Yeah, right," I mouthed silently, but then I had to smile. I was trespassing too. A guerrilla gardener, spying on a guerrilla wedding.

I tugged the bill of my cap lower. Several of the guests were using their phones to record the ceremony. Even if no one noticed me at the moment, I might show up in someone's video, crouching in the bushes like a criminal. My boss asked me and my fellow agents to keep up our professional appearance and behavior in public. I'd be in deep trouble if the whole thing went viral on YouTube and someone spotted me. And mentioned it to Betty.

Since I couldn't hear much of the preacher's address, I amused myself by imagining I was the bride. Wearing a lacy Jenny Packham gown. Carrying a lavish bouquet. I had no father to walk me down the grassy aisle, but I could walk with my groom, like my sister planned to do with Eric.

Mom was paying for Alexa's wedding, and boy, was it getting expensive. It was a good thing Mom had a steady paycheck from the school system as well as a nest egg from selling part of Grandpa's land. Alexa wanted all the fuss and feathers so she'd feel good and married. I wanted a traditional ceremony too, but I'd started a wedding fund years ago. If I paid for everything, Mom couldn't call the shots.

The first step, of course, was finding a groom. Didn't seem right that my kid sister had beat me to it. She was only twenty-two, four years younger than me.

Peering between the bushes, I studied the guests. They were a motley crew, most of them on the young side. Only a few of them had dressed up for the occasion.

I caught a glimpse of a tall man in jeans and cowboy boots. The people in front of him blocked my view of his face, but the rest of him reminded me of the hottie I often noticed at Java Town, a few blocks away. I was usually with Betty so I'd never said more than "Good morning" to him, but I always savored the scenery from across the room. I liked his voice too. It held a smile even when he was only ordering his coffee.

But was this the same man? I studied him more closely — what I could see of him. He was about the right height. His hair was right. Medium brown, neatly shorn. His clothes were right. So was his footwear, and not many men in Atlanta wore cowboy boots.

A man in front of him shifted his position, giving me an unobstructed look. Yikes. It was him. Mr. Boots himself.

I scrunched myself into a tighter ball. Again and again, my eyes made the pleasant transit from shiny boots to long legs to a nice, solid chest. From there, my gaze crawled up his necktie to his face. Ah, that face. I wasn't close enough now to see the details, but I remembered them. A cleft chin. A friendly smile. Green eyes with a definite twinkle.

After about ten visual trips up and down the manly person of Mr. Boots, I was breathing pretty hard. Then I quit breathing altogether. His eyes had locked onto mine.

I froze. Maybe it was my imagination. He was only inspecting the camellias.

He drew his eyebrows together.

Nope. He was inspecting me. Maybe he didn't recognize me, though. He'd never be able to pull me out of a lineup. Not in my professional persona, anyway.

I looked away, straining my ears to hear the couple's vows just so I'd have something new to think about. Something besides being busted.

Within minutes, the young preacher pronounced them husband and wife. They kissed to a smattering of applause and laughter.

"Ladies and gentlemen, I present to you Mr. and Mrs. —"

The name was too complicated to catch. With half my heart, I wished them well. With the other half, I wished Mr. Boots would have the courtesy to pretend he hadn't seen me.

The guests began to follow the giddy newlyweds back the way they'd come. I squeezed my eyes shut and prayed. *Dear God, please make him go away.*

I had a crick in my neck and my legs were falling asleep from crouching so long, but I was afraid to move. Afraid to peek.

I listened for signs of movement beyond the flower bed. Nothing but street noises. The clunking sounds of car doors shutting again. Engines starting up. Driving away.

I opened one eye to boots and blue jeans, smack-dab in the pansies.

I'd fantasized about meeting Mr. Boots, but not when I was a mess. Smelling like dirt. Sports bra smooshing my assets. An ugly shirt, trashed jeans, a camo baseball cap. And trespassing.

Once again, my eyes made the trip that should have been quite pleasant. Boots, legs, shirt, tie — and somber face.

Clutching my bag of weeds, I creaked to my feet and held myself as tall as I could, but I wasn't even eye-level with that cute little indentation in his chin. It tempted me to reach up and touch it.

He smelled delicious, and his sage-green shirt was crisp and spotless, but his stern expression reminded me of the cop who'd pulled me over for driving with expired tags. I offered a smile, hoping to coax one out of him.

"Good morning," I said.

He frowned harder. "Good morning."

Small green azalea bushes hemmed me in on both sides. Camellias blocked the rear. A tower of stubborn masculinity stood in front of me.

I took a tentative step forward. "Excuse me."

He didn't budge. "You won't rat out my friends, will you?"

"You mean . . . for using the church grounds without permission?"

He nodded.

I couldn't resist. "And without paying the church its fee?"

"How do you know they didn't pay? Maybe they dropped the money into the offering last week."

"Why all the stealth, then? Do they go to church here?"

"No. Do you?"

I hesitated. If he knew I was an intruder too, I would lose any leverage I had. But I wouldn't lie. "No."

"Why are you here, then?"

I held up the bag of weeds. "I'm weeding."

"When it's not your church?"

I shrugged. "So I'm a guerrilla gardener."

A slow smile produced a single dimple as tantalizing as the tiny divot in his chin. "Let's call you a trespasser."

"Takes one to know one."

He squinted at me. "I know you, all right. From somewhere. I've seen you at . . . at . . ." He snapped his fingers, twice, as if that would make his brain kick into gear.

I waited, hoping it wouldn't.

"Java Town," he said. "With an older lady. All dressed up, and both of you poring over your computers. Right?"

I sighed. Maybe I could swear him to secrecy. "Yeah. She's my boss. My broker."

"Real estate?"

I nodded. "She's very particular about her agents being professional at all times. If we should run into each other while she's there, I'd appreciate it if you didn't mention —"

"That you moonlight as a trespassing gardener?" His twinkle was back.

"I'm serious. I'm new to the business, trying to prove I've got what it takes. She's the one person who really wouldn't understand this whole thing."

"I don't either. Enlighten me."

It was too personal. I couldn't tell a stranger this was my time to think and pray. My time to commune with the God who'd once planted a garden and who'd told stories about fig trees and lilies and seeds.

I could share the short version, though. "Gardening is my escape when life gets crazy. I don't have a garden, so I borrow this one. I pull weeds and tidy things up. That's all."

"That doesn't sound too criminal. Tell you what, I won't tell if you won't."

"Deal." Remembering Betty's admonition

to see everyone as a potential client, I decided to introduce myself. "I'm Ellie Martin."

"Gray Whitby."

The name surprised me. There was nothing gray about him. He was life and color and fun.

"Hurry up if you want a ride, Graham," a man hollered from the direction of the parking lot.

"Hold your horses," he yelled back.

Graham? Graham Whitby. That sounded stuffy, like he was a duke or something. But my real name wasn't much better.

"I've got to run too." I edged closer. Another whiff of his yummy, masculine scent made me want to bury my nose in his neck or thereabouts, but I kept a respectable distance as I passed him.

He followed me out of the flower bed onto the lawn. We faced each other, and suddenly I was as tongue-tied as a seventh grader at a school dance.

He had no such issues. He smiled, his dimple showing its cute little self again. "Now I know who to call if I need a real estate agent."

Shoot. I'd broken one of Betty's inflexible rules: Never be without a supply of business cards. "I'd give you my card, but I don't have any on me. I'm online, though. Alioto Realty."

He opened a wallet as shiny as his boots, pulled out a card, and placed it in my grimy palm. "Here's mine. Call me sometime." He started walking backward across the grass. "By the way, you've got some real estate on your nose." He winked, turned around, and loped across the lawn toward his impatient friend.

I ran one finger down my nose. My finger came away smeared with orangey-red.

A shapeless trespasser with red dirt on her nose. So attractive.

Sighing, I tucked the card into my pocket without reading it. I wouldn't call him. He could track me down if he wanted to, but it wasn't likely.

Bracing myself for another day of fighting traffic and paperwork, I headed down the sidewalk toward my apartment and a shower.

Two

A thoughtful gentleman held the door for Betty and me as we exited Java Town after our regular mentoring session on Tuesday. Lugging our computer bags and our to-go cups, we moved down the sidewalk to chat in the morning sun.

Betty was in her seventies, but she carried herself like a beauty queen. Beneath her sleek gray hair and chic clothes, she was one tough businesswoman who would never let anybody out-negotiate her. She wouldn't botch a termite letter or forget to return an important call either.

"As always, I appreciate the help and advice," I said. "Thanks for catching my mistakes and making me look like I know what I'm doing."

"You're very welcome. And I do appreciate your abilities, you know. I wouldn't invest my time if I didn't believe in you."

"Thanks, Betty."

"You'll do the same for someone else someday. You're good, Ellie."

She wasn't one to hand out undeserved compliments, so her praise warmed my heart — which then overheated completely because Mr. Graham Whitby was striding around the corner just in time to catch me in the stylish gray trousers, red shirt, and proper support I'd donned with him in mind. Even Betty had said I looked especially nice this morning.

"Hey, Ellie," he said, walking right up to us. "Beautiful day, isn't it? If only I had a garden, I'd be out there enjoying it." He winked at me so blatantly that Betty couldn't have missed it.

I smiled at the same time I sent him a cease-and-desist order with my eyes, which made my face feel schizophrenic. "If you want a garden, we'd be happy to sell you one, although it might come with a house attached. Gray, this is Betty Alioto of Alioto Realty. Betty, this is Gray Whitby."

While they exchanged pleasantries, I tried to see him from her perspective. She would like him for being cheerful, courteous, and neatly groomed. She would even approve of his habit of wearing shades of green that emphasized his eyes. Today his shirt was forest green. He looked more like a model than a brilliant computer geek.

"Gray's an internet engineer with Kahlman International," I told her, quoting the business card I'd stuck on my bedroom mirror after I Googled his company.

"What a marvelous job," she said, and she was off, asking questions with the genuine interest that always made people enjoy answering. Her method produced much better results than my mom's heavy-handed interrogations ever did.

I stood there silently cataloging the facts as Betty drew them out of him. Gray was a graduate of Georgia Tech. His real love was history — American history in particular — but technology was a more lucrative field. He worked from home most of the time, and he lived at the Heather Glen Apartments a few blocks away. He loved Java Town as much as Betty did, although she preferred French roast and he liked the breakfast blend.

I knew it. Weeks ago, I'd noticed him filling his cup at the self-serve carafe of breakfast blend. It was my favorite too.

With her usual grace, Betty checked her watch and began to detach herself from the conversation. "Let me know how your showings go, Ellie. It was a pleasure to meet you, Gray."

"And you, ma'am."

She walked away, and I met his eyes. Warm magnets, they pulled me in.

"She doesn't seem like a tyrant," he said.

I checked to be sure she was out of earshot. "I never called her a tyrant. She's just a stickler for professional behavior."

"Your time off should be your own, though."

"It is, mostly."

He glanced at my to-go cup. "Do you have time for a refill and a chat?"

Wow, he moved fast. It was both exhilarating and scary. I really didn't know this guy — but I'd been wanting to.

"I wish I had time," I said. "But I have an appointment."

"How about dinner tonight?"

I blinked. "Tonight?"

"A girl's gotta eat sometime."

"True . . ." Now I was really glad I'd Googled his company and found his name on their website. He was who he said he was.

"What do you say? About six?"

I did a whirlwind assessment of my day. After the showings, I might have an offer to write up. Or I might be back at my computer, starting from scratch. Either way, a mountain of unrelated work awaited me too.

"I don't know what my day's going to hold," I admitted.

He raised his eyebrows. "Your job doesn't have an off switch?"

"Well . . ." A gust of wind whipped around the corner, rustling the trees with a tempting whiff of springtime.

"Live a little," he said with a grin. "You like Italian? I know a great little mom-and-pop place on Roswell Road. Except I guess it's more of a mama-and-papa place."

He was adorable. My mother's stories still floated around my head like nightmares, though. My father the rat had once looked adorable.

I knew what Betty would say too. *If a client flirts, never flirt back. Never mix business and pleasure.* But Gray wasn't a client.

"Okay," I said. "As long as you can be a little flexible on the time. Can I text you late in the afternoon when I have a better idea?"

"Sure. You still have my card?"

"Yes, and here's mine."

He took my card and studied it. "This only has the office address. I'll need to know where to pick you up."

Mom would have advised me to meet him in a public place with a friend in tow, but I wasn't quite that paranoid. Still, I didn't

369

want him to know exactly where I lived, so I gave him my street address but not my apartment number. "I'm at the Myrtle Gate Apartments. I'll meet you at the gate."

"That's easy to remember. The Myrtle Gate gate. Look for a black BMW."

"Ooh, nice."

"With well over two hundred thousand miles on it," he added quickly. "But it looks okay and it runs great. It'll do until I can buy my dream car."

"What's your dream car?"

"A Mustang convertible. Red."

"I'll look for a black Beemer, but I'll pretend it's a red Mustang."

"A brand-new one, please?"

"Of course. Brand new."

Like Gray. New, exciting, and fast.

I gave him a little wave. "Talk to you later, then." I walked away sedately enough, but I was skipping on the inside.

THREE

I'd managed to get away early, so Gray picked me up at six. It felt later, though, with nasty storm clouds bringing an early nightfall.

As I fastened my seat belt, I checked out the interior of his shiny black car. Either he'd tidied it for the occasion, or he was naturally neat. He wasn't too finicky, though, or he would have dealt with the thin layer of dust on the dash.

The dome light went out, leaving us in cozy darkness just as a downpour hit. The weather gave us something to talk about while he made the four turns that took us to I-85.

"How did your workday go?" he asked, eyeing the rearview mirror as he merged into a rush-hour slowdown made worse by the heavy rain.

"Parts of it were frustrating. The clients I took out this morning are too nice. They pretend to like every listing, even the ones that don't appeal to them. Or maybe they haven't figured out what appeals to them."

"I've figured out what appeals to me, and I'm not shy about making it known."

He wasn't talking about houses. I decided to let his flirtatious little remark hang there, unanswered.

He seemed entirely unperturbed by my silence. "Let me get this straight," he said. "You sell real estate but you rent an apartment?"

"Yep. If I sell enough real estate, maybe I can afford my own house someday."

"And if you —"

Lightning ripped a blue-white gash across the sky, and thunder crashed. I jumped and let out a puny squeak.

"Whoa, Nellie!" He leaned forward, scanning the sky. "That was close. What's it like on your side?"

Knowing he meant funnel clouds, I swallowed hard and peered out my window. "It's too dark to see much."

"The storm's coming from that direction."

"No kidding." Wind rocked the car, and a torrent of water covered the windshield. "How can you see the road?"

"I can't." He made a cautious move to the exit lane. "Turn on the radio for me, would you? The traffic and weather guys are the second button."

I did as he asked. Hyperventilating weather reporters delivered rapid-fire tales of woe. Downed trees. Flash floods. A possible funnel cloud sighted downtown. All of metro Atlanta was under a tornado warning, and the rest of North Georgia was under a tornado watch.

"And it's only February," he said with a laugh. He got off the interstate, made a couple of quick turns, and pulled into a Publix parking lot.

I took momentary comfort in the familiarity of my favorite grocery chain, but I didn't like the look of things. Waves of water sloshed across the pavement, turning it into a shallow lake. The western sky was a massive wall of black clouds.

Gray pulled out his phone and checked a radar map. "If we wait it out here, it'll miss us."

"Are you sure?"

"Yes, ma'am." He swiveled his head to follow the progress of a couple of intrepid shoppers dashing through rain and puddles toward the store.

A cop car drove through the intersection, lights on and siren screaming, followed moments later by a fire truck. More sirens wailed in the distance.

"Ever been through a tornado?" he asked casually.

"No. Have you?"

"Two. They're no fun." He unfastened his seat belt and turned toward me, his face peachy in the glow of the halogen lights. He was smiling.

We were hiding from possible tornadoes and the man was smiling?

"You think maybe you've been through two tornadoes because you don't try hard enough to avoid them?"

"It's okay, Ellie. In an hour, we'll be chowing down. Laughing about this."

"I hope you're right."

"I am." He leaned his head against his window and studied me. "So, what do you want to talk about?"

Fine. If he could be fearless, so could I. I could fake it, anyway.

"Are you from around here?" I asked.

"Yes, ma'am. I'm that rare bird, a native of Atlanta. Born and raised inside the Perimeter."

ITP, we called it at the office. The part of Atlanta that was encircled by I-285, it ranged from shacks to mansions.

"You're a city boy. In cowboy boots."

"Yes, ma'am. You?"

374

"A country girl, born and raised in Wynn-ville."

"East of here, right? Rolling hills. Big horse farms with white fences. Money."

It would be a cold day in the chicken fryer before I told him exactly where and how I grew up, but I could at least admit to being a farm girl.

"Parts of Wynnville are pricey," I said. "Right in town, it's typical suburbia, and on the outskirts it's a mix of new money and old working farms. I grew up on a working farm. I learned to drive a tractor before I learned how to apply mascara."

"I can't see you plowing the fields."

"I didn't. We used the tractor mostly to haul stuff around."

"This city boy has never driven a riding mower, much less a tractor." The smile fled his lips but still shone in his eyes. "And I've never worn mascara."

I laughed. "That's a relief."

He didn't answer, but he kept his gaze on me. Drinking me in.

My insides wobbled. I wasn't quite as afraid of the storm anymore, simply because he wasn't, but I was afraid of myself. I could fall hard and fast with this one.

I wasn't going to let some fast-moving charmer make a shotgun bride out of me, though. I would make better choices than my mom. Of course, if she'd made better choices, I wouldn't have been born. Sometimes that put a damper on my high-minded notions about personal morality.

A heavy gust of wind shook the car. The streetlights went out, followed in short order by the parking lot lights. The lights in Publix dimmed as if they'd switched to generator power.

The new darkness gave me cover. I didn't have to worry that he could see the bedazzlement in my eyes.

"Tell me more about yourself," I said.

"What do you want to know?"

Everything. "Start with the basics."

"I'm twenty-eight. Never married. I live alone. No roommates, no pets."

"Any siblings?"

"Two older brothers. A lot older. They made it their mission to keep me from growing up spoiled. If I wanted something, I had to earn it. If I had problems, I had to solve 'em myself."

I had failed Alexa in that respect. "Maybe I should apply that principle to my little sister, but if she has a problem, I try to help."

"I hope it goes both ways."

"It does, usually. She's a good kid."

I asked more questions, and he was free with his answers. He played guitar, rather badly, and he'd played soccer in college. He was a lefty. A semi-decent cook. He'd made good grades all through school, and he had a clean record except for a parking ticket. That dent in the rear fender of his car, though? He'd put it there. Backed right into a light pole.

He pulled the same level of information out of me. Never married. I'd made good grades too. After college, I'd worked for a mortgage company for a few years. I hated being cooped up in an office all day, so I segued to real estate. I liked to cook when I was in the mood, and my favorite coffee spot was my own patio.

"Java Town's breakfast blend?" he asked.

"How did you know?"

He laughed softly. "I noticed you a long time ago, Ellie. The first time I saw you, weeks ago — or maybe months ago, I don't remember — you were standing at that carafe. Filling your cup."

Wow. That might have sounded stalkerish, except I'd been watching him the same way. For a long time.

I closed my eyes in the darkness and enjoyed the gentle closeness of the diminishing rain tapping on the car. The comfortable silence. The sense of having made a new friend.

Or maybe my bad-guy radar was broken. It wouldn't hurt to keep asking questions.

"Tell me about your parents," I said.

"Oh boy." I heard the smile in his voice. "As my brother Tony puts it, our folks don't care what people think, and that's what makes them so much fun. Or, as Tony's wife puts it, they don't care what people think, and that's why they're so aggravating. They're good people. Just unconventional."

"Nothing wrong with that."

"Nothing at all. Now tell me about your family."

I gave him the slightly sanitized version, focused on Mom's gardening prowess instead of her paranoia. Alexa's wedding plans instead of her meltdowns. Eric's kind heart instead of his country-boy ways. I didn't mention chicken houses, but I mentioned Mom's fantastic fried chicken and home-made biscuits.

"She's a cafeteria lady," I added. "She loves to feed hungry kids."

"I want to meet her," Gray said drowsily. "Think she'd feed me?"

I wanted to postpone that drama as long as I could. "Sure, she would feed you," I said bravely, then changed the subject.

"Hey, the storm's about over."

Gray turned on the radio for the road closures. Accidents had shut down the interstate in both directions near us. Roswell Road was blocked by a fallen tree. Traffic lights were out everywhere.

He turned off the radio. "Can I give you a rain check on the Italian place and go to Plan B for tonight?"

"What's Plan B?"

He nodded toward the store. "The Publix deli. They have great subs. Messy and drippy and delicious."

"I love Publix subs." My stomach growled, and we both laughed.

"I think I'll take that as a yes."

My phone tootled Mom's ringtone. Instant guilt. I should have called to see how she'd fared in the storm. I dug the phone out of my purse.

"Mom, are you okay?"

"Yes, but are you? Channel 2 says there was a funnel cloud downtown."

"Everything's fine here. Did Alexa get home before the roads got bad?"

"She's home. Are you sure you're in the clear, baby?"

"Yes, it's barely sprinkling now. Thanks for checking on me, but I've got to run."

"I hope Eric's okay," Mom fretted. "Alexa

says he's over in Monroe . . ."

When Gray walked around to open my door, I was still sitting there, trying to escape the conversation. Mom was tenacious.

A distant roll of thunder inspired a solution. "Mom, we shouldn't be on the phone in a thunderstorm."

Gray laughed. "Or on a date."

"Who's that?" she asked.

"Bye!" I placed my phone in the console, where it could ring its little heart out, and climbed out of the car. Taking a deep breath of misty air, I looked around. I hadn't seen such a dark night since I'd moved to Atlanta, but the power outage had temporarily put us back several generations.

At first I could hardly see Gray, but then I saw him holding out his hand.

And I took it.

Four

We'd sat at a dinky table in the Publix deli for a couple of hours, staying long after the storm had passed. Then there were so many downed trees and road closures that a five-mile trip home took two more hours. The whole time, we didn't run out of things to talk about. We compared our churches and our jobs, our childhoods and our college years, our pet peeves and our preferences in everything from ice cream to computers. I hadn't laughed so much in years.

As Gray walked me to the door of my apartment, the love songs of frogs and crickets filled the chilly air. Moths flung themselves at the porch light like suitors desperate to win the object of their affections.

"I'd like to see you again," he said. "If that's all right."

"Of course it's all right."

"I'll take you someplace a little nicer than

the Publix deli. Can I call you tomorrow so we can compare calendars?"

"Sure." Feeling quite daring, I touched one finger to the cleft of his chin.

Shoot. Now I'd practically invited him to kiss me.

He moved closer, his eyes searching mine. Oh, those eyes. Warm and lively and kind — with a dash of mischief.

"Ellie?"

"Yes?" My voice sounded normal but my heart rate went into overdrive.

He cupped my chin in his hand. "May I?"

A good girl won't kiss on the first date, Mom scolded in my head. *A good man won't ask her to.*

I would consider that guerrilla wedding our first date, then. It was a stretch, but I didn't care.

"Sure," I whispered, tilting toward him on tiptoes.

He bent toward me, and our lips met in warm, delicious union. He encircled me lightly in his arms. His lips pressed mine a little harder.

The Mom-tape played again. *Watch out for the fast-moving, fast-talking charmers. They'll lead a girl astray every time.*

I pulled away, and his long-lashed eyes crowded Mom's warning right out of my head. "Thank you for dinner. Even with the storm, it was a wonderful evening."

"Unforgettable." He leaned in for another kiss.

I was starting to understand what Alexa meant when she said being in Eric's arms made her woozy.

I stepped back. "Well. Enough of that. Good night, Gray."

He smiled, took my hand, and kissed my fingertips. "Good night. Sleep tight. I'll call you tomorrow."

He walked to his car, but he didn't drive away until I was safely inside.

City men, they're all alike, Mom would have said. *They're like your father the rat.*

She always ran it together like that. Your-father-the-rat.

She would have said I was on the fast track to hell, doing exactly what she'd always warned me not to do. I had gone out with a man I didn't know. I'd kissed him on the first date. And I'd already agreed to go out with him again.

I would set clear boundaries, though. If he didn't respect them, it was all over.

I flopped onto the couch and stared straight ahead, seeing nothing but Gray, who was anything but gray. Gray, who kept me laughing even in tornado weather.

I couldn't tell Mom. Not yet. She would take all the joy out of it.

FIVE

Gray didn't call. He just showed up at the office a few minutes past ten. Fortunately, Betty didn't frown on visitors if their stays were brief. Every visitor, after all, was a potential client.

Unless my eyes deceived me, he was holding a tall to-go cup from Java Town and one of their gigantic cookies in its neat little paper wrapper. With the cookie hand, he managed to hold the door open for Rosie Kramer as she hurried out with her phone to her ear. She was late for an appointment, as usual, but she had time to give him an appreciative smile.

I did too. I took my fingers off my keyboard and applied every one of my brain cells to watching him walk toward me. I saw a lot to appreciate.

"Breakfast blend," he said. "And chocolate chip."

"Thank you, Gray. How thoughtful." I

took the coffee in one hand and the cookie in the other. "You know my addictions."

"Do you know my new one?"

My cheeks heated. To compensate, I tried to sound like a wary spinster in a Jane Austen novel. "Shouldn't you be at work, Mr. Whitby?"

"Nah. I can pretty much set my own hours."

He was too cute to resist. I motioned toward the comfy chair beside the desk.

He shook his head. "I'll only stay a minute — unless you'd like to show me some houses."

I'd seen his phone, and it was the priciest new model. His car had almost a quarter of a million miles on it, though. Was he prosperous or poor? In the market for a house or only teasing me?

"Are you looking for a house? Seriously?"

"Hello again, Gray," Betty said from somewhere behind me. "I hate to interrupt, but I need to borrow Ellie for a moment."

"No problem," he said.

Knowing what was coming, I abandoned the coffee, the cookie, and the man to follow Betty into her office. She closed the door but didn't invite me to sit.

"Ellie, you know my policy about agent-client romances. I'm sorry."

386

I wanted to argue. She owned the business, though, and I'd agreed to abide by her rules. "Yes, ma'am. I'll tell him."

"I knew you would understand. If you can sell him a home, please do, but don't date him until after the closing. After the closing, he's fair game. And, I might add, he's darling." She dismissed me with a prim nod.

I found Gray studying the full-color listing printouts on the bulletin board. "There's something you need to know."

He kept reading the listings. "You have a husband and seven children."

"Do I look old enough to have seven children?"

"No. So what do you need to tell me?"

"Either I can go out with you or I can show you some houses, but I can't do both. That's Betty's policy."

He faced me. "Why?"

"She thinks that if our, um, relationship goes sour, and then if anything goes wrong with the buying process, you could claim improper representation."

"I wouldn't do that."

"But you could." I closed my eyes briefly, recalling the approximate wording from her policy manual. "Because an agent is paid to perform a set of professional duties for every party to a transaction, a romantic entanglement with any one of those parties could blur the lines."

His eyes danced. "Romantic entanglement? I like the sound of that."

"Then find yourself a different agent."

"You'll get in trouble if you go out with me?"

"If I'm also representing you, yes. Not legal trouble or even ethical trouble, in my opinion, but I need to honor Betty's rules."

He finally seemed to be taking it seriously. "But then you won't get a commission if I buy a house."

It was awkward to talk about money. Maybe Betty's policy was wiser than I'd thought.

"If I refer you to another agent, I'll at least get a referral fee. It's not as much, but it's something."

He grinned. "You're willing to take a pay cut to keep going out with me?"

Heat flooded my face again. "Only if you take me to some *very* nice restaurants."

"I will. Let's start tonight. Dress up. We'll save the Italian joint for another time, and we'll save the house-hunting for later too."

I narrowed my eyes. "Didn't I just tell you I intend to abide by Betty's rules? And mine too, by the way."

He laughed softly. "I shouldn't tease you.

I'm not looking for a house. I only wanted to stop by and say hey."

"Are you only teasing about the nice restaurant too?"

"No, ma'am, I'm not. May I go ahead and make reservations for tonight? About eight, maybe?"

"That sounds good." I fought the urge to ask which restaurant he had in mind.

"I'll see you at eight, then. Have a great day, Ellie."

"You too."

After he'd walked out, I tried a careful sip of the hot coffee. He'd added cream, no sugar, just the way I liked it.

I had to decide what to wear to dinner. That question seemed considerably more important than the papers on my desk. I slogged through them, though, enjoying my coffee, nibbling at the cookie to make it last, and grinning like an idiot.

Six

By the end of February, Gray had taken me to several incredible restaurants, which meant piling up a bit of credit card debt for new outfits. I started running again in March so I wouldn't be a blimp before swimsuit season, but my old running shoes were worn out. So one sunny day when I was off work until noon, I walked down Peachtree on a shoe-shopping expedition. The Bradford pear trees were decked out in sweet perfume and white blossoms like brides in their dresses. It would have been a perfect day to decide I was in love.

But smart women didn't fall in love too quickly. They simply didn't. Therefore, having known Gray for only about six weeks, I wasn't in love. I was only . . . smitten. And it was all his fault for being ridiculously lovable.

Everyone at the office loved him too, and we'd all grown accustomed to his habit of bringing me sweets and coffee. If I was busy, he passed the time browsing the listings posted on the bulletin board.

He could have qualified for a mortgage. I'd learned that he drove a high-mileage car not because he couldn't afford car payments but because he hated debt. He wasn't far from his goal of buying his dream car, nearly new, with cash.

A stunning window display caught my attention. A wonderland of lace and glitz, it made Canon in D start playing in my head.

"Oh no," I whispered. "Don't."

I ordered my feet to keep moving down the sidewalk, but the attraction was too strong. Like a lemming over a cliff, I followed half a dozen chattering women into a consignment bridal boutique.

The store carried new, sample, and consignment gowns. Faint floral scents hung in the air along with subdued classical music. Peach-colored couches scattered across the store provided seating for small armies of women who'd accompanied brides that day.

I had no army. No ring. No fiancé. I was just there on a lark. Really.

A saleswoman approached me. "May I help you?"

"I'm just browsing, but . . . I love some of the Jenny Packham gowns I've seen online.

They're out of my price range, though. Do you have any used ones?"

"We have a lovely Jenny on consignment, and I think it's about your size."

She led me to an ivory gown with an exquisitely detailed bodice, short sleeves of delicate lace, and a slim and graceful skirt. As glamorous as anything from the era of *The Great Gatsby,* it was still ladylike. Not even my mother could call that neckline immodest.

"I love it," I breathed, investigating the peekaboo back.

"Isn't it beautiful? And the ivory is perfect with your coloring."

It's not white, Mom said in my head. *People will think you don't deserve to wear white. Do you?*

But I didn't want to be like her, worrying about what people might think.

The saleswoman checked her watch. "I have some time before my next appointment if you'd like to try it on."

"Really? May I?"

"Of course. Follow me."

In a daze, I trailed her and the gorgeous gown into a luxurious dressing room. My common sense spoke up briefly: I'd better ask the price before I fell in love with the dress. Actually, I'd better have a groom before I fell in love with the dress.

While the woman straightened the gown's skirt and rhapsodized about Jenny Packham's timeless sense of style, my phone rang. I pulled it out of my purse and glared at it.

It was one of my clients, a guy who seemed to think I lived for the joy of driving him and his cranky wife all over Atlanta to tour houses that somehow never met his high expectations.

But until noon, I wasn't working. I let his call go to voice mail, knowing he was hot on the trail of another house he wouldn't buy anyway.

As for me, I was hot on the trail of a man I wanted to . . . well, not buy.

Marry.

There. I'd said it. Not out loud, but I'd said it.

SEVEN

Sometimes I counted off the time on my mental calendar: February, March, and now we were well into April, but I still hadn't known Gray long enough to let him get wind of my secret hopes.

Every time he came over, I made sure the bedroom door wasn't open more than a crack. If he saw what I'd tucked into the frame of my mirror, he would know exactly what I was thinking.

Next to his business card, I'd added a few photos of the two of us together. He'd seen them, of course, but I couldn't let him see the image I'd found online.

After my visit to the bridal shop, I'd added a picture of the Jenny Packham gown, printed off the company's website. Daily, I begged God to keep some other woman from buying the used gown. Wedding fund or not, I couldn't afford it new.

Today, I felt slightly guilty about taking a

Saturday off, but it wasn't enough to dampen my mood. The other agents could snag any new walk-in prospects. I had several deals about to close and a couple of listing leads. I deserved a chance to play.

I was dressed and ready for breakfast with Gray and then a visit to the High Museum, one of my favorite destinations since a field trip in the fifth grade had introduced me to Matisse. Now, though, I wasn't a lonesome, knock-kneed kid from the country.

I grinned at the happy woman in the mirror. For weeks now, I'd managed to see Gray almost every day. We'd hiked Stone Mountain, we'd driven up to the mountains to see the spring wildflowers, and we'd shared so many meals I couldn't count them.

I'd told him he didn't have to keep taking me to expensive restaurants, so he'd toned it down. We'd had pizza at his sparsely furnished apartment and watched an old John Wayne movie. We'd had burgers at the Varsity and an authentic Chinese meal on Buford Highway, and we'd finally hit the little Italian place on Roswell. We'd even gone to his parents' house for chili and corn bread.

Gray's parents were almost as much fun as he was. Like him, they enjoyed good food. "Good," not necessarily healthy. I smiled, remembering his mother's response when I raved about her chili. She'd laughed and told me she just dumped ingredients into the pot and hoped for the best. "Comes out different every time," she'd said, and I'd begun to understand where Gray had learned to fly by the seat of his pants.

Wind and rain lashed my bedroom window. Even if we hadn't planned a breakfast date, I couldn't have worked in the church's flower beds today. And if anyone had planned an outdoor wedding, they'd need Plan B.

My thoughts drifted to Alexa's desperate search for the perfect but affordable gown. Every gown Alexa loved, Mom hated. According to Mom, they were too low cut, too tight, or not white enough. Her daughter deserved a white-dress wedding, so her gown had to be pure white. Not ivory. Not cream. White.

It wasn't too early to call Alexa for a progress report — and to tell her about Gray, finally. I had to get over my superstitious notion that telling her might jinx everything.

I picked up my phone and tapped her name. She answered right away, sounding glum.

"Any luck on the dress hunt?" I asked.

"Mom found one last night that doesn't offend her." Alexa offered an unenthusiastic description of a garment that might have escaped from 1980. "I have barely enough time to get it fitted. Most girls have their dresses six months ahead of time. Mom doesn't understand how it's done these days."

If Mom didn't understand, it was probably because Grandpa had made her throw a wedding together in a hurry, before she started showing. But that wasn't what troubled me at the moment.

"You don't sound excited about the dress, Lex. Is it really what you want?"

"No, but she's paying for the wedding so I have to cater to her whims."

"Well, at least she approves of Eric."

Alexa snorted. "Sometimes I wonder. It must be nice to have your own place without your snoopy mother listening to your phone calls. And her house rules are awful. I wish I hadn't moved back home."

Poor Lexie. Times were tough, and jobs were scarce. So far, her college education had only won her a low-paying job at a customer service call center.

"I'm sorry, but hang in there. It's not long until the wedding."

"Seems like we've already been waiting forever." She sighed. "I know, I shouldn't complain. At least I've already found my guy."

"Maybe I've found mine too."

"*What?* Who? When? Where?"

"His name is Gray Whitby. He's an internet engineer."

"A geek, huh?"

"He's brilliant and gorgeous. Not at all geeky."

"Seriously? Where did you meet him? At church, I hope. Mom thinks that's the only way to meet a decent man."

"Well, it was . . . at a church. Sort of. I met him at a wedding."

"Ooh, that's romantic."

I grinned, remembering the particulars. "Anyway, things are moving along pretty fast. I've met his parents —"

"Met his parents? Do you realize how huge that is?"

"Yes, but Mom can't know that I've met his parents before I've even told her about him, so don't say a word."

"I won't. Oh, Ellie, remember all those awful questions she asked when you brought what's-his-name over? Justin?"

"No, that was Jason. Justin was . . . you know. My prom date."

"Oh, wow. I'd almost forgotten about that."

I certainly hadn't. "Anyway, Gray's taking me to the High Museum today. There's a display of Western art. An indoor adventure for a rainy day, he calls it."

"Fun. Send pics if you take any. When are you gonna tell Mom?"

"Soon. You'll love him. He's a sweetheart. And so funny. You know the verse that says a merry heart is like a medicine? Well, Gray is more like truth serum. Laughing gas. He gets me laughing and then he coaxes all my secrets out of me . . ." I blinked, startled to realize my voice had turned dreamy and trailed away.

Alexa snickered. "You sound like you're head over heels."

"Hmm. I wonder why."

"I'm so happy for you." Her voice quavered.

"Stop it," I said, laughing but nearly crying too. "I don't have time to blubber. Gray will be here any minute."

I said good-bye and applied a quick spritz of perfume. It was a far better fragrance than the stench that gagged my date for senior prom when he came to pick me up. Poor Justin. He'd grown up in town, and his nose had never met a chicken farm up close and personal.

I'd never shared that humiliating story with anyone I'd dated, but I might tell Gray. He would get a kick out of it. He knew I was a country girl, but he didn't know just how country. He didn't know how far I'd come.

When I moved to Atlanta after high school, it was my declaration of independence, intended to send a signal to Mom: *You don't run my life anymore.*

I'd sent the signal, but somehow she'd never received it.

Hearing Gray's knock, I ran to greet him.

EIGHT

By the time Gray and I finished browsing the High's *Go West* exhibit on loan from a museum in Wyoming, the rain had let up. Hand in hand, we walked the wet sidewalk in search of a restaurant. Glancing down at his brown boots ambling along beside my white sandals, I nearly laughed as I finally put it all together.

The boots. His fondness for old black-and-white Westerns. His excitement about the exhibit's paintings and sculptures by Frederic Remington and Charles Russell. Even the longed-for Mustang, or "the pony," as Gray called it, made it clear. The city boy yearned to be a cowboy. It was an endearing peek into the part of his heart that was still eight years old.

He stopped to read an outdoor chalkboard menu for a trendy little café. "Good thing the museum closed at five. I'm starved."

"That was the plan. Big breakfast, no

lunch, early supper. We'll survive."

"Barely." He shot me a quick smile and went back to perusing the menu.

"Have you noticed that most of our time together is centered on food?" I said.

"Have you noticed food is central to life?" He kissed my forehead. "So I keep feeding my girl."

He'd never called me that before. Pleasant shivers ran down my spine.

"The wait's too long here," he said. "Let's see what's in the next block."

We walked on and stopped at the corner. While we waited for the green light, he consulted the weather forecast on his phone.

"No rain tomorrow, and the azaleas are blooming," he said. "Let's hit the botanical gardens tomorrow after church."

"That would be fun, but since I'm spending today with you, I need to visit Mom tomorrow."

"Why can't she visit you sometimes? It'd save you an hour and a half on the road."

"She's afraid to drive in Atlanta."

"Come on. She wouldn't even have to get on the interstate. It's not that scary."

"To her, Highway 78 is scary."

The light changed, and we crossed the street.

"I can go with you, then," he said as we

reached the curb. "We'd have the drive time together, and then I can finally meet her."

"Not until I've warned her about you."

He gave me a puzzled frown. "You still haven't told her we're dating?"

"Um, no."

"And why did you use that word, *warned*? Is something wrong with me?"

"Nothing. It's her problem, not yours."

Gray tugged me out of the stream of pedestrians and faced me. "I not only told my folks about you, I wangled a dinner invite so you could meet them — weeks ago — but you haven't even *warned* your mother about me? Why?"

"Sometimes she's a little too protective."

"Mama Bear won't be happy that Baby Bear is seeing a man?"

"Well . . . I told you she married young and it didn't last, didn't I?"

"Yes, you mentioned that."

"It was a shotgun wedding. She was barely eighteen and pregnant."

"With you?"

"Yes, and she's afraid I'll follow her bad example."

"You're not a teenager, though." He looked away and then returned his troubled gaze to my face. "You're one of those women who can't cut the apron strings."

"I am not."

He folded his arms across his chest. "Prove it."

"Fine. I'll drive over to Wynnville tonight, by myself —"

"Tonight? We're going out tonight. We *are* out, right now."

"It's barely past five. If you'll drop me off at my place, I'll be at Mom's house in time for supper. I'll tell her about you tonight, and that leaves tomorrow free so we can go see her together after church." I stopped to breathe. "And I'll introduce you."

He studied me a little too long. "All right. Which church in the morning? Yours or mine?"

I was about to say it didn't matter, but I reconsidered. "Let's go to yours."

Because the services at his church started later and ran longer, our time with Mom would be a merciful tad shorter.

NINE

What a contrast. I'd spent the day in a glistening, modern museum with Gray. Now I would spend the evening at my childhood home, a small brick ranch on the outskirts of Wynnville. Birdbaths, birdhouses, and feeders littered the front yard, but they'd soon be keeping company with masses of April flowers.

Mom could coax almost anything into bloom, thanks to an inexhaustible supply of well-aged fertilizer and an ideal microclimate. The L of the house blocked her flowers from the wind, the sun-warmed bricks held their heat throughout the day, and a well-placed drain pipe from the roof kept the plants watered.

A small red barn stood abandoned behind the house, and behind the barn lay the grassy field she'd sold a few years ago. Grandpa's three gigantic chicken houses used to stand there, reeking to high heaven.

He and his chicken houses were long gone, but the guilt trip he'd laid on Mom remained. She'd ignored his lectures about the big bad city and the wicked men therein, and she'd fallen for the first one who'd set his sights on her.

Crossing the yard, I allowed myself a cynical smile. The scenario had possibilities for a country song.

My country mama was a shotgun bride . . . It had a nice rhythm and an easy setup for a rhyme.

A wicked city man came and took her for a ride . . . Maybe even Mom would think it was funny.

"Nah," I said under my breath. She wouldn't think it was funny that I was dating a smooth-talking city man either. To Mom, Gray would look all too sophisticated.

Worldly. That was the word she would use. She'd called me worldly too, when I went off to college and dared to grow up.

My stomach was in knots before I'd crossed the yard and climbed the cement steps to the porch. The welcome mat proclaimed *God Is in Charge.* He tried to be, anyway, but Mom gave him a run for his money.

Alexa opened the door, her dark curls in need of a trim. "Hey, El. Mom's in the kitchen, cooking up a storm."

At least Mom and Gray had that in common. They both loved good food.

I sidled into the big country kitchen. Mom stood at the stove, stirring a mess of greens with fatback. She'd set pieces of fried chicken on a wire rack to drain over paper towels, and the aroma of fresh biscuits wafted out of the oven. It was amazing that she could eat like that and still keep her trim figure.

She looked up, her cheeks flushed with heat. "Hey, hon. You're just in time."

"How can I help?"

"Set the table for three, baby, and keep me company."

As I plunked three old Corelle dinner plates around the scarred kitchen table, I eyed her. Evalina Bliss Martin still looked too young and pretty to be the mother of two grown daughters, but when men gathered around her like bees to nectar, she shooed them away. Once her no-good husband had abandoned her with a six-year-old and a toddler, she'd sworn off men.

All through supper, while Mom and Alexa wrangled about appropriate attire for the rehearsal dinner, I tried to drum up the courage to mention Gray. I could only imagine the conversation descending into a nightmarish showdown involving accusations of loose living in the city.

After supper, we moved to the living room, and Alexa and Mom started arguing about the filling for the cake. Mom didn't like any of the choices. My theory was that she'd been deprived of a nice wedding herself, so she wanted to live vicariously through Alexa's.

Finally Alexa rubbed her eyes like an exhausted child. "I'm so tired of all the fuss."

That was funny, considering she was the one who wanted the fancy nuptials. "Skip the fuss and have a guerrilla wedding." I was only half joking.

Alexa frowned. "What's that?"

"That's when you show up somewhere like a park, without reservations, and pull off a quick ceremony before you get kicked out."

"That's awful," Alexa said. "I would never want that."

"Me either, but I happened to see one once, and it was beautiful." I described the guerrilla wedding I'd witnessed but left out the part about hiding in the bushes — and meeting Gray. "It was lovely and natural, and . . . relaxed."

Mom let out a dry laugh. "If you want

natural, watch the Nature Channel. That doesn't even sound like a wedding. People drifting hither and yon with their guitars. La la la la la! Let's strew some flowers. Let's pretend we're fairies."

Alexa widened her eyes at me to show her solidarity but kept her mouth shut.

I shook my head. How on earth could I bring Gray into the conversation without stirring up more negativity? He'd blown into my life like a spring storm that left me in dazzling sunshine, my lungs filled with rain-washed air and my feet itching to dance. But Mom frowned on dancing, and she frowned on anything that resembled love at first sight.

Alexa cleared her throat. "Anything new in your life, sis?"

As if she didn't know.

"Actually, yes. I've met a very interesting man."

That got Mom's attention. "What's that got to do with the price of eggs?"

Oh, sheesh, Mom and her old-timey expressions that made no sense. "I was only answering Alexa's question."

"A man, huh? Is it serious?"

"Um . . . we're getting there."

"Out of the blue, you're serious about some stranger?"

Hoping to look relaxed, I clasped my hands over my knees. "He's not a stranger to me. He's my boyfriend. I'm his girlfriend. Isn't that a nice, healthy, all-American relationship?"

"Sounds like trouble."

"He's a good man. If you'll give him half a chance, you'll love him as much as I do." I hadn't meant to let that dangerous word slip out.

"Love," Mom said slowly. "If you just met him, it's too soon to be talking about love. Lust, maybe."

"Relax, Mom. I've known him for a while. And we're not doing anything to be ashamed of."

I might as well have added, *Unlike you and Dad.*

Stiff silence fell over the room. Alexa picked up her phone and started texting someone, her thumbs flying. Mom took a gardening magazine from the coffee table and pretended to be absorbed in it.

"His name is Graham," I said. "Gray for short. I'd like to bring him over tomorrow so you can meet him."

Mom closed the magazine and slapped it onto the table. "Got a picture?"

"Lots." I grabbed my phone and scrolled through photos from the museum until I found the best one: Gray, standing in front of a gigantic horse sculpture, grinning at the camera. "Here. Isn't he cute?"

Mom leaned over to see. "Handsome is as handsome does. Your father the rat was handsome too."

"That doesn't make Gray a rat. Please don't treat him like one."

"I'll mind my manners." She picked up her magazine again. "But it pays to know a man before you get too involved. If I'd known your father a little better, I would have run."

"Then I wouldn't exist."

She laughed. "I'm glad you exist, baby. You and your sister both. But be careful."

"I *am* careful, Mom." I caught Alexa's eye and sent her a silent plea for help.

My loyal ally set down her phone and leaned forward, twisting her hands together. "Mom," she said softly. "Remember how you scared Ellie's last boyfriend away with all those embarrassing questions? You'd better not do that to Gray."

That wasn't even enough to make Mom look up from her magazine. "I said I would mind my manners," she said. "But it's my responsibility to protect my children when they need protection."

"We're not children," I said. "We're adults."

Mom didn't answer.

Alexa and I sighed in unison. She picked up her phone and resumed texting somebody — Eric, probably.

I picked up my phone too, and scrolled through photos of Gray — always smiling — and imagined him right there in the living room, getting acquainted with my ultraconservative mother. He wouldn't be smiling long.

TEN

I had warned Gray that Mom might treat him like a criminal, but he'd laughed it off. Now that we were sitting in her driveway and he'd killed the engine, I felt obligated to give him one more bit of advice.

"Brace yourself," I said as he frowned at his phone and started texting somebody. "She doesn't trust men. Especially good-lookin' men like you."

"Mmm," he said, deaf to the warning and to the compliment.

"Doesn't your job have an off switch?"

He didn't seem to hear me quoting his line back to him either. I let out a huff of exasperation. Sometimes he called his phone his "precious." I wanted to snatch it out of his hand and throw it in the nearest birdbath.

"Excuse me?" he said, his eyes still on his precious.

"Your job. Your phone. Turn it off, please?

413

It's Sunday."

"Mmm," he said again, his thumbs skipping all over the tiny keyboard. He was the fastest texter I'd ever seen. Faster even than Alexa.

"Mom will get your attention soon enough even if I can't," I said.

He hit Send, and his eyes finally connected with mine. "Excuse me?"

"This could get interesting, okay? Mom is something else."

He smiled and leaned over to kiss me. "She can't be worse than my parents."

"Wrong," I whispered as I climbed out of the car.

Mom already stood in the doorway, giving him a squinty-eyed once-over. We climbed the steps and survived the initial introductions without any drama.

"We won't eat until Alexa and Eric can get here," Mom said. "Come on back."

She led us through the house to the screened-in porch out back. She settled into the middle of the wooden porch swing, leaving Gray and me to sit across from her in cushioned chairs separated by a small table. As much as I wanted to hang on to him for reassurance, the table made it impossible.

Actually, Mom's presence would have made it impossible anyway.

414

After an awkward silence, Gray dived in. "I'm looking forward to meeting Alexa and her fiancé."

"Eric's a nice young man," Mom said. "A friend of the family. We've known him for years. He and Lexie practically grew up together."

"That's great," Gray said. "I appreciate hometown friendships too, but my hometown happens to be Atlanta."

Mom gave him a skeptical look. "What do you do for a living?"

"I'm an internet engineer."

"You're doing all right? In this economy?"

"Yes, ma'am," he said, respectful but uncowed. "I'm doing fine."

While Mom kept the swing creaking like the hinges of an old door, she asked more questions but didn't delve into anything too personal. Maybe she'd actually listened to my pleas and to Alexa's gentle admonition.

Starting to relax, I studied him. How could such a gorgeous guy be so down-to-earth too? So genuine? Sometimes he drove me nuts with his last-minute plans for anything from a concert to a hike, but just as often, he was happy to hang out at my apartment or his, swapping the ordinary news of our ordinary days.

Mom planted her feet firmly on the floor,

stopping the swing's movement. "Is Ellie your first girlfriend?"

"Mom!" I stared at her. "He's twenty-eight years old. What do you think? He's not my first boyfriend either."

Her cheeks turned pink. "I suppose —" Her phone buzzed. She pulled it out of her pocket and had a brief conversation consisting of monosyllables. "That was Alexa. They're almost here. I'll go finish up. Y'all stay put." She went inside.

Gray crooked his finger. "Don't stay put."

Quite the rebel when Mom wasn't looking, I sat in his lap. He made up for lost time, smothering my face in kisses.

I pulled back. "Whoa there, John Wayne. Slow down."

"Yes, ma'am." He regarded me solemnly, nearly cross-eyed because we were only inches apart. "Thanks for protecting me from Mama Bear. She's scary."

"I tried to warn you, but you weren't listening."

From out front came a loud rumble that could only be Eric's truck. Glad that we wouldn't be Mom's sole target much longer, I stood up.

"Eric and Alexa are here. Come on. I'll introduce you."

I led him down the steps into the backyard

and around the house to the front. We rounded the corner by the snowball bush and stopped short.

Alexa and Eric stood beside his big silver truck, their lips locked. Unaware of their audience, they clung to each other like lichens to rock.

She was lucky. She'd known him all her life. She knew his flaws as well as his good points. She knew his parents, his siblings, his crazy aunt. There weren't any unknowns. Chances were very slim that blond, brawny Eric would be anything but a good and loyal husband.

Gray nuzzled my ear. "Should we tell 'em to slow down?" he whispered.

"They're engaged," I whispered back. "Mind your own business."

He laughed, startling Alexa and Eric out of their embrace and into a slightly awkward round of introductions.

The awkwardness lasted right into the meal, starting with Mom's long-winded prayer. A minute into it, I peeked up at Gray. He was staring at her as she droned on. And on.

"And dear Lord," she continued, "I just ask you to keep my precious daughters safe from worldly evils. I just ask you to keep them in the old ways, the good ways."

Gray's lips started moving as if he'd started his own prayer to counteract hers. A faint giggle slipped out of me.

She paused briefly and continued, louder. "And, Lord, I just pray, Lord, that you'll help my girls to make good choices and turn away from evil." She drew a deep breath. "In Jesus' name, amen."

Amid the soft chorus of amens around the table, I caught an almost inaudible "Wow" from Gray. I hoped Mom hadn't heard it.

Although she didn't interrogate him further, she didn't warm up to him either, in stark contrast to her motherly attitude toward Eric. She trusted Eric as much as she would ever trust any man.

After supper, Mom stayed at the table and watched as the rest of us divided the cleanup chores. She kept quiet except to toss me an occasional word of instruction, as if I hadn't grown up knowing how she ran her kitchen.

"Relax, Mom," I finally snapped. "I know you don't use soap on your cast iron."

"That doesn't mean you'll do it my way. You've learned some fancy new habits in the city."

Gray shot me a worried look. I only clamped my mouth shut and handed him another pot to dry.

When the kitchen was spic and span,

Alexa hung her dish towel over the handle of the oven door. "We hate to run, but we have to meet with Eric's mom to go over her guest list again."

If it was only an excuse to escape, I didn't blame them. "Have fun."

"Tell your folks hey for me, Eric," Mom said.

"Yes, ma'am, I'll do that." Eric took Alexa's hand and tugged her toward freedom. "Thanks again for lunch."

"Anytime, honey. You're part of the family now."

Being part of the family didn't keep him and Alexa from making a swift exit. They were driving away before I'd dried my hands — and Mom was eyeing Gray like something the cat might have sicked up on the floor.

He gave me a brave smile. "We'd better hit the road too." He turned toward Mom. "Thank you for the delicious meal, Mrs. Martin, and it was a pleasure to meet you."

"You're welcome," she said tonelessly.

I hung my dish towel beside Alexa's. "Bye, Mom, and thanks."

"You're welcome," she repeated.

I started to follow Gray out of the kitchen, but Mom jumped out of her chair and grabbed my elbow.

"You still don't know him," she whispered in my ear. "Be careful."

I hugged her, mostly to cover the way she'd latched onto my arm. "Yes, ma'am," I said, loud and clear. I wasn't going to whisper in front of Gray, but I would have a few things to say to her later.

I caught up to him and practically dragged him out to the car. About to open the door for me, he turned to face the house.

"Now I know why you didn't want me to meet her earlier," he said. "You were afraid she'd scare me away."

My laugh was shaky. "You're so perceptive."

He didn't laugh. His frown suggested that my tactic might have backfired.

ELEVEN

Gray and I were halfway home, with Atlanta's elegant skyline already looming ahead of us, and he'd hardly spoken ten words. It was very unlike him.

We had to talk about it sometime. Might as well get started.

I glanced toward him. "So, you survived meeting my mom."

"Yes, indeed. She's a great cook."

"I knew you would appreciate her cooking, but . . ."

"Yeah, but." He sighed. "Why is she friendly toward Eric but so unfriendly toward me?"

"We've known Eric forever, but you came out of nowhere. And you're a fast-moving, fast-talking guy from the city. To Mom, that makes you too much like my dad."

"But I'm not him."

"No, but she'll take some convincing."

"If she thinks giving me dirty looks will

scare me off, she's wrong, but she'll make us miserable the rest of our lives if we don't stand up to her."

Had he heard himself? The rest of our lives? He might as well have mentioned marriage. It should have made me shiver in anticipation, but I slumped in my seat and tried not to cry.

"It's not my place to deal with it, though," he added. "She's your mother."

"I know." My voice cracked. "You can't fix the problem for me."

"I wish you hadn't kept it from me for so long. We're a team. I'm on your side."

"Now there are sides? You want me to choose between you and her?"

"No, but I don't want her to sabotage us."

That familiar ringtone came from the depths of my purse, and I started digging for my phone. "Speak of the devil."

"We were just there," Gray said. "What could she possibly need?"

His tone made me hesitate, phone in hand. "Well . . ."

"Let it go to voice mail," he said.

"She'll wonder why I'm not picking up. She'll worry."

"Oh, you're worried that she might worry?"

I hit Ignore and slid the phone into my

purse. "There. She'll live."

"And so will you."

I felt cut off, though. Disconnected. As if the phone were the umbilical cord and Gray had snipped it. Who was he to talk, though? He couldn't live without his phone.

But his mother didn't call him all the time.

I glanced out my window at a strip mall that had fallen on hard times. Most of its storefronts were vacant, the parking spots empty. The place looked as dismal as I felt.

Gray reached for my hand. "You okay?"

His instant awareness of my mood nearly brought me to tears. "I'm fine," I said lightly. "But it's kind of painful to keep hacking away at the apron strings."

"I've never had that problem with my parents. We've never lived in each other's pockets."

"Lucky you."

He squeezed my hand. "I am lucky, Ellie. I have you."

There he went again, saying things that should have made my heart turn somersaults.

He pulled off of Highway 78 and made a couple of turns. As we passed his apartment complex and then Java Town, I tried to imagine being married. Would I move in with him, or would he move in with me?

My apartment was bigger, but his backed up to Lenox Park. We could go running there in the evenings. Have coffee on his balcony in the mornings, or walk to Java Town. Together. We would even pay our bills together. That would be a relief. I'd been living a bit beyond my means.

He slowed for a red light near the little white church. "Done any weeding lately?"

Hearing the smile in his voice, I smiled too. It was good to have the meeting-Mom thing behind us. "No. You keep me too busy. Have you seen your friends lately?"

"The guerrillas? The bride and groom? No. I don't know them well."

"Really? It was such a small wedding, I thought they'd only invited family and close friends."

"I know him from work, but working from home so much, I don't see him often. I'd never met her. They weren't getting any love from their families because there was already a baby on the way. So . . . when he invited me, it just seemed right to go."

No wonder he'd asked me not to rat out his friends. They had enough troubles.

I wished Mom would see this side of Gray. His kindness. But she would only see that he socialized with people who put the bed before the wed, as she would put it.

As if she had any room to talk.

"Your friends looked happy," I said. "I hope it lasts."

"I do too." He hit the gas as the light turned green. "I wonder what the minister there would think of a guerrilla wedding on church property."

"He probably wouldn't approve. I suspect he's pretty conservative. I've seen him a few times, from a distance, and he looks like an old country preacher."

"You've never spoken with him?"

"No, and I hope I never will. It would be awkward to explain."

He laughed softly. "You told me you pull weeds to escape when life gets crazy, but I think it's to de-stress from time with your mom. Or to shore up your courage for the next visit."

"You're probably right. So, are you gonna start weeding with me?"

"Nah. She doesn't scare me. Much."

My heart was lighter by the time we arrived at Myrtle Gate. He punched the code at the security gate, drove to my apartment, and walked me to the door. Inside, I dropped my purse on the floor. Gray pulled me close and made all my worries evaporate like mist in the sun.

When we were in the middle of an especially enjoyable smooch, Mom's ringtone chimed.

"Again?" he murmured against my lips. "Ignore."

"But I have to talk to —"

He released me and stepped away, frowning, while the phone repeated its insistent tune from the floor. "If you have to talk to your mother at this particular moment —"

"That's the whole point. I have to talk to her right now and tell her to bug off. It's gonna get ugly, so you might as well go home." I tried to steer him toward the door.

He resisted, sneaking in one last kiss. "Okay, then. Call me later — and good luck."

As soon as he was out the door, I grabbed my phone. "Mom, please. I have a life."

"I was worried. When I called before, you didn't pick up."

Gray was already backing his car out, and I waved good-bye through the window. I'd hated to send him away, but this was my battle. Not his.

"Gray and I were having a conversation," I said. "Is there a problem?"

"Watch your attitude. I only want to remind you to pick up that guest book for Alexa."

"Is that all? I'm sorry, but you have to stop

living in my pockets." It felt good to use Gray's phrase.

"I'm your mother. I have a right to be involved in your life."

"But you can't run my life. Especially when it comes to Gray. I'm an adult. I make my own decisions."

"You're rushing things. Walking into a trap. He'll hurt you like —"

"No, he won't. He isn't Dad. He's Gray, and I love him."

"Listen to me, young lady. You're saying the same things I said to your grandfather. He said I was rushing things. I didn't believe him. Well, we all know how that turned out."

"That doesn't mean it'll turn out the same for me and Gray."

"I've warned you. That's all I can do." Mom's voice hardened. "Maybe you shouldn't bring him next time you come for Sunday dinner."

"If he's not welcome, I'm not coming."

Mom grumbled something and hung up on me.

I tossed my phone onto the couch and paced the living room, my heart pounding and my hands shaking. I felt as if she'd slammed a door in my face. And in Gray's. That hurt even worse.

TWELVE

With my hands itching to get busy, I stood before the flower bed and took an invigorating breath of morning air. Between April's rainy weather and my frequent breakfast dates with Gray, I hadn't visited my secret garden in a month. I missed it.

I missed weekend dinners with Mom too. I still saw her fairly often, but meeting to discuss wedding details with her and Alexa wasn't the same as sitting at the table with them.

For Alexa's sake, Mom and I had entered an uneasy truce. We simply didn't talk about Gray. The strain of it was wearing on me, though.

I tried to shake off my gloom. It was going to be a sunny day. The dogwoods were finished, the azaleas were fading fast, and someone had replaced the cold-loving pansies with heat-loving pink petunias. Petunias were risky because we could still have a killing frost, but it wasn't my garden. Or my church.

Church. That was an issue Gray and I had to settle. He didn't exactly like my church; he said the worship band was all glitz and no substance. But his church was too informal and home-churchy for me, and the services went too long. He argued in his amiable way that the first-century church was home-churchy too. Sooner or later, we would figure it out.

Fairly sure the old parson wouldn't be out and about so early, I knelt by the petunias. Getting my hands in the dirt again made me feel . . . grounded. Smiling at my bad pun, I pulled my first weed in a month.

It was obvious that the groundskeeper didn't use chemicals. That was healthier for the honeybees — and for me — but combined with the rainy season, it gave the crabgrass and dandelions an advantage in their mission to conquer the world.

Within minutes, calm descended.

I still had some questions for God, though. Big ones. I hadn't heard any answers.

Sometimes I wondered if I was stupid to ignore Mom's advice — like she'd ignored her father's advice. Gray was a good guy, though. I'd set my boundaries, and he respected them. Sure, we had to fight each other off sometimes, but we never let it get too steamy. We could exercise self-control like the adults we were.

I hadn't seen any red flags in our relationship. Gray loved God and his family. He was a considerate boyfriend, a good son, a conscientious employee. A wise manager of money, he knew when to pinch pennies and when to be generous.

As far as I could tell, impulsiveness was his biggest flaw. He trusted his instincts, and once he'd made a decision, he moved fast. His impetuous streak showed even in the way he drove. He wasn't overly concerned with the letter of the law, sometimes fudging on the speed limit or parking with the nose of his car in a no-parking zone.

He'd even put a dent in my car the first time he drove it. When he'd lifted his hands in a beguiling "forgive me" gesture, I'd wanted to strangle him and hug him simultaneously.

"Now we have his-and-hers vehicles," he'd said with a boyish grin. "They match. One dent each."

Of course, he took care of the car repairs. Then he'd said we would save money on car insurance when we were both with the same company. And there it was, another hint that he was thinking about marriage, spoken as casually as a mention of rotating his tires.

It wasn't a decision to make lightly, though. Too many marriages didn't last. Gray might abandon me someday like Dad abandoned Mom. Impulsively, without warning.

I sat back on my heels. Staring up at white clouds drifting across a blue sky, I tried to remember Dad, but I only recalled the caricature Mom had made of him. A smooth talker. A player. Gray wasn't that kind of man, though. I trusted him. I loved him. He was worth the risk — wasn't he?

Brooding over everything, I worked until my bag was full. Getting to my feet, I surveyed the petunias. Beautiful — but weeds still lurked here and there. They were part of the curse of a fallen world, along with thorns and mosquitoes —

"Good morning!"

I whirled around. The old clergyman stood a few feet away, his face shaded by his broad-brimmed hat.

Trapped, I attempted a cheerful smile. "Good morning."

"I was starting to wonder if I would ever catch you at it," he said.

"I'm sorry. I should have asked permission."

"No, no. You're welcome anytime. The fella who takes care of the grounds says there's an angel doing some of the work for him. Why do you do it, though?"

The line I'd rehearsed so often came easily. "When life gets crazy, pulling weeds helps me relax."

He tipped his hat higher on his head, bringing cherubic features into the sunlight — round cheeks, a gentle smile. "But why are you so secretive about it?"

"It would have been odd if I'd knocked on your office door and asked permission to pull weeds."

His laughter was as contagious as Gray's. "No odder than pulling weeds without permission. But maybe you like to bend the rules a little."

"Not usually. I just like gardening."

"I'm no gardener, but I love flowers. Sometimes a garden's better than a cathedral for worship and prayer, and I'm happy to share this one." He made a sweeping gesture that took in the whole property.

"Then you wouldn't be upset if somebody borrowed this spot for a sneaky little sunrise wedding?"

His eyes twinkled. "You have a date in mind?"

I laughed. "Not at all. Back in February, I

happened to be here when somebody did just that. They call it a guerrilla wedding. It's part of a trend to save money."

"That doesn't surprise me. Getting hitched used to be simple. Inexpensive. A short ceremony in Mother's parlor, perhaps, with everybody in their Sunday best, and then a wedding trip to the next county. None of this Cancun business." He peered at me more closely. "Do you know this couple?"

"No, but I stuck around to watch. It was beautiful."

"Good. I hope they'll be as happy as my wife and I have been for nearly fifty years."

I tried to imagine Gray at seventy or eighty, still smiling. Married to me — or to someone else?

"How did you know you'd found the right person?" I blurted.

He fiddled with his wedding band and smiled as if he were reliving the moment his bride had placed it on his finger. "It was simple. I was young and foolish and madly in love." He looked up. "This person you're contemplating. Do you love him?"

"Yes."

"Ah. You didn't even hesitate. That's a good sign. It doesn't need to be complicated, dear. If you love him and you want to marry him, well . . . marry him."

I smiled at the simplistic advice. "He hasn't asked me."

"I think a woman should be at liberty to pursue a man, if that's what the situation calls for. I can even back it up with Scripture. Do you know the story of Ruth and Boaz?"

Now he had me laughing. "Yes, but threshing floors are in short supply these days."

"Who says you need a threshing floor?" He chuckled and checked his watch. "I'd better be on my way. Remember now, Adam and Eve ran and hid when they heard God walking in the cool of the day, but this isn't Eden, and I'm not God. So please don't hide from me."

"I won't. Not anymore."

"Good." He stuck out a gnarled hand. "I'm Pastor Michael."

I shook his hand. "I'm Ellie. Glad to meet you."

"I'll see you around, Ellie. God bless you." He turned and limped up the rise that Gray had taken at a lope when his impatient friend had called his name.

I reached out to groom an azalea of spent brown blooms that had once been bright white. By the time I'd tucked them into my bag, my mood had darkened again and I knew exactly why.

Out of that entire conversation with Pastor Michael, one particular phrase kept rattling around in my mind: *A short ceremony in Mother's parlor, perhaps.*

Of course I didn't want to get married in Mom's living room, but when I tried to imagine our families gathered around Gray and me, sharing our joy, I could only visualize Gray's parents, Alexa, and Eric. Mom wouldn't even want to be there.

THIRTEEN

A week after I met Pastor Michael, my romance with Gray was cruising along at warp speed, my dealings with Mom were still strained, and I was just about sick of the real estate business.

Humans are constantly shuffling the ownership of their properties when God is the true owner anyway. We all live on the top layer of the earth like ants clinging to a beach ball, and it is God's beach ball. I wouldn't blame him if he decided to brush off the ants, take his ball, and go home.

That was what I wanted to do. Go home. It was only early afternoon, but I was running on empty and impatient for Gray to show up with lunch as he'd promised. Either he was stuck in traffic or he'd forgotten to check the clock. That happened a little too often.

When he finally arrived, I had a hunger headache and a bad attitude. Trying to hide them, I led him to the sunny courtyard behind the building, where we sat on the wrought iron bench and indulged in a kiss. A quick one. We were in full view of a number of windows, including Betty's. At least nobody could see our faces. Just our backs.

Gray gave me a searching look, then reached into a bag from the Publix deli and pulled out two half subs wrapped in paper. "Something tells me you're not having a great day."

"You're right. My closing in Decatur ran overtime because the buyers were late, so I was late for an appointment all the way up in Mari-flippin'-etta."

"You're cute when you're trying not to cuss."

"Thanks so much."

"You're welcome." He smiled, unwrapping my sandwich for me. The Ultimate on whole wheat, as I'd requested. He passed it over.

"Thanks, Gray." I could hardly wait to sink my teeth into it.

"I have an idea to make a rough day a whole lot better. Ever heard of Hard Labor Creek? Out past Social Circle?"

"Isn't it a state park?"

"Yeah, with miles and miles of horse trails.

One of my college buddies called today. He's trailering his horses there for a trail ride the day after tomorrow. He's had two cancellations. Think you can clear your calendar?"

"No. Sorry. That's the day Mom needs a ride to Midtown so she can pick up her dress for the wedding. She'll have to try it on and make sure the alterations are right."

The excitement faded from his eyes. "And you're her chauffeur."

"You got it." The very thought intensified my headache.

"You'll have to pick her up in Wynnville, haul her to Midtown, haul her back to Wynnville, and drive home. That's almost four hours on the road."

"Yep. I'm not looking forward to it."

He shook his head. "Why can't she get over her phobia about driving in Atlanta? Or why can't Alexa take her? For Pete's sake, it's her wedding. And we might never have another shot at a trail ride."

"Alexa doesn't have a flexible schedule like mine." I brushed a dangling streamer of lettuce from my sandwich, took another bite, and thought cranky thoughts while I chewed. "Spontaneity's great, but why do your plans always have to be last-minute?"

"Two days' warning isn't last-minute. My

438

friend called me with a kind offer, which you are spurning."

"Because I already have plans."

"To pick up a dress your mother won't wear until June. It can't wait a week?"

"I'm trying to patch things up with her. I can't bail on the fitting, especially if it's to go gallivanting with you."

"Obviously, she doesn't like anything that involves you and me together."

"Making her cancel her appointment just so I could be with you would only make it worse. Mom says —"

"Mom says this, Mom says that. How does she do that? Even when she's miles away, she butts in. She's always hanging over us."

I pictured a gigantic Mama Bear balloon, worthy of the Macy's parade. Floating above us. Spying on us. It wasn't a pleasant picture, but I was too grumpy to argue. I shrugged and took another bite.

"The trail ride is a unique opportunity," he said. "And the weather will be perfect."

"Sorry, Gray. Enjoy yourself if you go, but I'm not going."

"I don't want to go alone."

"Then don't go."

He wrapped up his half-eaten sandwich and returned it to the bag. "You've really thrown a monkey wrench into my plans."

"What about my plans with Mom? You want me to reschedule a fitting she's had on her calendar for weeks? So I can hang out with a horse?"

"And with me," he said. "You're forgetting that part."

"I see you all the time, but I don't see much of Mom. When I do, Alexa's there too. I need some time with just Mom and me so we can talk."

"You and I need to talk too." His eyes were blazing.

"Whoa! Don't spring a last-minute idea on me and then lose your temper when I can't join you. Get a grip on your spontaneity. See, this is one of the reasons Mom would say we need to slow down."

He got to his feet, a muscle ticking in his jaw. "You want to slow down? I guess I've misinterpreted things." He blew out a sharp sigh. "Okay, we'll slow down. I shouldn't have presumed —" He shook his head. "I'm sorry."

"I am too. The timing —"

"Yeah, it's the timing. Bye, Ellie." He walked back inside without giving me a good-bye kiss.

I'd lost my appetite but not my headache. I stuffed my sandwich back into the bag too.

Then I gave him thirty seconds to exit the building before I called. He didn't pick up.

Suddenly chilled in spite of the sun, I texted. Still no response. I threw the remains of both sandwiches in the trash and returned to my desk.

I called, texted, or emailed every time I had a spare moment. He never responded. Gray, the man who called his phone his "precious," the man who responded quickly to all forms of electronic communication, was ignoring me.

By quitting time, I was a wreck. Betty noticed, and no doubt she'd seen him striding out of the building only minutes after he'd arrived. When I gathered up my things for the trip home, she gave me a sympathetic smile.

"Whatever it is, he'll get over it, dear. They always do."

"I'm not worried," I said with a phony grin. "Have a nice evening."

I walked out, holding my briefcase to my chest like a shield. I had places to go. Tears to cry. But I wouldn't track him down. He knew where to find me.

FOURTEEN

I had never visited my secret garden so late in the morning. The steady roar of rush-hour traffic drowned out the birdsongs, and the mosquitoes were already out. I didn't care.

I'd called in sick, my tear-clogged voice making me sound as ill as I claimed to be, but I knew Betty would see right through my story. Everyone would.

I kept imagining finality in Gray's tone when he said good-bye. Surely he wouldn't break up with me like that, though, leaving me in the dark. But he'd left me. No doubt about it.

Mom was right. That was what men did.

I yanked at a dandelion. The root broke off in the ground.

I hadn't slept all night. I'd paced and cried and paced some more, trying to talk myself into calling or texting again, but I'd already tried that. And I wouldn't go pound on his door. That would smack of desperation. I'd brought my phone, though, just in case.

He would go on the trail ride in the morning. Wearing a cowboy hat and a happy grin, he would be so darned cute.

He might meet some other woman. A friend of his friend. A woman who could afford to be spontaneous because she wasn't stuck driving her perfectly capable mother around Atlanta. And because I'd said something about slowing down and he'd heard it as "Go away," he would feel unattached. Available.

Would he forget me that quickly? Really?

A mosquito bit my arm. I slapped hard, stinging my arm and leaving a smear of blood. The minor hurt brought the tears back. I let my shoulders shake but I wouldn't let myself cry out loud.

Something rustled in the grass behind me. Pastor Michael's footsteps, maybe. I didn't want to talk to him when I was a mess of tears and snot and misery. I didn't want to talk to anybody. Not even —

"Ellie?"

Gray. I froze, holding my breath.

"When you didn't come to the door, I thought you might be here," he said.

I kept my eyes on the pink petunias. "Why didn't you call?"

"I broke my phone yesterday. Threw it halfway across the parking lot."

He'd thrown his precious?

Still on my knees, I maneuvered myself around to see him. He loomed over me, his face unshaved and his shirt rumpled. The same shirt he'd worn yesterday.

"You slept in your clothes?"

He gave me a wry smile. "You slept?"

"No." I wiped my nose on the shoulder of my shirt. "I'm sorry, Gray."

"I am too."

He didn't move closer, though. He only looked down at me from his considerable height. We were nearly in the same place where we'd first met. I was wearing the same trashed jeans. Should've been wearing the same flannel shirt to ward off the mosquitoes.

I sat on the ground and wrapped my arms around my knees. "I never said I wanted to break up or anything like that. I only said Mom would want us to slow down."

"And that worries me, El. I wish she felt differently about us."

I studied the filthy toes of my gardening shoes. "I do, too."

"But I do see what you were saying about needing to stick with your plans," he said. "You were right."

"No." I got to my feet, pulling my phone from my back pocket. "I'll tell her I can't drive her tomorrow. We're doing that trail ride."

"Too late," Gary said. "My friend found some other people who were free to go."

I felt sick. "I'm sorry. I'm sorry I ruined your chance to do something that meant so much to you."

"You have no idea." His twisted little smile only made me feel worse.

Not knowing what to say, I looked down at my phone and ran my dirty fingers over its glossy surface. I tried to imagine Gray hurling his phone across the parking lot. I'd never seen him that angry. Not even close.

He pulled the phone out of my hand and tucked it into the back pocket of my jeans. "We don't want any calls right now. I want to talk about something that would give us more time together. Lots more time."

"What's your idea?"

He took my hands in his. "I'd planned to bring it up on the trail ride, but this is a nice spot too."

I searched his eyes. "Nice spot for what?"

"Well, I wanted to ask if you think we should spend our lives together."

Suddenly shaky all over, I could barely speak. "Um . . . what?"

445

"Will you marry me?"

What?

His eyes became pools of lost-puppy grief. "You're supposed to say 'yes,' not 'what,' Ellie."

Wait. That was why he'd wanted so badly to go on the trail ride? He'd decided to propose — on horseback? Of all the goofy, impractical, adorable impulses . . .

My vision blurred. I blinked hard and focused on the love in his eyes. And the apprehension. He wasn't sure I loved him back. My heart hurt with wanting to prove that I did.

"Ask me again," I whispered.

A mockingbird trilled at the very moment Gray spoke. "Will you marry —"

"Yes!"

The bird hadn't finished its trill before Gray wrapped his arms around me and bowled me over. Laughing and crying, we nearly suffocated each other with kisses, right there on the scratchy lawn.

Gray propped himself on one elbow and studied me. Gently, he ran his thumb over my left cheekbone and then my right. "How did your face get so muddy?"

"Water plus dirt equals mud, city boy."

"I'm sorry I made you cry. I never want to do that again." He cupped my cheek in one hand and bent to kiss my forehead. "I wish I had a ring to give you, but I didn't want to buy the wrong style."

"The ring can wait. But I won't make you wait to marry me."

I started crying for no good reason. He put me in his lap and held me close, his scratchy, whiskery face pressed against mine. A splash of sunshine settled over my shoulders like a benediction.

I'd found my gown. I'd found my groom. Now I only had to find the courage to tell my mother.

FIFTEEN

That evening, we made quesadillas at his place. All through the cooking and the eating and the cleanup, I dreamed of the day we would share one apartment or the other, and we wouldn't part at the end of the evening.

He sank into his couch, found the remote, and turned on his wall-mounted TV. A cowboy was riding into a black-and-white sunset with his woman snuggled into the saddle with him.

"That could be us, riding into the sunset," he said. "Together. You want to get married on horseback?"

I sat beside him, not wanting to be a party pooper again but utterly unenthusiastic about inviting horses to our wedding. "Well, um . . ."

"Just kidding. I don't care how or where we get married. Could be in a hot air balloon. In gorilla suits. As long as we're to-gether."

I smiled, imagining a hot air balloon land-ing on the manicured lawn of a country club somewhere. In gorilla suits — tuxedo black for him and bridal white for me — we would make our grand entrance and take to the dance floor. Dancing in fake gorilla feet couldn't be any worse than dancing in heels.

I needed to try on the Jenny Packham gown again. If it was as amazing as I remem-bered, I would buy it. And I wanted to start gathering ideas for color schemes. Flowers. Music and food. Everything that would make our wedding beautiful — but afford-able. The gown would take a big chunk of my wedding fund.

"I wonder if we can put everything to-gether in time for a fall wedding," I said. "I hate to wait even that long, but I don't want to steal Alexa's thunder."

"What's her wedding date again?"

"The second Saturday in June, if she and Mom don't kill each other first. I'm glad I have my own money so I won't have to do things Mom's way."

"What? I'm marrying a rich chick?"

"No, but I started a wedding fund when I was eighteen. It's not a lot, but it'll be enough if we focus on the important things, not on all the frou-frou trappings."

"Sounds good. We don't want to get trapped in the cogs of the 'gom.' "

"The what?"

"The G-A-W-M," he spelled. "The Great American Wedding Machine. The industry that bamboozles millions of people into spending their wedding dollars on over-priced merchandise produced by exploited workers."

I wrinkled up my nose. "Are you going to be a wedding Scrooge?"

"Probably not, but if your mom tries to talk you into all the trappings, tell her no."

"Easier said than done."

"It's only one little syllable. Practice with me, sweetheart —"

"No."

"Very good."

"No. I meant — you know what I meant."

Now he had me laughing again. The conversation deteriorated but the snuggling picked up steam. After a few minutes, we shoved each other away.

I laid my head chastely on his warm chest and enjoyed the steady thudding of his heart. "Did I ever tell you I met the preacher at the secret-garden church?"

"No. Did he run you off?"

"No, he introduced himself as Pastor Michael. We had a nice chat, and he advised me to marry you."

Gray chuckled. "He's brilliant, obviously."

"Yes." I sighed with contentment. "I can't wait to marry you, Gray."

"Likewise."

"I'll finally get to change my last name, too. I've always hated it."

"Martin? What's wrong with that?"

"It sounds like an aerospace company. Ellison Martin. Like Lockheed Martin."

"Ellison? That's different. I like it, but I thought Ellie was short for Elizabeth."

"I never told you my real name?" I straightened up, meeting his eyes. "You know what my mom would say?"

"Sure. She'd say we don't know each other well enough to get married."

"Yep." I leaned against him again. "Maybe we should keep it to ourselves for a while. Give her some time to adjust to the boyfriend-girlfriend stage first."

"You don't want to tell her we're engaged?"

"Or your folks either, to keep things fair. Just for a little while."

"But I want to tell the world."

"I do too, but can you imagine telling Mom we're engaged when we've only known each other since February? Can you imagine her reaction?"

"I'm afraid I can." He laughed. "Maybe we can plan the whole wedding before she even knows we're engaged."

That crazy idea brought up a whole new passel of problems, but I had no time to consider them. We were already indulging in a whole new passel of giddy smooches.

Sixteen

Eric and Alexa had found an apartment on the south side of Wynnville. On the last Saturday of April, Mom and I met them there for the grand tour of the empty rooms. The place was old and small, but it had its charms, not the least of which was its distance from Mom's house.

Mom and I left the lovebirds there with their cleaning supplies and the stars in their eyes, and we headed back to Mom's house to work in her flower garden. That was part of my plan for patching things up. Taking her to her dress fitting had helped too, although I was still careful not to mention Gray if I didn't need to.

"Your garden is so beautiful," I told her, leaning over to smell the last of the late daffodils.

"It'll be even better when all the roses and peonies come in. I wish Alexa would let me do her bouquet, at least. The florist charges an arm and a leg."

"You won't have time. You'll be too busy being the mother of the bride."

The mother of two brides, actually. She just didn't know it yet. I hid a smile, feeling like a shaken-up seltzer bottle about to explode with joy.

Being secretly engaged was the most fun I'd ever had. Gray and I might be anywhere, with anyone, talking about anything from politics to potholes, and suddenly our eyes would meet and we'd struggle to keep from laughing. Sometimes, though, our happy secret didn't seem real. I would wake in the middle of the night and ask myself if I was delusional. My ring finger was still bare.

I smiled, remembering Gray's not-so-subtle attempts to learn my preferences in ring styles. Knowing how frugal he was, I'd dropped hints that I would be happy with something small and simple. I never wore anything flashy.

He set a good example with his frugality. He'd inspired me to get serious about freezing my credit card purchases, no easy task with Alexa's wedding on the horizon. I'd had to buy my maid-of-honor dress and the expensive undergarments that made it work. Then shoes and jewelry. Shower gifts. A wedding gift. I couldn't skimp on my baby sister even though I'd had a closing fall through, depriving me of a commission I'd counted on.

"Look at that big ol' swallowtail," Mom said.

I turned to see the yellow-and-black butterfly wafting toward us. It hovered indecisively over a red peony, then lit on a spray of small ivory roses.

"Beautiful," I said.

Ivory roses would be perfect with the Jenny Packham gown. I'd checked on it, and God had heard my prayers. It hadn't sold yet. I wanted to show it to Mom and convince her that an ivory gown didn't brand a bride as less than virtuous, but I had to bide my time a little longer — and then let her think I'd just found the dress.

"Alexa's big day is coming up too soon," Mom said with a heavy sigh. "I'll be alone again. At least she won't be far away. I sure wish you lived close."

"I'm not far. You should come over sometime. How about this weekend?"

"It's not the distance. It's the traffic. Those crazy drivers. That crazy interstate. Every time, I get lost or I nearly get in a wreck."

"Back when you met Dad, didn't you drive back and forth all the time?"

"Sure, but it was an easy drive then. I can't handle I-285 anymore. It's eighteen lanes wide in some parts, and that one ramp, the high one at Spaghetti Junction —" She shuddered. "It's ninety feet in the air."

I suspected she was exaggerating, but I'd never looked it up. "You won't be anywhere near Spaghetti Junction. Just stay on 78 forever, make a few easy turns, and you'll be there. Why don't you come over on Sunday afternoon? I'll take you to Gray's apartment so you can see where he lives — it's just a few blocks away — and then we'll take you out to eat."

I held my breath, afraid she still wasn't ready to accept Gray's place in my life.

She gave me a worried squint. "That close? I hope you're not over there at all hours. I'm afraid that's how Alexa will be too. If I've told her once I've told her a hundred times, just because Eric's moving into the apartment doesn't mean they can start playing house."

"I know, but I wish you would lighten up a little."

"She's a kid. Kids need some guidance."

"She's an adult." I pointed at a clump of jade-green hens-and-chicks, their succulent rosettes growing so close together that they

456

smashed each other. "See how crowded the hens-and-chicks are? That's how Alexa must feel. She's one of those chicks, trying to find room to grow."

"Baloney. She's got plenty of room." Mom touched a fingertip to one of the small green rosettes. "This old hen will be glad when the wedding's over."

"Old hen? Mom, you'll be the prettiest mother of the bride ever. You were stunning at your fitting, and you didn't even have your hair done."

"Huh. I only know I've had enough of your sister's meltdowns. When it's your turn, I hope you'll keep your head on your shoulders."

"I'll try."

That was the closest she'd come to acknowledging that Gray and I might get married. I wanted to blurt it out, then and there, but that wouldn't have been right. He had to be part of the happy announcement. I could hardly wait.

SEVENTEEN

Mother's Day had come and gone. Gray and I had spent the day with our respective mothers, and we still hadn't shared our news.

On a Wednesday afternoon halfway through May, I washed dishes at his kitchen sink while he caught up on work in the living room. Once the heat and humidity arrived, Atlanta would hum with air conditioners. For now, Gray kept his windows open so we could hear songbirds and enjoy the sweet scent of jasmine from a neighboring balcony.

The next few weeks would be crazy. Alexa had two bridal showers, her final fitting, and umpteen appointments to confirm this and that. As her maid of honor, I was in the thick of it and so was Mom. Although Mom and I were on reasonably good terms again, tensions between her and Alexa were rising. I stayed out of it whenever I could.

Gray's computer chimed as he shut it down. "There," he said. "That'll hold 'em until tomorrow."

"Good." I'd given up trying to understand exactly what his job entailed. I only knew his company had recently given him a generous raise to keep him from being poached by a competitor.

I wished I had some extra money too. I'd had more bills lately, for everything from a new radiator to a new computer, and I hadn't earned many commissions. I needed to devote more of my time to drumming up prospects.

Once we were married, I wouldn't have to worry about money. Even though I planned to go on working, his income could support both of us — and a family someday too.

I imagined a toddler in tiny jeans and miniature boots. Mr. Boots Junior. Or Miss Boots, maybe.

I scrubbed the starchy residue of pasta from Gray's beat-up metal colander. When we went public with our engagement, a decent colander would be one of the first items I'd add to our gift registry.

I was tired of living in limbo. I wanted a ring on my finger and a date on my calendar. Without a date, we couldn't make real progress on our plans.

"Gray?"

I heard his bare feet padding across the kitchen floor. His hands snuggled around my waist, and his lips brushed my right ear.

"You called?" he murmured.

"Mm-hmm." I rinsed the soap off the colander and stuck it on the drying rack. "It's weird to be so involved in Alexa's plans without saying a word about ours."

"Do you think it's time to fess up?"

"I do. Even if we kept it a secret for months, my mom would still say we're rushing things. Besides, I'm excited and I want to tell everybody."

"I do too." His lips tickled my left ear. "We can tell my folks before they run off to their Wednesday night church thing, and then we can go tell your mom and Alexa."

"You mean tonight? Right now?"

"Why not? Got cold feet?"

"About marrying you? Never." I wiped my wet hands on my shorts and turned around, his fingers skimming my midriff. "It's just . . ."

"I know. Mama Bear is scary."

"And she'll think we just got engaged. It's almost a lie."

"We'll tell her the whole truth, then. We'll admit we've been engaged for a while." He shrugged. "What's the big deal?"

"We've only known each other since February. If we admit we've already been engaged for a while, it'll only look more scandalous to her."

"Maybe she won't ask for details," he said hopefully.

"Oh, she will. And then she'll say it still isn't official because we don't have a ring and a date."

"Guess what? She's wrong. Come on. Let's go for broke." He scooped me off my feet so suddenly that I shrieked. "I'm practicing for when I carry you over the threshold. We're getting married!"

He spun in a circle, whirling me into dizzy giggles that almost made my worries flee. Almost.

EIGHTEEN

We interrupted Gray's parents in a cheek-to-cheek tango in their living room, but they showed no signs of embarrassment. When we shared our news, they whooped and hollered, welcomed me into the family, and proposed a toast with sweet tea. After visiting for an hour, Gray and I hit the road for Mom's house.

Alexa's car was in the driveway when we arrived, and the roses and peonies were blooming in happy profusion. We ran through the yard, paused on the porch for one quick kiss for luck, and walked right in. Alexa's lacy white wedding binder lay on the couch along with a few leftover invitations.

"Mom," I called. "Alexa. Where are you?"

Then I heard them in the kitchen. Yelling. Their volume and pitch rose with every word.

"He did not!" my sister screamed.

"He did too!" my mother screamed back.

"Oh boy," I whispered. "One of Lexie's famous meltdowns."

Gray's eyes were wide. "Maybe I should wait outside."

"Good idea. I'll come get you when they've calmed down."

He escaped to the porch, and I entered the kitchen. Mirror images of each other, Mom and Alexa stood at opposite ends of the table, their hands clenched into fists at hip level. Alexa's cheeks were streaked with tears and mascara.

"Hey there," I said. "What's going on?"

They glanced at me and resumed their argument, nearly drowning each other out. None of it made sense, but it was something about the apartment. Something about Eric. A huge disappointment.

"Call it what it is," Mom shouted. "It's immorality."

I sucked in my breath. If Eric was cheating on my little sister, I would rip his heart out. Shove it down his throat. Pull it out his butt.

"What happened?" I asked. "Mom, Lex, what's going on?"

Alexa stared out the window, her chest heaving. "She nagged me with nosy questions until I confessed."

"Confessed what?"

"Go ahead, Mom. Tell her."

Mom turned toward me, tears on her face too. "They put the bed before the wed, so the wedding's off. Or at least the big church wedding is off."

"*What?* Why?"

She turned back to Alexa. "I warned you. I told you not to spend so much time there. No chaperones. No accountability. All the temptation in the world."

"Can you blame us? You never give us a moment's privacy here." Alexa grabbed a paper napkin from the table and blew her nose. "Okay, so we messed up. It's none of your business."

"Yes it is, missy. I won't pay for a white-dress wedding now. You can't stand there in church, in front of God and everybody, and pretend you deserve a white dress. It's hypocrisy, that's what it is."

"Who's the hypocrite? You *had* to get married. At least I'm not pregnant."

Mom murmured something unintelligible. "I should've known a good-lookin' boy like him would lead you astray."

"Maybe I led *him* astray. Ever think about that?" Alexa snatched her purse from the counter and ran out, slamming the front door so hard that Mom's prized collection

464

of delft blue plates shook on their narrow shelf.

Oblivious to their peril, Mom aimed her angry gaze at me. "What do *you* want?"

"Some common sense. Some kindness."

I heard Lexie's car spitting gravel. In her blind rage, she might have run right past Gray without seeing him, but he couldn't have missed seeing her.

I put my hands on my hips and braced myself for battle. "I don't care what they've done, Mom. You can't renege on paying for —"

"Watch me. God won't bless couples who don't keep themselves pure, so I can't either."

"Excuse me? Where's the grace? Sure, it would have been best if they'd waited, but that's no reason to call off the wedding."

"There'll be a wedding, all right. A quickie. Tomorrow I'll drag 'em to the courthouse."

"You think they would let you? Get real."

"I won't pay for a white-dress wedding. It'd be a charade." Mom sniffled. "I tried so hard to raise godly girls."

I ached inside, remembering Alexa as a little girl at our cousin's wedding in Savannah. Awestruck by his bride's beauty, she'd started dreaming of her own wedding. But not like this. Never like this.

I choked back a sob. "You're not paying for my wedding either. I don't need a dime from you, thank you very much, and I'm buying an ivory dress. Not because I don't deserve to wear white, but because it's my dream dress. And Gray's my dream man."

Mom's mouth dropped open. "What are you talking about?"

"I'm marrying Gray." I started crying in earnest.

This wasn't the way I'd wanted to tell her. Gray wasn't even in the room. He was outside somewhere, probably wanting to run from me and my crazy family.

"I guess you're shacking up too," Mom said sorrowfully.

I blushed, not because I was guilty — I wasn't — but because her fixation on the topic was embarrassing. "Don't even go there," I said between clenched teeth.

"Oh, Ellie." She wiped a tear away. "You are, aren't you?"

"No, I'm not! But back to Alexa — you can't cancel anything. The invitations already went out."

"We can call people." She muttered something. "I'll lose my deposits."

"You're worried about your deposits when Alexa's heartbroken?"

"She should've thought about that before she messed around."

"Who are you to judge? You were no angel. Neither am I. Gray and I try to behave ourselves, but I'll admit I'm looking forward to — to — consummating our relationship. Sorry, but I'm human. News flash, Mom: God loves humans."

"Humans can be mighty messed up, and now you're marrying one you hardly know? Doing the same thing I did?"

"It's not the same. I know him. I trust him. I love him. We're engaged."

Mom glared at my left hand. "I don't see a ring."

"We didn't get that far yet. Deal with it." I walked out, breathing hard, but I managed to shut the door in a civil manner.

Gray stood on Mom's lush lawn, facing the spot where Alexa's car had been. I could only imagine what he thought of my family now. He would love them for my sake, but that didn't mean he would ever understand them. Or even me.

As I hurried through the yard where my sister and I had played as children, I remembered teaching her a new song when she was three or four. She'd picked it up right away. For days, she'd walked around singing it at the top of her lungs.

Jesus loves me, this I know, for the Bible tells me so.

I couldn't stand to let her think Jesus stopped loving her when she and Eric fell to temptation.

They are weak, but he is strong. Yes, Jesus loves me . . .

I wouldn't tell anyone else about Alexa's private troubles, but Gray needed to know the basics. He would be far more merciful than Mom.

"Gray," I called, and he wheeled around. "We have to find Alexa. She's probably on her way to Eric's place. Can I drive?"

He tossed me his keys, and we ran to his car.

NINETEEN

While I drove, I brought Gray up to speed. "I can't believe Mom sometimes," I finished, still fuming.

"Yeah, I'd say her reaction is a little over the top."

"A little? It's downright un-Christian. I was so mad, I told her I don't need her money for our wedding."

"You told her we're getting married?"

"It kind of slipped out." Slowing for a stop sign, I glanced at him. "I'm sorry."

He was frowning straight ahead. "It's okay."

"No, I shouldn't have said anything. It should have been a happy moment, like it was when we told your mom and dad."

"A together moment."

"That too. I'm sorry, Gray."

"It's okay," he said again, a little too quietly.

When we reached the apartment, he

elected to wait in the car. My sandals made a racket as I ran up the metal stairs. Stopping at 2D, I knocked on the door.

"Lex? It's me."

A long silence ensued, but she must have heard me. Through the thin walls, I could hear her blowing her nose.

I knocked again. "I'm alone."

"Mom's not with you?"

"No. It's just me."

Alexa opened the door, her eyes puffy and her nose red. "What am I gonna do?"

"It'll be okay." I shut the door and hugged her.

She cried while I massaged her back, the magic trick that had always stopped her meltdowns when she was five or six. It didn't calm her now.

Eric had turned the apartment into a bachelor pad. A Georgia Dawgs T-shirt hung over a chair in the dining nook, and he'd crammed a weight set into one corner of the living room. So far, the room had no feminine touches except their engagement photo flanked by stubby white candles on a thrift-store coffee table.

"I don't even know how it started," she said, her speech garbled with tears. "I'd come over here just to get away from Mom . . . and . . . things happened. I wish we'd waited, but it's too late." She gulped. "I'm so, so sorry."

"I know, Lex."

"I wanted to be one of those beautiful, happy brides," she sobbed.

"You still can be."

"Not if Mom won't pay for it."

I kept remembering the couple from the guerrilla wedding. With a baby on the way, with no support from their families, they'd still had a joyful, romantic ceremony.

"A simple wedding can still be beautiful," I said. "You don't need the fuss and feathers. You only need each other."

"But if we just run down to the courthouse, everybody will think we *have* to get married."

"Who cares what people think? It doesn't matter."

She collapsed on the couch and started bawling again.

I couldn't stay dry-eyed either. Even if I could help them put together a scaled-down version of their original plans, it would feel like second best. And Alexa, the sentimental one who felt everything deeply, would never get over that wound. She would think *she* was second best.

I knelt beside the couch. "Forget everything Mom said. God still wants to bless you. He doesn't love you any less than he did before. Okay? You and Eric can forgive yourselves because God does. And you can move on."

"With a cheap, ugly wedding. Because I'm cheap and ugly."

"You are not. You're precious and beautiful. To God, to Eric, to me."

No matter what I said, she only cried harder. I had to think of something. I couldn't let her start her marriage with a bundle of shame on her slender shoulders. With "condemned" stamped on her tender heart.

Dis-grace. No grace. That wasn't God's way.

Mom had a lot of nerve.

I was in the middle of imagining what I'd say to her when inspiration struck. I had the resources to salvage Alexa's happiness.

It was crazy. It was perfect.

It was going to hurt.

I imagined Alexa exiting the church on Eric's arm, smiling, celebrating vows that started not with past mistakes but with the present.

From this day forward . . .

Go for broke, Gray had said. Boy, would I be broke.

I took a deep breath and exhaled, letting

go of that fabulous Jenny Packham gown and so much more. A good photographer. A good band. A nice reception menu. Alexa mattered more than all of it put together.

"Lexie, you can still have the wedding you've planned. Remember my wedding fund?"

She nodded in the middle of a sob.

"It's yours," I said. "I'm giving it to you."

She gasped. "You can't do that."

"Yes, I can."

"Why? Why would you want to?"

"Because you need to know how much you're loved. No matter what."

She pressed her lips together to keep from crying, the same way she'd done as a toddler in trouble. "Ellie, no."

"Yes."

She slid off the couch to sit beside me on the carpet. "You mean it? You're giving me the money?"

Unable to speak, I could only nod as my dreams dissolved . . . but light gleamed in my sister's eyes.

She hugged me fiercely. "You're the best, El. I — I don't know what to say."

I didn't either, and I sure didn't know how I would explain it to Gray. I pulled away from her hug. "Call me later, because unless Mom comes around, I'll have to take over her to-do list."

"She won't come around." Alexa's chin wobbled, but then a dazzling smile lit her face. "Thank you, Ellie."

"You're welcome." I scrambled to my feet. "Chin up, sis. Everything's going to be fine." I left her sitting on the carpet in a puddle of sunshine.

Outside, one hand on the stair rail, I looked down at the parking lot. Gray leaned against his shiny old car with his shiny new phone to his ear. He was probably calling his brothers with our news.

In all the drama, I'd forgotten to tell Alexa I was engaged too. Maybe that was for the best, because I didn't want to talk about it now.

Holding my head high, I walked down the stairs. Paying for my sister's wedding was the ultimate in standing up to Mom. Gray would be so proud.

TWENTY

Gray didn't start asking questions until he'd pulled onto the main road. "How's she doing?"

"She's all right. I, um, helped her out a little." I wiped my eyes. "I offered my wedding fund."

"To Alexa?"

"Yes." I let out a shaky laugh. "She couldn't believe it."

"I can't either." Gray drummed his fingers on the steering wheel. "Clarify, please. How much did you offer?"

"All of it."

"The whole thing? You gave her your entire wedding fund?"

"You want me to stand up to Mom, right? Well, I did. Not just with talk but with action too. Alexa will have her dream wedding after all."

"I see," he said lightly. "And what about yours?"

"Ours? Well, it . . . it'll still happen."

"How?"

"Um . . . a courthouse wedding? There's nothing wrong with that. We've talked about outsmarting the GAWM, right? It's supposed to be about the vows. The relationship."

"Isn't a relationship supposed to include some communication?"

A cold knot of fear weighted my stomach, reminding me of a day when I'd lost my footing on the way down Stone Mountain. If I made one wrong move, I would slip and slide straight to disaster.

I tried to sound chipper. "Isn't that what we're doing? Communicating?"

"After the fact. After you've made a big decision. Without me."

"If I did something impetuous, well, look who's talking."

He punched the accelerator and swerved around a slow-moving farm tractor.

I grabbed my armrest. "Slow down!"

He didn't. He swooped around a couple of curves and made an abrupt turn into a brand-new park on the outskirts of town. He pulled smoothly into a parking space and shut off the engine.

"Alexa and Eric could have solved their own problems," he said. "You're not responsible for their happiness."

"Too late. She already accepted the offer. Very gratefully." My voice shook. I was beginning to feel my own losses.

"I should think so." He shook his head. "Why can't she borrow money? Why can't Eric help? Or his parents? Is everybody broke? Nobody has good credit?"

"You're the guy who hates debt. Now you want Alexa to go into debt?"

"There must have been another way."

I watched through the windshield as three teenage boys kicked a soccer ball around on the grass. "It's not just about the money."

"No kidding."

"It's about love. And forgiveness."

"Yes, and your kindness is commendable. Your priorities are skewed, though."

"But you're the one who doesn't want all the frou-frou trappings. Fine. We can't afford them now, so what's the problem?"

"You still don't see it?"

I was starting to. I'd saved for a wedding for years. Now that I'd finally found the right man, I was back at square one. Saving. Waiting. Except for the money I'd just promised to Alexa, I was nearly broke. Even if I cut corners everywhere, I couldn't pull off a wedding with no money.

I swallowed hard, remembering what I'd

told him: *I won't make you wait to marry me.*

"It won't take long to save enough money for a simple wedding," I said. "And maybe you could help out a little?"

"Sure, I could." He pulled the key out of the ignition. "Tell me, though. How would you feel if I gave my entire wedding fund to my sister, if I had one, without talking things over with you first?"

"You have a wedding fund?"

"That's beside the point, but yes. I pulled money from the pony fund for rings and the honeymoon. Because you're more important than a car."

I absorbed that in silence for a moment. "And you're more important than Alexa's fuss and feathers, but come on, Gray. You're always telling me to stand up to my mom. Now that I did, you're mad at me. It's not fair."

He let out a sharp sigh. "There's your mom again, affecting everything. If she hadn't overreacted, you wouldn't have overreacted either. We'd still have a happy announcement to make — together — and we'd still have our own wedding to plan."

"We still have a wedding to plan."

"Do we? I can't compete with your family. They always come first."

"No, they don't."

He stared straight ahead, his silence chilling me. He pulled his phone from his pocket and dropped it into the console.

"Gray?" I said timidly.

"I need some time to cool off." He climbed out, shut the door, and strode toward a walking trail that would lead him into the woods and out of sight.

I grabbed the door handle, prepared to charge after him, but the fact that he'd left his phone behind made me reconsider. He didn't want to talk.

TWENTY-ONE

Forty minutes later, Gray came back. He'd cooled off, all right. We drove back toward his apartment in chilly silence. Between road work, accidents, and a natural gas leak at a business on 78, every route was slowed to a crawl. Thanks to one of Atlanta's epic traffic jams, we were stuck together for two miserable hours.

I didn't know if we were still engaged or not. He'd never given me a ring, so he couldn't take one back.

It was eight thirty and the sun was setting when he parked a few spaces from my car. We climbed out and faced each other over the roof of his.

"Well," I said, "after all your talk about the importance of communication, you haven't communicated a thing for two solid hours."

"I don't know what to say."

"That makes two of us." I ran to my car,

climbed in, and slammed the door.

I'd never made the short trip home in such a terrible, brakes-squealing hurry. Home again, I ran inside and slammed that door too, wishing Gray could hear it from blocks away. Then I whispered an apology to my neighbors and threw myself down on the couch for a good long cry.

It was three in the morning and I was on my second box of tissues when it hit me. Plan A had crashed and burned, but Plan B might fly.

Gray thought he'd fallen to the bottom of my priority list, so I had to put him at the very top. Except I needed to run the idea past him first. I certainly couldn't do it without him.

It wasn't a conversation I could entrust to a phone call. I wasn't even sure he would take a call from me, anyway.

I brushed my teeth, scrubbed my face, and put on my prettiest shirt, and then I grabbed a jacket and drove back to his apartment. No lights shone from behind his blinds. I didn't want to wake him.

I couldn't find a parking space near his car, so I parked as close as I could and walked back in the spooky darkness.

Sometimes he was careless about locking up his shiny black BMW. Sure enough, the passenger door was unlocked. I settled into the familiar seat and hit the lock button.

The car wasn't a threshing floor, and Gray wasn't there anyway, and we weren't Boaz and Ruth. Besides, we were already betrothed — or at least I hoped we still were. But Pastor Michael would have understood what I was trying to do.

Do you love him? It doesn't need to be complicated, dear.

I wiped my eyes. I didn't have time for more tears. I had to flesh out Plan B, fast. With almost no money.

I loved Gray. He needed to know how much.

TWENTY-TWO

I woke to the sound of Gray's key unlocking the car door. He slid behind the wheel, scowling, with shadows under his eyes and stubble on his chin.

He jumped when he saw me. "What did you do? Sleep in my car?"

"Sort of. We have to talk."

He nodded. His grim expression didn't change.

I blew out a breath and prayed for courage. "You're usually so laid-back and light-hearted, so it's extra scary when you get upset."

"I think I had good reason to be upset," he said quietly.

"You did, and I want to change the way I handle problems with Mom and Alexa. I love them, but I won't put them ahead of you again. I can't go back on my word about the money, though. It's too late for that."

"I know." He shook his head. "I don't

want to come between you and your sister or your mom."

"I know you don't. What's more important is that we can't let them come between us."

His expression softened but his eyes were still wary. "I like the sound of that."

"We need to stand up to Mom. Together. We can stand up to the GAWM while we're at it."

"Sounds interesting."

"You have no idea how interesting." With my fingertip, I touched the divot in his chin. Then I slid my finger up to his lips and held my breath.

He kissed my finger, and I started breathing again. I could ask him.

"Are you doing anything on Saturday, Mr. Whitby? You want to get married?"

He blinked. "What?"

"You're supposed to say 'yes,' not 'what.' Will you marry me? On Saturday?"

"*This* Saturday? The day after tomorrow?"

"We can have a guerrilla wedding, sort of. We don't need the frills. What's important is that we'll promise to love each other from this day forward. That's all we need. Oh, and a marriage license. And a preacher and a place. And of course we'll want some friends and family there."

He raised his eyebrows. "Are you the same

woman who complained that two days wasn't enough warning for a trail ride?"

"Yes, but I'm learning to fly by the seat of my pants. My mom will say we're doing something rash —"

"Of course she will," he grumbled. "She thinks we've been engaged for less than twenty-four hours." His dimple was trying to surface, though.

I gave him an innocent look. "Are we still engaged? Last night I wasn't quite sure."

"Be sure, baby. Be very sure. But we won't be engaged long, because I intend to marry you ASAP."

The front seat of his car wasn't especially comfortable for a celebratory embrace, but we managed. For quite a while. Then we got back to business.

I squeezed my eyes shut, trying to recover the long to-do list I'd been engraving on my brain through the wee hours. "Are you okay with Pastor Michael's church? In the garden, I mean?"

"Sure, if he'll have us."

"I know he will. But where can we have a reception, spur of the moment?"

"For how many people?"

"I don't know. Twenty? Maybe thirty?"

"My parents' backyard, then. A picnic."

"Brilliant."

"Can we serve Publix subs?" he asked hopefully. "In honor of our first date?"

"Why not? We can get a cake there too. Publix has the best cakes. We'll invite people by phone or text or email. Whatever works. I'll ask Lex and Eric to help. Can we draft your folks too?"

"Sure. They'll roll with it." Gray leaned over and gave me a long, delicious kiss that made my head reel. "Do I have to wear a tux?" he murmured.

"Did you kiss me like that just to make me dizzy so I'll say you don't have to wear a tux?"

"Yes," he said, deadpan, and did it again. Longer.

"Wear your favorite suit." My imagination jumped to a hotel room somewhere. I would enjoy the privilege of making that suit come off.

"Can I wear my boots?"

"Of course you can. You're my Mr. Boots."

"That sounds like something you'd call a cat. Never mind. What else do we need?"

"Not much. We don't need attendants. We can ask friends to take pictures and video. I haven't even thought about music."

"My brother plays guitar," Gray said. "Much better than I do."

"That'll work. And we don't need a florist.

The church's flower beds are in full bloom."

"Isn't the groom supposed to provide the bride's bouquet?"

"Yes, but I'd like to ask my mom to bring a bouquet from her garden."

"In her current frame of mind, do you think she will?"

"If she won't, I'll carry a handful of dandelions." I made myself smile. "We'll still be just as married."

"We'll need to arrange a few days off work. How about a short honeymoon now and a long one later?"

"Works for me. And then which apartment will we come home to? Yours or mine?"

He laughed. "What a dilemma. As long as we're together, I won't care." He lifted my left hand to his lips. "This hand needs a ring on it. A couple of rings."

"They can wait. They're only tokens."

"I'll take care of the tokens," he said with a mischievous smile.

"Perfect. Thanks." I'd hardly heard him, though. My mind was already on other problems.

Gray had several handsome suits to choose from, but I had nothing that even resembled a wedding dress. Worse, I couldn't expect Mom to make my bouquet. Most likely, she wouldn't even show up.

TWENTY-THREE

Thursday and Friday had passed in a blur that included my mother's horrified reaction. "*This* Saturday?" she'd yelled. "Are you pregnant?"

She tuned out my protestations of innocence. She wasn't amenable to my request for a bouquet from her garden either, but I was still holding out hope that she would soften — in the next few minutes. We were nearly out of time.

My wedding day had started at a mad pace at dawn. At five minutes to eleven, I stood on a rise overlooking the secret garden, bright now with roses, hydrangeas, and peonies. Maybe it wasn't too late to ask Gray to pick a few blooms for me — if he had something to cut the stems with.

But when I turned around to see where he'd disappeared to, he was walking toward me with a nosegay of miniature white roses, about the right size for a flower girl to carry.

"I picked these in my mother's yard and stashed 'em in my car," he said. "Just in case."

My eyes watered in gratitude for his thoughtfulness and in sorrow over my mother's absence. "Thanks, Gray. It was sweet of you. It's not quite time yet, though."

"But your mom missed her ride with Eric and Alexa —"

"Deliberately. I know. Maybe she's taking a cab."

I was whistling Dixie, though. Mom must have decided to boycott my wedding.

"Come on," he coaxed. "It's tradition. Carry the roses from your groom."

I took the nosegay. I wanted flowers from my mother, though. I wanted her there.

She would have approved of the pure white fabric of the street-length frock I'd found at a thrift store, but she wouldn't have approved of the style. Strapless. A little bit low cut. I wasn't crazy about it myself, but it didn't matter. I would only wear it for a few hours, and then I would get on with life. With my *husband*. The word made my heart flutter with excitement that almost banished the sorrow.

Gray was scrumptious in his gray suit and sage-green shirt. His mother had pinned a pink rosebud on his lapel. She'd tried to talk him out of wearing his brown boots, saying they didn't go with the gray, but he'd stuck to his guns.

I leaned around the shrubbery to spy on our friends and relatives. Like the guests at the wedding back in February, they'd assembled in a loose semicircle on the lawn. Gray's parents were there with his brothers and their families. Alexa and Eric, holding hands. My favorite cousin, all the way from Savannah with his wife. Betty, chic in a pale blue suit. And Gray had invited his friends, the guerrilla couple. Her baby bump showed now, and they were still smiling.

Ours wasn't quite a guerrilla wedding because we had permission to use the church grounds. The garden I'd invested in for years, like I'd invested in my wedding fund, never dreaming I would turn it over to my sister.

Pastor Michael stood in front of the flower bed that had once been my hiding place. He'd donned a more respectable black suit today, and he was bareheaded. He looked like an amiable cherub. An angel. He'd said we didn't have to pay a cent, but Gray had already taken care of a generous stipend for him.

When Pastor Michael caught me peeking,

he grinned. I gave him a quick wave and stepped back so no one else would see me.

Taking a deep breath, I studied the simple but beautiful engagement ring Gray had put on my finger the night before. Its short solo run was nearly over already. He had wedding bands in his pocket, ready to go.

He pulled out his phone and turned it on.

"Turn that thing off, please," I said.

"It's on mute. I was just checking the time. It's eleven, El."

About to cry, I turned my back on him — and there was Mom, trotting across the grass in a pink dress I'd never seen before. She clutched her keys in one hand and a bright mix of flowers in the other — pink and white and yellow. I could hardly see the bouquet through my tears.

"Mom! You drove?"

"I drove." She gave my dress a sharp glance. "Sorry to cut it so close — oh!" She stopped short. With stricken eyes, she regarded the white nosegay. "I'm too late."

"No, you're not. Thank you. What a gorgeous bunch of flowers."

Hesitantly, she held them out to me, and I took them. Fragrant roses. Peonies. A few late daffodils. The pale, freckled green of Lenten roses, not roses at all but a lovely accent. She'd even included a few jade-

491

green hens-and-chicks.

"I notice you made a little space between the hen and the chicks," I said.

"I did. Just a little." She smiled. Our eyes met and held for a long moment.

"It's perfect, Mom."

Except there I stood with one bouquet in each hand, one from my groom and one from my mother. I didn't want to hurt Mom's feelings when things were still dicey between her and Alexa, but I couldn't let Gray think I preferred Mom's flowers to his.

He stepped forward. Moving my hands together, he merged the two bouquets into one. "There," he said, giving me a wink. "Now it's perfect."

Ignoring him, Mom curved her hand around my cheek. "My little girl. My baby. All grown up."

Careful to keep from squishing the flowers, we hugged each other. Then she wagged a finger at Gray.

"If you don't treat my daughter like a queen, you will answer to me."

"Yes, ma'am. And to God."

His grave expression terrified me. What were we doing? How could fallen and fallible humans like us make such huge promises?

But Jesus loved fallen, fallible humans. He loved weddings too. He'd told stories about brides and grooms. He'd been a wedding guest in a dusty village called Cana —

"Honey, where do you want me?" Mom's question jolted me back to the present.

"Why don't you stand with Lex and Eric?"

Her lips tightened, and she cast a skeptical look across the grounds to our waiting guests. She let out a huff, squared her shoulders, and set off across the lawn.

No one else had to know she'd arrived in the nick of time. It was traditional for the mother of the bride to be the last one to walk the aisle before the wedding party.

It would not be traditional for the mother to snub her younger daughter, though.

Alexa and Eric stood toward the left side of our assembled guests, while Gray's family, whom Mom had never met, stood on the right. I held my breath and prayed.

She drifted to the right, then slowed her pace and edged to the left. Then back to the center. Back to the right. Finally she veered left. Holding her head high, she took her place a few yards from Alexa.

With Eric tagging along, Alexa moved closer and held out her hand.

Mom took it.

Able to breathe again, I looked up at Gray

and laughed, the flowers shaking in my grip. I was a happy mess. A muddle of nerves and tears and joy.

Pastor Michael caught my eye and raised his eyebrows. I nodded. He nodded to Gray's oldest brother, who strummed a single chord on his guitar. Silence fell. Even the traffic noises seemed to fade away as he began to play a simple song made elegant with precision and embellished with grace notes.

Jesus loves me, this I know . . .

Gray offered his arm. When I took it, the nerves fled but the joy remained. Steady and sure, we walked together across the lawn to the Eden I'd tended for so long. To our new friend, the minister I used to hide from.

I wasn't wearing Jenny Packham, but then, I wasn't Jenny Packham. I was Ellison Martin, moments from marrying Graham Whitby.

Graham and Ellison Whitby. People might think we were stuffy, like a duke and duchess or something.

It didn't matter. Nothing would matter as long as we were together.

We stopped in front of Pastor Michael. He smiled at us, then opened his black book and swept the small crowd with his kind and merry eyes.

"Dearly beloved," he said, and I knew he meant it with all his heart.

So did I. And Gray's happy grin made me feel exactly as a bride should feel.

Blessed and beloved.

DISCUSSION QUESTIONS

1. Raised by a worry-wart mother, Ellie is normally cautious and responsible. What was your first clue that she sometimes breaks the rules or takes risks?
2. Getting married may be one of the biggest risks a person can take. If you think Ellie rushed into her commitment to Gray, what do you wish she had done first?
3. Pastor Michael's advice to Ellie is straightforward: "If you love him and you want to marry him, well . . . marry him." But how can any of us know for sure when love is real?
4. Young, self-focused Alexa doesn't deserve the sacrifice Ellie makes for her. Why does Ellie choose to make this sacrifice anyway?
5. If a bride asked your advice about

her wedding, what are the essential elements that you would encourage her and her groom to focus on?

ACKNOWLEDGMENTS

I'm grateful to so many people, starting with my family, friends, and readers. I appreciate your love and your prayers. I also want to thank my editor, Becky Philpott, who is utterly professional but also so much fun to work with; my agent, Chip MacGregor, whose wisdom I always need; and Deeanne Gist, Rob and Susanne Krouse, and Suzan Robertson for their invaluable feedback. I love you one and all!

ABOUT THE AUTHOR

As a little girl in California, **Meg Moseley** used to pretend she was a novelist while she pounded the keys of her grandmother's typewriter. Now the author of *A Stillness of Chimes, Gone South,* and *When Sparrows Fall,* Meg lives with her husband near Atlanta and never stops dreaming up ideas for contemporary fiction. Visit her website at http://megmoseley.com/.